The next thing Lindsey knew, Zane was saying her name softly through the darkness, a gentle, low, seductive sound

Slowly she opened her eyes, and he was there, in the soft shadows of the room. He was bending over her and the child, close enough for her to inhale the scent of soap and freshness that clung to him.

"How is he?" Zane whispered.

"Sound asleep."

"It's a miracle," he said, and smiled at her. That was seductive, too, almost as seductive as his soft "Thanks to you."

She had to get out of there. She was off balance, and wasn't at all sure how to regain her balance with Zane. She was shaking just thinking about how much she wanted him to kiss her. A man who had the power to destroy every dream she had for the day-care center.

Dear Reader,

Welcome to Harlequin American Romance. With your search for satisfying reading in mind, every month Harlequin American Romance aims to offer you a stimulating blend of heartwarming, emotional and deeply romantic stories.

Unexpected arrivals lead to the sweetest of surprises as Harlequin American Romance celebrates the love only a baby can bring, in our brand-new promotion, AMERICAN BABY, which begins this month with Jacqueline Diamond's delightful *Surprise, Doc! You're a Daddy!* After months of searching for her missing husband, Meg Avery finally finds him—only, Dr. Hugh Menton doesn't remember her or their child!

With Valor and Devotion, the latest book in Charlotte Maclay's exciting MEN OF STATION SIX series, is a must-read about a valorous firefighter who rescues an orphaned boy. Will the steadfast bachelor consider becoming a devoted family man after meeting the little boy's pretty social worker? JUST FOR KIDS, Mary Anne Wilson's new miniseries, debuts with *Regarding the Tycoon's Toddler....* This trilogy focuses on a corporate day-care center and the lives and loves of those who work there. And don't miss *The Biological Bond* by Jamie Denton, the dramatic story of a mother who is reunited with the child she'd been forced to give away, when her daughter's adoptive single father seeks her help.

Enjoy this month's offerings, and be sure to return each and every month to Harlequin American Romance!

Wishing you happy reading,

Melissa Jeglinski
Associate Senior Editor
Harlequin American Romance

REGARDING THE TYCOON'S TODDLER...

Mary Anne Wilson

TORONTO • NEW YORK • LONDON
AMSTERDAM • PARIS • SYDNEY • HAMBURG
STOCKHOLM • ATHENS • TOKYO • MILAN • MADRID
PRAGUE • WARSAW • BUDAPEST • AUCKLAND

To Walker Scott Levin
For all the joy and wonder you bring into my life
XOXOXO

ISBN 0-373-16891-8

REGARDING THE TYCOON'S TODDLER...

Copyright © 2001 by Mary Anne Wilson.

This edition published by arrangement with Harlequin Books S.A.

® and TM are trademarks of the publisher. Trademarks indicated with
® are registered in the United States Patent and Trademark Office, the
Canadian Trade Marks Office and in other countries.

Visit us at www.eHarlequin.com

Printed in U.S.A.

ABOUT THE AUTHOR

Mary Anne Wilson is a Canadian transplanted to Southern California where she lives with her husband, three children and an assortment of animals. She knew she wanted to write romances when she found herself "rewriting" the great stories in literature, such as *A Tale of Two Cities,* to give them "happy endings." Over a ten-year career, she's published thirty romances, had her books on the bestseller lists, been nominated for Reviewer's Choice Awards and received a Career Achievement Award in Romantic Suspense. She's looking forward to her next thirty books.

Books by Mary Anne Wilson

HARLEQUIN AMERICAN ROMANCE

495—HART'S OBSESSION
523—COULD IT BE YOU?
543—HER BODYGUARD
570—THE BRIDE WORE BLUE JEANS
589—HART'S DREAM
609—THE CHRISTMAS HUSBAND
637—NINE MONTHS LATER…
652—MISMATCHED MOMMY?
670—JUST ONE TOUCH
700—MR. WRONG!
714—VALENTINE FOR AN ANGEL
760—RICH, SINGLE & SEXY
778—COWBOY IN A TUX
826—THAT NIGHT WE MADE BABY
891—REGARDING THE TYCOON'S TODDLER…*

*Just for Kids

LynTech Corporation
Corporate Towers
Founder: Robert Lewis

20th Floor—Executive Suite
Zane S. Holden, Chairman & Co-CEO
Matthew R. Terrell, President & Co-CEO
Rita S. Donovan, Executive Assistant
Jackson D. Ford, Executive Senior Vice President

19th Floor—Legal Department

18th Floor—Accounting and Financial

7th through 17th Floors—General Services,
See specific floor directory

6th Floor—Just For Kids Day Care Center
Lindsey Atherton, Child Care Director
Amy Blake, Child Care Coordinator

3rd through 5th Floors—
Marketing and Public Relations

2nd Floor—Security and Maintenance

Lobby Level—
Information, Conference Rooms and Employment
Opportunities

Chapter One

"What am I supposed to do with a child?"

Zane Holden stared hard at the city of Houston, twenty stories below his office at LynTech Corporation in downtown Houston. The question held the very real annoyance and impatience he felt over this interruption to his schedule.

He turned to Edward Stiller, an attorney from Florida, and watched the slender, gray-suited man shrug. "Sir, your wife is dead—at least, I mean, your ex-wife."

Zane was still trying to grasp the idea that Suzanne was gone. That she and her new husband had died in a multiple-car crash in southern Florida. The man sat in one of two leather chairs that faced the huge executive desk cluttered with paperwork. "You already said that," he said. "And I am very.sorry that Suzanne and Weaver were killed two days ago. But we haven't been married for more than two years. I haven't even talked to her in all that time. Now you're here. Explain it to me so I can get a grip on this."

"I told you, I'm only here because I'm executing her wishes."

Zane moved back to his chair and sank down into the

high-backed chair. "That's what I don't get at all." He ran a hand over his face, as impatient with the man as he was with the odd mixture of feelings he was experiencing. Suzanne was dead. It didn't seem real somehow. No more unreal, though, than this man babbling on about the child she had had with Dan Weaver. A child she had been carrying even before their divorce was final.

Stiller set a slim briefcase on the desk, pressing perfectly manicured fingers on the expensive leather. "I thought of calling, but felt you needed to be told this in person. There is so much to decide."

Zane tried to focus on what the man was saying, instead of on Suzanne. He didn't know if he'd ever loved her. Love was something he never gave much thought to. But he did know that now she was irrevocably gone, and that created a deep ache inside him. Then regret.

All she'd wanted was a family. And that was what he hadn't wanted. So, she found someone who did. Dan Weaver. A man Zane had seen only once, in their attorney's offices when they signed the divorce papers. He couldn't even hate the man then. Weaver hadn't broken up their marriage. By then Zane had realized there had never been a real marriage to break up.

"Before we decide anything, Mr. Stiller, explain to me how I ended up as the executor of the estate. You're telling me that Suzanne never changed her will? She never thought it was important enough, even with the child involved, to change it?"

The man snapped open the briefcase. "Mr. Holden, I don't know what was in her mind, or what her intent was, but she didn't change it." He took out a thick sheaf of papers and glanced at them. "I checked it very carefully." He closed his briefcase and dropped the papers on top of it. "You can have it checked yourself—but I can tell you, it's valid."

Zane ran a hand roughly over his face and tried to push away that feeling of regret. It didn't have a place in his life. He wouldn't regret their marriage, or their divorce. He wouldn't waste time on regret. And he wouldn't waste time putting off what had to be done.

"This child of hers—?"

"A boy, Walker Scott Weaver. Almost two years old. Lovely child, from what I've heard. He luckily was with a sitter when…" He coughed slightly. "Well, he's safe, still with the sitter, until he can be resituated."

Zane never thought about children. They didn't have a part in his life. But today was very different. First, there was another request for more money to fund programs at the day care center run by the company. He glanced at the yellow paper on his desk. The last request for funding from the director of the day care center, L. Atherton. The third request. And the third rejection.

He looked back at Stiller. The day care decision was cut-and-dried. But this child that Stiller was talking about—Suzanne's son…he knew this wasn't going to be as simple.

He looked at Stiller. "This is ludicrous," he muttered, and reached for the phone. He punched in a two-digit extension, and, when Stiller was about to say something, he held up his hand. His secretary answered the phone.

"Marlene, get a hold of Mr. Terrel and ask him to come to my office as soon as he can. It's urgent."

As he put the phone back on the cradle, he looked at Stiller and asked, "What about grandparents?"

"There are none."

"Aunts or uncles?"

"We don't really know, but we don't believe so."

Suzanne had been an only child, like him, and her parents had been gone for years, but Zane would have thought Weaver had family somewhere. "No distant cousin?"

"It's a matter of form to look for any living relatives in a case like this, and my office staff is on it. But right now, it's up to you to make arrangements for the child. The wording of Suzanne's will is not exact, but the intent is clear."

"Wording?"

He motioned to the stack of papers. "I'll paraphrase, but there is a clause that the executor, you, will have full control over all matters of her life. The child is certainly a 'matter,' and as such, you are in charge of him, or at least his fate." He spread his hand on the will. "What do you want to do?"

There was a sharp knock on the door, the barrier opened immediately and Matthew Terrel was there. The man was built like a linebacker, all muscles and lean strength, and looked nothing like the corporate lawyer and co-C.E.O. of LynTech. He was dressed all in black, his blond hair the only lightness about him at that moment. His face was grim.

Matt was the closest thing to a good friend that Zane had had for the past seven years, and Zane trusted him completely. He'd know what to do about this. "Matt—" Zane motioned to Mr. Stiller. "Edward Stiller, he just got here from Florida."

Matt crossed the room, his dark eyes narrowed, his hand held out to the attorney. "Mr. Stiller," he said in his deep voice. "Matthew Terrel." He shook hands with the man, then looked at Zane. "What's the emergency?"

"Listen to what Mr. Stiller has to say, then we'll get to work."

Matt moved closer, sank down in the other leather chair

and sat forward, leaning toward Mr. Stiller. "Okay, bring me up to speed."

While Stiller and Matt talked, Zane stood and went back to the windows. He listened to the two men as he frowned at his image bouncing back at him in the floor-to-ceiling windows. He saw a tall, lean man who'd stripped off his gray suit coat, unbuttoned his dark vest and rolled up the sleeves of his dress shirt—his maroon tie having been discarded two minutes after he'd arrived at work this morning. He looked tense, with eyes that were shadowed and unreadable. *A cold man,* Suzanne had called him. He hadn't argued the point. To think she wanted him anywhere near a child was ludicrous. It's the last thing she would have wanted.

If you don't want children, then we don't have a future. Her words that last day rang in his memory.

Then his words, the bare truth. No games. No empty promises or lies. "I've never wanted children. I don't want them now."

Suzanne had backed away from him—the memory was a blur now, but her words remained. "You're self-centered and obsessed. And I made a terrible mistake marrying you." Then, as she was leaving, she'd added, "God help the child if you ever slip up and one appears in your life. You're as cold as stone."

Now her child *had* appeared in his life. It was wrong, very wrong—as wrong as his thinking he could be married.

Suzanne had never guessed at the anger that had been there in flashes when they broke up, the bitterness over the fact that he'd done something so badly that she'd had to leave. He hated failure. He hated admitting defeat. But he'd learned a long time ago to cut his losses. So he had. She'd found Weaver, and Zane had gone back to work—

"Zane?"

Matt's voice got him to refocus on the present, and he
spoke without turning, choosing instead to look at the re-
flection of Matt in the glass. Matt was getting to his feet,
but not moving from the other side of the desk. Stiller was
sitting forward with his briefcase open on the desk again.
Matt had the will in his hand.

"It's ridiculous, isn't it?" he asked Matt.

Matt shrugged. "Ridiculous or not, the wording's solid
in the will. As it stands, you're all the kid has until they
can find a relative."

"Suzanne wouldn't have wanted me within twenty feet
of any child she had. You know that."

"She obviously didn't think she'd be gone at thirty, or
that this situation would become a reality. She probably
meant to change her will. She just didn't get the chance.
There has to be someone out there, a relative of some sort
that will take the child and raise him. But for now..." Matt
exhaled. "What do you want from me?"

Zane turned to the two men, but looked right at Matt.
"What do you figure my options are?"

"You could fight it—argue that you're divorced, you no
longer have any part in Suzanne's life in any way, shape
or form, and you refuse to get involved, despite the will."

"And if I do that?"

"The boy will go into foster care with the county or
state, until they find a home for him...*if* they find a home
for him."

His last glimpse of Suzanne had been in the attorney's
office, she'd been obviously pregnant and holding onto Dan
Weaver's hand. There hadn't even been anger by that time.
She'd wanted everything he hadn't wanted, but even if
there hadn't been real love there, if there was such a thing,
he knew that he'd cared about her. Despite what Suzanne
had thought, he had cared.

"Option B?" he asked.

"Pay to have the boy taken care of until a relative can be found."

He frowned at Matt. "Okay. That's doable, very doable."

Matt glanced at Mr. Stiller. "How about that? A nanny or a service or a baby-sitter, to take care of the boy? That would work, wouldn't it?"

Mr. Stiller closed his briefcase. "It's up to Mr. Holden. I'll have the child brought out here, and take care of making final payment to the baby-sitter out there. Then Mr. Holden can—"

"Brought out here?" Zane cut in. "As in bringing him to the west coast?"

"Exactly," the man said, looking right at Zane. "He can't stay in Florida."

"Why not? We can do what Matt said—get a nanny to care for him—"

"Well, if you or Mr. Terrel or your representative wants to go to Miami and take care of things, we can—"

"We can't. You do it. I'll pay for it."

"That's very generous of you, sir," the man said with a shake of his head. "But I'm an attorney with a small staff that is already stretched to the limit, and I don't have the time to do that sort of thing. Perhaps you can find someone else to do it out there?"

Zane looked at Matt, and the big man shrugged. "That's too damn complicated. It'll take up a lot of precious time just getting there. Then there's setting it all up and monitoring the situation—"

"Whatever you decide on, you have one week to do it," Mr. Stiller said abruptly. "The sitter can keep the boy until next Monday. He'll have to be situated by then."

"Option C," Matt said to Zane.

"Which is?"

"Bring him out here. Set him up with a nanny at your penthouse at the hotel or wherever. That's a hell of a lot less complicated than trying to do this long distance."

Zane realized right then that he had no desire to see the child, much less live with him, even temporarily. But he knew that Matt was right. It was logical. And how hard could it be?

"Okay, we'll do that." He looked at Mr. Stiller. "Make all the arrangements for the trip, then contact us with the details. I'll pay for everything. We'll keep a discussion of what Suzanne left for the child for later. Just continue the search for a relative."

"Of course," the man said, snapping his briefcase shut, then gripping it by the handle as he glanced at Matt. "Who will be handling the legal aspects of this situation?"

Matt glanced at Zane. "What about the legal department?"

"I want to keep this close to home," replied Zane. "I'll owe you if you make sure things are set up properly."

Matt nodded, then looked at Mr. Stiller. "My office is two doors down on the right. I'll meet you in there in a couple of minutes."

Matt showed the man out, then closed the door after him. Zane sank back down in his chair. Matt was studying him narrowly as he came back to the desk. But he didn't sit down this time. He looked down at Zane.

"Just what you needed, huh?"

"I knew this acquisition would be trouble, but it's a hell of a lot more than I ever dreamed it would be." He looked down at the clutter on his desk, the yellow memo catching his eye. "It seems Mr. Lewis had a soft heart and an open wallet and never heard of the concept of saying no to anyone. No wonder no one around here understands that the wallet left with him and that there isn't any more money being passed out.''

"Are you okay, Zane?"

He motioned at the work he needed to do. "I would be, if I could get some uninterrupted time to get this done.''

"I wasn't talking about this business," Matt said. "I was talking about Suzanne's death.''

There was no obvious reproach in his tone, but Zane felt it nonetheless. "It was a shock, but it's the past—at least, it was until Stiller showed up.'' He sat back in his chair. "I appreciate your taking care of the paperwork for me.''

"What about the arrangements for the kid?'' Before Zane could say anything, Matt held up both hands, palms out. "No, I do not do that. Corporate things? I'm your man. Finding a nanny? No way.''

"Then, who?''

Matt snapped his fingers. "I know. Rita. She's got kids. She knows about those things. She'll do it.''

Matt's personal secretary was working overtime as it was, with all the work involved in the LynTech restructuring. "Will she have time for it?''

"She's such an efficient secretary that she's ahead of me half the time. No problem.'' He smiled, a lopsided expression. "Who would have thought being your business partner, president and co-C.E.O. would get me involved in a nanny search?''

"Certainly not me,'' Zane muttered, and looked down at the papers on his desk and spotted that annoying yellow page again. He reached for it. "One last favor before you go and talk to Stiller? Could you give this to Marlene on the way out and ask her to make sure this gets sent to Atherton at the day care center?''

Matt took it and frowned as he glanced at the paper.

"For Pete's sake. What is this, your third denial for funding?"

"Number three. This Atherton person who keeps sending them up—won't take no for an answer. Obviously a proponent of the old 'squeaky wheel gets the grease' theory. But there isn't any grease. And there won't be. Maybe he'll take the third strike and realize he's out of luck."

"Let's hope so," Matt said as he turned and headed for the door.

"Let me know what Rita finds," Zane called after him.

"Sure, no problem," Matt said over his shoulder, and then he was gone.

Zane sat back in the chair and refocused on the work in front of him—work that had been put there just before Mr. Stiller had shown up.

Since he'd taken over LynTech from the founder of the corporation, he'd all but lived at the office. LynTech, the core company in a conglomerate that did everything in computer technology from production to service to communications, was going to become lean and mean. Then Zane could break up the network and sell off the pieces for more than the total value of the whole. It was something he'd been doing for years with companies in trouble. He knew that LynTech was a gold mine, but it was going to take a hell of a lot of digging to get to the gold.

He started sorting through the financial reports, scanning the figures. Then he took out his gold pen and began to cross out figures, recalculating. In a few moments everything about children was forgotten.

Monday night

WHEN THE DREAM came to her, Lindsey Atherton had the clear thought that for as long as she could remember, the only constant in her life had been that dream. It had first started when she was too young to be able to tell anyone, and had stayed with her. At twenty-seven, she still had it. She'd never understood it, and she'd never figured out how to stop it.

When she was little, it had always started with her in complete darkness, nothing around her as she floated alone. No sounds, no contact with anything or anyone, and no sensations except total and complete safety.

She'd felt safe at first, snuggled into the blackness, embraced by the shadows. A tiny place that was all hers. A welcome place—until the sounds started. The faint jiggling of a doorknob, the click of a lock, then the creak of hinges. It was then that everything changed. Lights exploded around her and robbed her of the safety she craved.

When she was little, she was certain it was the boogeyman who had found her in her safe place—that he'd come to get her. But as she got older, the dream changed. There was no boogeyman. And the darkness didn't mean safety anymore. It meant she was cut off, isolated. And the noises outside were those of a person. Someone about to rescue her.

She never knew who it was. She just knew that whoever was there had found her, and she was going to be okay. But that never happened. There was hope when the sounds came, when the creaking of hinges echoed through her. Then the light.

But there was no one there.

When the dream came that night, it was the same, except that when the light came, she had a flashing vision of someone—a shadow backed by the brilliance. She reached out, but there was nothing. She was wakened suddenly, cut off again, isolated. And it hurt. It was a dream, but she woke breathing hard, thinking that if she had just been able to keep the dream going, she would have seen who was there.

But she couldn't. She woke suddenly, violently, and she bolted upright in bed, the sounds of her gasping breaths echoing in the high-ceilinged bedroom area of her loft. Moonlight filtered in through the high, transit windows, and she could make out the dark outlines of the furniture. There was the opening in the partial walls that led out to the living area. She was alone.

She scrambled out of bed, padded barefoot across the floor to the bathroom, and fumbled for the light switch by the door. The illumination from an old-fashioned tulip fixture over a pedestal sink and mirror made her blink at first. It exposed the claw-footed tub, the old-fashioned shower stall and the tank-topped toilet. And it exposed her.

She saw herself in the mirror, and gripped the sides of the sink. Her cap of blond hair was mussed around a decidedly pale face. The only color she had was from her eyes, a deep amber hue with smudges under them. Quickly, she turned on cold water, splashed her face with it, and was unnerved that her hands were shaking.

This was stupid. She had that dream so often, it was in some ways like an old friend to her. But she never got used to the end. And now that was changing. She was certain she'd caught a glimpse of someone. She shook her head, then grabbed a white towel and pressed it to her face.

She wasn't six years old anymore, locking herself in a closet because that was the only place she felt safe. And she wasn't a teenager anymore, dreaming of a knight in shining armor rescuing her and whisking her away with him. She was an adult who was making her own life, doing her own rescuing by working hard, getting an education and trying to make a difference in the world.

She'd fought so long to find the stability she now had.

She had a good life. She loved her job, and being alone was okay. It was fine. It was what she wanted. She tossed the towel to one side and went back into the bedroom area of the loft, but instead of going back to bed, she crossed to an old-fashioned desk by the far windows. She snapped on the lamp on the scarred wooden surface, sank down in the padded office chair and raked both hands through her short hair.

She wasn't going to sleep again tonight, so she'd get something done. The first thing she saw was the request forms for funding. She reached for the yellow sheets of paper, found a pen, then started to fill in the fourth form she'd completed in the past month. The other three forms asking for more money for programs in the day care center at LynTech had all brought rejections from the new powers-that-be—the last one just hours old. But she wasn't giving up.

She methodically filled out all the spaces again, almost knowing by heart what to put in each place. Mr. Lewis had loved the program. He'd brought her to LynTech to build it and fine-tune it, and he'd been behind her a hundred percent. But he was retired now, and the company had been bartered off to the highest bidder.

The head man, a person called Zane Holden, didn't love anything but money. He didn't care about anything but the bottom line, and the word was that a lot of jobs and programs were going to be eliminated. She hesitated, then, on a line that said, Reasons for Request, she printed, *The well-being of the children of the employees of LynTech Corporation.*

Well-being? She could have put safety, happiness, security and helping them not have horrible dreams. So many reasons. She sat back. "To keep the boogeyman away," she whispered. But a man like Zane Holden wouldn't know about boogeymen, or children who lived with the fear of being alone. No, he wouldn't understand that. Not many people did.

And improved work performance for the parents, she added, knowing she was trying to appeal to the only thing Holden seemed to care about. Then she scrawled, *L. Atherton, Project Director* on the bottom and dated it.

Number four. Maybe that would be the charm. She put the papers in her folder, set them by her purse, then went back across the space, avoiding the bed and heading for the bathroom again. A hot shower, a book to read. She could get through the night. Then, first thing in the morning, she was going to submit the request again. But this time she was going to do it in person. No more company mail and waiting days to find out.

She stripped off her sleep shirt, turned on the shower and stepped under the hot water. As she turned, the light from the bathroom seemed to stream into the shower stall, cutting through the shadows, like in the dream. She shook her head, then lifted her face to the spray and closed her eyes.

She needed to concentrate on life, and what she had to do. As the water streamed around her, she went over and over what she was going to say to Zane Holden when she finally met with him. The rumor was that he didn't have a heart, but she didn't buy into that. He just didn't understand.

If she said the right thing, if she put things in the right way, she knew that he'd understand the importance of what she was doing. She'd talk until he saw her point of view. And after all, it was for the children. Even a heartless man had to care about the children.

Chapter Two

Wednesday

Lindsey found out it was easier said than done to get a face-to-face appointment with Zane Holden. She persevered through frustrating phone calls to his office, and being told he was "unavailable." But she refused to take no for an answer. Stubbornness. That had always been one of her saving qualities. A quality that had helped her survive everything she'd gone through. What she had, she'd fought for—and the funding for the center was something she'd fight for.

Finally, she got some satisfaction when Zane Holden's secretary capitulated slightly with "I'll see if there's any way to work you in."

Lindsey tasted a degree of victory when the woman came back on the line. "Mr. Holden can see you for a brief meeting tomorrow morning at nine o'clock."

A brief meeting? She'd take anything she could get. "Thank you. I'll be there," she said, hung up the phone in her office at the center and let out a cheer. "Yes!" she yelled and raised both hands, curling them into fists over her head.

"Shhhh, keep it down."

She turned and found Amy Blake, her coordinator, at the open door of the small office. The tiny woman, dressed in jeans and a pink sweater, her long dark hair pulled back from a fine-featured face in a single braid, had her arms full of stuffed animals.

"Oh, sorry. I thought you were gone," Lindsey said.

"Taylor's still in the nap room, and I'm letting her sleep while I pick up a bit. What's going on?" She came farther into the room as a smile grew on her face. "Come on, tell me. That sounded like a victory yell. We've got funding? We can get a new van? Start the Mommy and Me program?"

"No, we don't have any of that—at least, not yet. But I have a meeting with Mr. Zane Holden, head of LynTech, tomorrow at nine in the morning."

"That's great," Amy said, but the smile wasn't as big now. Lindsey knew that Amy had more to lose than she did if the center had to make drastic cuts. She barely made enough now to support herself and her daughter. But being employed here was the only way Amy could be with her tiny daughter and still work.

"At least I can talk to the man face-to-face instead of through notes. It took me forever to convince his secretary, 'the human iceberg,' that I needed to see him in person." Her sense of victory was starting to fade under nervous anticipation of the meeting. "I've got prep to do before the meeting."

"You know everything inside and out."

"I'd better," she sighed as she smoothed the brown slacks she was wearing with a beige silk shirt. She looked around her cluttered office. Boxes and bare board shelves didn't make it look very professional, but it was usable. Organization was not her strong suit, but she had to be completely in control for her meeting. "I need to go over the figures to make them look better. Maybe take away a few little things to make him think I'm compromising. But I'll get the most important things, believe me. I'll try to get you more money, too."

"If you can do that, it would be terrific."

Lindsey couldn't spot her clipboard with her list of what they needed, then remembered she'd had it out in the play area. "I'll give it my best shot," she said as she moved past Amy and into the hallway to head for the main part of the center. She stepped into the space with clouds painted on the pale blue ceilings, walls alive with murals depicting various fairy tales, and dividers that looked like rows of giant crayons.

It was quiet now, but for ten hours a day the center was alive with children who desperately needed the care, children whose working parents knew that their children were close by and well taken care of, and children who weren't coming home to empty houses and hiding in closets just to feel safe.

She spotted her clipboard on one of the tiny mushroom tables near the napping area on the far side of the room. "What to cut," she whispered as she crossed to pick it up. Then she sank down on one of the mushroom-shaped stools by the flower petal tables in the story area. It was an awkward place to sit with her leggy five-foot seven-inch frame. But the only adult chair in the playroom was a rocking chair filled with children's toys.

Amy was there, talking quickly in a low voice. "Do you think he'll go for it? He's rejected three attempts."

She stared at the lists she'd made. It would be hard to cross off anything, but she could start with a few of the extras. The new storybooks. The new sleeping pads. They could make do for now. But they did need the stove for the kitchen area, and they needed a better van for transporting school-age kids to the center so they could wait here for their parents to get off work.

"I'm going to get everything I can," she said, "even if the meeting is going to be 'very brief.'"

"If anyone can talk Mr. Holden into giving us the funding, it's you. Look what you did with Mr. Lewis. He didn't even know about day care centers until you met him and convinced him to start this place."

"He was anxious to make things better for his employees, not just worried about how much profit he could make. I just wish he were still here, instead of running all over Europe chasing that daughter of his." She grimaced up at Amy. "Last I heard, he was in France with her celebrating her third engagement in three years and no marriages. Now, that has to be some sort of record."

Amy shook her head. "I heard she'd gone through tons of colleges, too, and got kicked out of most of them. She's running her parents a merry chase."

"And I think she's part of the reason he retired and sold out to the Holden group." Lindsey exhaled. "Tell me, what's the point in getting a corporation like this, then cutting it up into little pieces and selling the pieces off to the highest bidder?"

"Money, Lindsey. It's the money. It's called doing business for a profit."

Lindsey wrapped her arms around herself in a hug, rubbing the flats of her hands on her upper arms. "I don't care what it is, as long as it doesn't ruin this program." She looked at the other woman, as dark and tiny as she was leggy and blond, her face tight with concern. "I won't let anyone destroy this program."

"They've already started the layoffs. You might not have a choice."

Lindsey hadn't had a choice about not having parents, or being in foster homes, or being alone and scared, but she'd had a choice in making a life for herself when she was old enough to be on her own. And she had a choice now.

"No, I've got a choice. I can fight or I can give up. I'm not giving up. I'm not going to let Zane Holden ignore us any longer. For better or worse, he'll have to deal with me in person."

"Isn't that like trying to reason with the Big Bad Wolf? All he knows is killing and eating." Amy smiled. "I don't mean he's a killer, but you know what I mean. He's ruthless."

"Do you think he has kids?"

"Do people like that breed?"

Lindsey laughed at that, and it felt good to find humor in something at that moment. "Forced sterilization is against the law," she said. "But, God help his kids. If they don't perform up to expectations, he probably has them downsized."

A tiny voice came from the other room: "Mommy?" Amy turned and called out, "Taylor, Mommy's out here, in the playroom." She looked back at Lindsey. "I need to get her, then head on home. How about you?"

"I have to face the Big Bad Wolf, and I'm not going to end up as his dinner. So, I have to have a good battle plan in place. I think I'll be here for a while."

"Don't stay too late. You've looked tired all day." She frowned at her. "Are you sleeping okay?"

Lindsey shrugged away the dream that disrupted her nights. "I don't sleep well at the best of times, but I know what we need around here. I'll get everything I can for the kids."

"I know you will. If anyone'll fight for the kids, you will. It's a shame you don't have any."

Lindsey shrugged that off, too. "Some have kids, some help kids, some do both. I think I'm meant to help." She pushed aside the idea of her own kids. She didn't even have the prerequisite—someone she loved enough to want to be with forever. A child deserved parents that wanted to be parents, not parents forced to be parents. "Tomorrow morning at nine, Zane Holden had better be ready for me."

"Well, word is his co-C.E.O. runs interference for him. You'd better watch out for him. His name's Terrel. I don't know his first name, but he sounds as if he's built like a linebacker. You know the kind—no neck, huge?"

Lindsey stood, caught a glimpse of herself in an acorn-shaped mirror. She really should wear a suit tomorrow, something very businesslike. Something Zane Holden would take seriously. There was no way he'd take her seriously looking like this, in casual clothes, with fine blond hair that insisted on curling at the worst moments, no make-up and freckles. Freckles definitely didn't engender confidence or fear.

"Okay, if I have to, I'll go through Terrel, but Mr. Holden is going to listen to me."

"Mommy?"

Lindsey looked around at a tiny little girl in a rumpled pink pinafore, standing in the arched doorway to the napping room. Taylor looked just like her mother—a two-year-old version with wispy dark hair, dark eyes heavy from her nap, and clutching an oversize white teddy bear that had seen better days.

She ran over to Amy, who scooped her up and hugged her. "I'm sorry, honey. I was talking. We're going home now."

"And I'm going to get to work," Lindsey said, brushing

the child's silky hair with her hand. "See you both tomorrow."

Amy looked over the child in her arms at Lindsey. "Is there anything I can do?"

"Just cross your fingers," Lindsey said. "And hope that the Big Bad Wolf is all bark and no bite."

"We'll go out the back after I get my things in the kitchen," Amy said. "Good luck."

Lindsey watched Amy head into the back area, and, moments later, heard the back exit click open, then shut. In the silence, she took the clipboard back to her office, and, as she passed a mural of Little Red Riding Hood and the Big Bad Wolf on the way, she stopped.

She and Amy had painted it, and the Big Bad Wolf was looking a bit worn and not so threatening, with chips in the color at his legs, and scuff marks where tricycle handles had brushed against him over and over again. The poor old thing looked pretty vulnerable to her.

She tapped the wolf on its painted snout just above his toothy snarl. "You won't know what hit you when I get through with you," she said. And hoped she was right.

Thursday

ZANE SAT ALONE in his office, the drapes still pulled to shut out the glare of the morning sun. In the dusky light with the blue flicker of the computer screen to his right, he stared into the shadows…thinking. He did his best thinking alone in the morning, before the full blast of the day hit him. He swiveled slowly back and forth, and admitted he did most things in his life alone. He always had.

Suzanne had known that and complained about it. Now her child was cluttering up things, making him trip over logical thinking and rational reasoning. If there were two things he valued in his line of work, they were ration and logic. Lead with the head, he'd always thought, and shove emotions out of the way.

He turned away from the stack of papers and computer, stood and crossed to open the drapes. But before he could pull back the fabric, there was a flash of light behind him.

"Hey, Zane," Matt said. "I thought you'd be at things early."

He turned without opening the curtains toward the big man who, once again, was dressed all in black, from a turtleneck sweater to slacks and boots. "I've been here since six. I was just going to call you to work out a time as soon as possible for us to meet with Sol Alberts's people." He undid the buttons at the cuffs of his gray dress shirt and slowly rolled the sleeves up as he talked. "I have a good feeling about Alberts's group. A real good feeling."

"Okay, let's do it. Tomorrow. I'll make time."

"Great. Now, what's up with you?"

He came over to the desk. "I was just going to update you on the nanny situation."

Matt didn't look pleased as he dropped down in one of the two chairs by the desk. "I thought you said it was under control," Zane said.

"That turned out to be a bit of an overstatement. Rita's on it, doing interviews, but it appears that none of the nannies that have been sent out so far from the agency is right for this situation."

He sat forward, elbows on the desk. "How can a nanny that's trained to be a nanny not be right?" Zane didn't have the patience for this right now. "What about that woman who showed up yesterday afternoon—the one I saw talking to Rita in the hallway by your office with that silly hat and sensible shoes? She looked like a real Mary Poppins type."

"More like Attila the Hun, according to Rita." Matt leaned forward. "Listen, I don't know one end of a kid from another, but Rita's got three children. She knows what she's doing. That's why I asked her to take care of this for you. And she says that none of the applicants so far is acceptable."

"You trust her judgment?"

"Implicitly."

Zane exhaled as he sank back in his chair. Strong fingers raked though his slightly long, brown hair, and his gray-blue eyes narrowed. "Then, let her do her job. We have until Monday. How hard can it be to find a glorified baby-sitter? I had a dozen nannies when I was a kid—and a nanny's a nanny. My mother never had any trouble finding one."

"According to Rita, the first one was a ditz, another one thought that painting a child's face blue and dancing in circles would free his spirit. Another older lady wasn't up to the stress of a two-year-old. One was acting like a drill sergeant."

"Then came Attila the Hun?"

"She was about number five, I think."

Zane clasped his hands behind his neck, lacing his fingers together and staring hard at the shadowy face of his friend. "How are you with kids?"

Matt smiled immediately. "I told you, I don't know one end from the other. I never go near the little people. I like the way they look from a distance, but I don't like the way they act. Besides, I'm an attorney turned co-C.E.O.—at least, I was last time I looked."

"No chance of making an addendum to your job description?"

"None. Rita's got some interviews today, so she'll probably hit upon someone who she thinks is right for the job.

I just wanted to tell you this isn't easy and it's eating up a lot of time.''

"Yeah, I know. And we don't have extra time right now. Not with the Alberts group showing interest."

"That's my point."

"Well, when Rita meets the kid's flight on Monday morning, there has to be a nanny at the penthouse—a wonderful, intelligent, caring nanny who bears no resemblance to Attila the Hun."

Matt grinned at him. "This is crazy."

"Tell me about it."

The phone rang, and Zane reached for it. "Holden."

"Ron Simmons here. Have you got a minute?"

"Sure, hold on," he said, then hit the speaker button. "Okay, I'm here. Matthew Terrel's in the office, too."

"Good. I need input on the figures you sent over. Is there any chance you can come by for half an hour, no more?"

Zane looked at Matt, who shook his head. Zane sighed, then pointed to himself. Matt nodded. "Sure, your office?"

"Yes, over on Grammercy. I'll see if I can get someone from Alberts over, too."

"Great, see you as soon as I can get there."

He hung up, then sat back. "The first nibble on our offer."

Matt stood. "Let me know what happens," he said, then headed for the door. But before he could leave, he turned. "Zane, it's sunny out. Open the curtains."

"I'm leaving, anyway. Meet me back here after lunch, and we'll talk?"

"Sure, your office or mine?"

"If the nanny candidates are meeting with Rita at your place, come on up here. We'll have more privacy."

"Okay, see you then," Matt said, and left.

Zane rolled his sleeves down, buttoned the cuffs, then

reached for his jacket and briefcase. He headed out of the office. As he passed the reception area, he stopped long enough to lay his briefcase on the desk and to talk to his secretary. "Cancel appointments for the next two hours and reschedule anything important." He slipped on his jacket as he spoke. "Route any calls that you need to, to Mr. Terrel. Just hold down the fort," he said as he checked his inside pocket for his gold pen and cell phone.

He smoothed his vest, then picked up his briefcase, but before he could head back into the office to take his private elevator down, she stopped him. "Mr. Holden, all the elevators are down, even yours. One of the maintenance men just came in to say they'd be shut down for an hour."

"Oh, great." He headed for the outside door and the stairwell beyond the useless elevators. At least it was all down for the twenty flights.

Thursday

THE MOST IMPORTANT DAY of her life, and it had been messed up for her before it even got going. First, the dream came again, taking away her sleep. Then when Lindsey had finally gotten back to sleep, she'd almost slept through the alarm. She'd been so preoccupied with the paperwork to present during her meeting with Zane Holden, she'd forgotten the only suit she owned was stained from finger paint and still at the dry cleaners. She'd missed her bus to work and had had to call a taxi—and the final blow had been the elevators.

The future of Just For Kids was in her hands, and she was in the stairwell of the building trying to get from the sixth floor to the twentieth floor in five minutes. She hurried up, the envelope with her printout in one hand, her purse in the other. She prayed Mr. Holden would cut her some slack if she was a few minutes late.

It was probably his doing that the elevators were down. "A servicing problem," the maintenance man had told her when she'd stepped out of the day care center to head up to the corporate offices.

"Service problem, my eye," she muttered. It was Zane Holden's cuts—him and his "lean and mean" program to make the company more viable.

She'd agonized over her lists far into the night. She hoped she'd done them right. That they wouldn't be so much that they'd put him off, but that they would be strong enough for her to get what the center needed. An echoing click of her heels rang with each step on the metal stair treads as she passed the landing for the fifteenth floor. Five more floors. A bit more time to go over in her mind what she was going to say to Zane Holden, *if* she had any breath left when she got there.

Thank goodness she was used to the stairs. Every day since she'd hired on as director of the day care program, she'd taken the stairs for the exercise. But not because of broken elevators—at least, not until today.

"Damn it," she muttered, annoyed at this edge of frustration that was becoming an almost permanent thing since the company had changed hands. The man and his people had come into the company and upset everything, including all her plans for the kids.

She went over again what to say. *"Hello, Mr. Holden. I want your money."* That brought a slight smile to her face, a welcome reprieve from the ever-present tension. *"Just give me a blank check. Trust me, I'll make good use of it."* That sounded good. A blank check. She smiled again as she turned right, stepped onto the next landing. Then, as she turned to start up the next flight of stairs, she realized she wasn't alone in the stairwell. At the same time, she ran directly into someone coming down.

What little air she had in her lungs rushed out on impact, and for a breathless second she was surrounded by heat and confusion and muttered oaths. Her purse and the envelope went flying out of her hands, and she was losing her balance, flailing for support. She gulped air at the same time that two hands grabbed her by her shoulders. In the next second she was on her feet, breathing and steady. Then she looked up at a man, into a face that seemed to be all plains and angles. Gray-blue eyes made her breath catch again with their intensity.

Thankfully, he let her go right then, and he became a blur as he dropped to his haunches in front of her. She looked at him, at strong, ring-free hands picking up an expensive-looking briefcase laying by her well-worn purse and envelope.

She quickly stooped to get her purse. "I'm so sorry. I didn't see you there, until it was too late. I was so lost in thought, I wasn't watching." She got her purse, but when she reached for the envelope, he had it, and her hand tangled with his.

She felt heat, then the contact was gone, and she drew back. "I've got this appointment, and I was hurrying and I didn't look where I was going. This place is getting so screwed up, isn't it," she said as she stood and swiped at the only businesslike clothes she'd been able to find—tailored navy slacks and a plain white silk shirt.

"What's so screwed up?" he asked, the sound of his voice making her look up at him. This time she saw the whole man.

He was tall, four or five inches taller than she, wearing a perfectly cut dove-gray suit, a vest, a shirt in a lighter shade of gray, and a muted burgundy-colored tie. It all defined a whipcord leanness in the man. She looked higher. She saw a wide mouth with a disturbingly sensuous full bottom lip. Then she looked again into those eyes—eyes that were narrowed in a clean-shaven face touched by a suggestion of a tan. Gray or blue eyes, she couldn't tell exactly.

What she did know was that there was an intensity in the man, making him seem as if he was in motion even while standing still. That there was a subtle edge to him that she couldn't quite define—nor could she figure out why it made her so self-conscious.

His gaze flicked over her briefly before he looked her right in the eyes again.

Nerves. That was it. She was all nerves today. From lack of sleep and frustration and broken elevators and running up stairs and thinking of facing Zane Holden. No wonder an attractive man who seemed able to look right through her was upsetting her equilibrium.

He was speaking again, and she had to focus to understand that deep voice. "What were you saying about it being screwed up?"

"Screwed up?" she asked blankly, then remembered. "Oh, I meant the company, LynTech. I'm sorry. The elevators aren't working. They said it was for service, but from what I've heard, they were probably told to shut them down every day for a while to save money. Anything to cut costs."

She looked down at the envelope still in his hand. "That's mine. I dropped it."

He held it out to her, and she took it back. "Thanks."

"Cutting costs is bad?" he asked.

"No, of course not. But the word is, he's cutting and cutting. God knows where it'll stop."

"Him?" he asked, apparently as fond of single-word

questions as she was of rambling. It was as unsettling as it was oddly attractive.

"Zane Holden and his cohorts."

"Cohorts?" he asked, a flash of what must have been a smile touching his mouth. It was a shockingly endearing expression that lasted for less than a heartbeat before it was gone.

"Okay, *associates,* or whatever you want to call the lot of them. They bought the corporation from Mr. Lewis, a nice old man. Everyone loved him. Then he retired." She frowned, focusing past this man in front of her and thinking about Mr. Lewis and his unconditional support for the day care program. "Now Holden and his…associates are in charge and making cuts everywhere they can, I guess. I've just talked to a few employees, and I know that there've been layoffs. When Mr. Lewis owned the company, there were never any layoffs. But now, well, things are changing, or at least being altered drastically."

"Everything changes in time," he murmured.

Time! She glanced at her watch. She was out of time, wasting what little she had talking to this man. And she had no idea who he was, even. She'd said more than enough. "Oh, shoot," she muttered.

"What?"

"I had an appointment and I'm late. I need to get going." She wondered something that came out of nowhere. What would he look like if he smiled—a complete expression that lingered? The man was distracting her from what she had to do, and that bothered her a lot. She didn't allow distractions in her life, especially not from someone with eyes that she could get lost in…if she let herself. And she wouldn't, she decided firmly.

But that resolution lasted only until those blue eyes flicked over her again. Their impact was not diminished.

"And you're who?" he asked in a low voice.

"I'm late," she said, snatching at reason and logic, and making herself move past him. "Sorry," she called back as she hurried away and up the stairs.

She heard a soft, "No problem," and as she rounded the next corner, she glanced back for just a moment. He was still there watching, and it jolted her. She gripped the handrail, looked away from him and climbed faster, fighting the oddest feeling that she was running away, instead of hurrying toward her appointment.

Chapter Three

But by the time she got to the twentieth floor, the man was forgotten. She stepped out into a lavishly appointed area. Paintings on the wall, carpet underfoot and wood accents everywhere—they were a far cry from tile floors and a Big Bad Wolf with chipped paint.

She stopped to catch her breath, to center herself and focus. And since there was no blue-eyed man anywhere around, she gathered her composure quickly. Then she headed down the corridor to a massive door with a discreet plate on it: Z. Holden.

Bracing herself, she stepped into an even more lavish area and crossed to a marble desk facing the door in the reception room.

"Lindsey Atherton to see Mr. Holden," she said to a woman as plain as the space around her was lavish. A navy dress, no makeup and very short gray hair were untouched by jewelry or frills. When she spoke, it was the cold voice Lindsey remembered from the phone conversations.

"I'm sorry. Mr. Holden had to cancel."

Lindsey closed her eyes for a brief moment to get whatever control she could find. All of this hurrying for nothing. Running into that man. And Zane Holden wasn't here, anyway. "But I had an appointment."

"He got called away. He said to reschedule."

She grabbed at anything. "I'll wait."

"No, he won't be back for quite a while."

The woman opened a leather-bound book in front of her, and Lindsey could see it was an appointment ledger. Names and notes in every hour frame were highlighted with different colors—red, blue, green and yellow. The hour blocks were all filled up to five in the afternoon.

"Let's see," the woman was saying as she ran her finger over the pages. "If you wish to reschedule, he could work you in...hmm, uh, let's see." She flipped some pages. "How about two weeks from yesterday at eight-thirty in the morning." She looked at Lindsey. "Should I pencil you in?"

She knew her jaw was clenching, but she nodded. "Yes, please, pencil me in."

She watched the woman write. "Atherton" in a space, then highlight it with yellow. She didn't think she wanted to know what a "yellow" appointment meant. Instead, she handed the envelope to the woman. "Could you please see that Mr. Holden gets this?"

The woman's expression stayed neutral as she took the envelope, laid it on the desk by a stack of letters, then date and time stamp it. She looked back at Lindsey. "Is there anything else I can help you with?"

"No, I guess not," she said, then turned and left before she did or said something totally irrational.

She hurried out into the hallway and back to the stairwell. Inside, with the door closed, she fought every urge in her to scream at the top of her lungs. Weeks to wait. Two full weeks. Until the day before Thanksgiving. She inhaled deeply, exhaled, willed herself to calm down, then headed back downstairs.

She went slowly, taking the time to get a grip on herself

doors, then turned to go to the elevators. ...e in a maintenance uniform, on his knees ...en panel to one side, working on something ...'t tell me—they're down again?'' she asked ...ached him.

...ack on his heels with a huge screwdriver in his ...looked up at her, his middle-aged face flushed ...efforts. "No, ma'am, they're working fine," he ...I'm just doing some fine-tuning on them."

...od. It seems they never work when you need them

...e got to his feet, pushed the screwdriver into a tool belt ...was wearing with grease-smudged overalls, then picked ...a rag and rubbed his soiled hands with it. "You and ...veryone else complaining about them." He lowered his voice. "Even him up there," he said, rolling his eyes upward.

"Him?"

"Holden. One of the big guys. He was just saying he wanted them kept in good working order, as if we'd been trying to keep them in *bad* working order."

"Mr. Holden's still here?"

"Yeah, that guy and Mr. Terrel—they're around at all hours. They work all the time."

So, he was here. And she knew, according to his appointment ledger, that he stopped appointments by five. She wasn't going to go home and eat with a cat. Not when Zane Holden was still in the building and possibly available. Maybe she wouldn't have to wait two weeks to see him, after all.

"Thanks," she said to the man. "Thanks a lot."

He looked a bit confused, but nodded and smiled. "You're real welcome, ma'am."

She pushed the up button on the nearest elevator, and and the mixture of frustration and anger churning inside her. All a group of two- to five-year-olds needed was a furiously frustrated caregiver. When she got to the landing where she'd collided with the stranger, she paused; something laying in the corner of the top step caught her eye. She stopped, crouched down and saw a gold pen. A very expensive gold pen.

She picked it up, fingered the smooth coolness and read the brand. Her heart sank. It had to be his, and it must have cost at least two hundred dollars. He'd had on a suit that must have cost a lot more than the pen. And he'd been coming down from the upper levels of the building.... Her heart sank.

"Damn it, damn it, damn it," she muttered as she pushed the pen into her purse and sank down on the top step.

He didn't just work here. He had to be an executive. An executive who had to know Zane Holden. "I'm dead," she breathed. All the things she'd said about Holden to him. She couldn't even remember now *what* she'd said. It was all a blur. But it hadn't been good. She knew that for sure.

Twenty-seven years old, and she still hadn't learned not to talk to strangers. Especially strangers coming down from the executive level. A flashing memory of those gray-blue eyes came to her, the intensity there, the way he asked her about Holden, the way she'd said something about a screw-up.

She didn't think she'd told him her name or why she was here, or where she was going or that her appointment was with Holden. She was sure she hadn't told him anything like that. At least, she hoped she didn't.

She stood, pushed the pen in her purse and tried to think positive thoughts. He didn't know anything, except that she was complaining—and any number of employees were complaining these days. *Every* employee was complaining. She was part of a very large crowd.

So, if she ever met up with the man again, she'd give him back his pen. He probably wouldn't even remember her. She had a feeling about him—he was the sort of person who had so much going on in his life that a clumsy woman in a stairwell who crashed into him wasn't memorable. Not for a man like that.

Friday

MATT STUCK HIS HEAD in Zane's office just before six and said, "Dinner anyone? I'm heading out at seven."

Zane sat back and tossed the cheap pen he'd had to use today onto the papers. "No, I've got too many loose ends here. One of them is finding that pen you gave me for Christmas. It's gone."

"I'll get you another one when we finish up here," he said.

Zane hated losing something like that. "If it works out, I'll get you one, too."

"So, no dinner?"

"Dinner, but not with you. I'm meeting someone at eight."

"Business?"

"Half and half. Karen Blair. She's a publicist for Schlesinger and Todd. She's good at what she does. I've seen her work, and I've been thinking that LynTech could use some good publicity for a change."

"You can say that again. Wait until those cuts hit the light of day."

"Everyone shares in the cuts equally," Zane said. "We'll face the angry hordes when we have to."

"Okay. Oh, Rita had to [...] yesterday morning, so s[...] ing to take those, and [...] see you tomorrow," [...] hind him.

The room felt [...] it be a major product[...] found them easily, one a[...] to boarding school. It wasn't [...] fill, he thought as he reached for [...] it on a higher beam. The light made [...] ning a hand roughly over his clean shave[...] up the cheap plastic excuse for a pen, and [...] he hated losing things.

LINDSEY SPENT THE DAY doing schedules and tryin[...] ure out how to make the stove in the kitchen work[...] bit longer. But she kept thinking that waiting two weeks[...] speak to Zane Holden was two weeks too long. When she[...] looked up at almost six-thirty, she knew she couldn't go home for the weekend and put this out of her mind.

Two weeks? She couldn't wait. There was too much at stake. So on impulse she called up to Zane Holden's office on the off chance that he was still at work. All she got was a voice-mail response. She hung up on the synthesized voice, then stood, turned off the lights in her office, got her purse and went out into the deserted play area.

Everyone was gone. Everyone had things to do. *She* was going to go home to her cat. She'd make a meal for one. Watch some television. Go to bed. Have a dream. Wake up, and come back here tomorrow to do the touch-up painting on the murals. "Boy, a really exciting life," she said as she crossed the room, turned off the last light and stepped out into the corridor.

the car was there immediately. "Have a good night," she said as she got in.

"You, too," he called after her as the doors shut.

"That's the plan," she muttered as she pushed the button for the twentieth floor. "That's the plan."

As the elevator started upward, she felt her heart start to hammer in her chest. She wasn't dressed right. It was Friday—dress down day—which meant she was in jeans, a plain white shirt and chunky boots. And she had no makeup on.

She caught herself. All that didn't matter. It didn't matter that she wasn't dressed up. *She* didn't matter. This was an opportunity. And she was going to take it. She had to take it.

She steeled herself. There was so much at stake, but she had always been a fighter by necessity and knew that you didn't wait for an opening to magically appear. You made the opening, then you struck when the iron was hot.

This was her opening. It didn't mean that she liked it or that she wasn't afraid to take on the powers that be, but she had no choice.

ZANE HAD BEEN in a hurry. He'd worked longer than he'd intended to, and by the time he looked up it was six-thirty. Karen Blair didn't do "waiting" well, and he didn't want to have to test her on that—not before he found out what she had to say about the company's PR issue.

He'd grabbed his jacket and briefcase, then headed down the hall to Matt's office to drop off more figures he'd ironed out. He went through his partner's empty outer office and into Matt's personal space. The room was supposed to be a duplicate of his, a matching C.E.O. suite, but he never ceased to marvel at the almost Spartan condition Matt could maintain anywhere he went. Despite the thick carpeting, the wood touches and elaborate metal-and-glass desk, there wasn't a thing out of place. The massive desk held only a silent computer and a phone system. And Matt was gone.

The man didn't own anything, despite all the money he was making. He didn't "collect personal paraphernalia," he'd said once. He lived out of a suitcase, in a hotel room, and drove rental cars and worked. Zane knew Matt grew up poor, got to college on scholarships, passed the bar exam, and had real brains for business. And another thing he knew for sure—Matt was one of very few people that Zane trusted, really trusted.

As he tossed the paperwork on the pristine desk, he heard the sound of a door opening. Matt wasn't gone, after all. Zane crossed to the door and stepped out of the inner office, but he wasn't facing Matt.

There was the hint of a flowery scent in the air, a scent he remembered from somewhere. Then he saw a woman in the open doorway, and he remembered. The first time he'd seen her he'd had a flashing impression of a slender wisp of a woman in dark slacks and a white top, just before she'd crashed into him in the stairwell. Then, as he'd grabbed her to keep her from falling, there had been a sensation of fine bones, heat, softness, before she spoke and everything had shifted.

A woman who had no use for Zane Holden and his "cohorts" had been a blip on his day at the time. But now she was here, and in the harsh overhead lights he took in details. Jeans defined slender hips and long legs, a shirt tucked in at the slim waist, hinted at high breasts. Then he looked up into her face. Incredible amber eyes were huge with shock, and sudden color flooded her face, emphasizing the fact that she wore no discernable makeup and that she had freckles, real freckles. A woman who blushed and had freckles. He almost smiled. Then he remembered what

she'd said about him. He didn't smile. Instead, Zane went
a bit closer, flicking his gaze over her feathery blond cap
of hair, her straight nose, those freckles, pale pink lips
softly parted with surprise—then back to her eyes.

"It's you," she breathed. "Oh, shoot, I'm so sorry. I
never should…" She bit her pale bottom lip. "I really owe
you an apology for what I said the other day," she said,
then started fumbling in her purse. "I didn't know who you
were and I was just saying things, and…" She was talking
quickly as she rummaged in her purse, then suddenly said,
"Aha. Here it is."

She pulled something out of her purse, then held it up
to him. His gold pen. "Where in the hell did you get that?"

"You dropped it on the stairs when we…when I ran into
you." She came closer, and held it out to him. "I found it
and didn't know who you were."

That color came again. She was blushing, which made
her freckles vivid. When was the last time he'd seen someone blush? He didn't have a clue.

"Anyway, I kept it and was going to give it back, and
now…" Her voice sort of faded.

He glanced at the pen in her hand—a hand with slender
fingers, no polish, short, oval nails and no rings. Then he
shifted his briefcase to the same hand holding his suit coat
and took the pen. He was vaguely aware of a sense of heat
in the rich metal. Her heat. "I was looking all over for it."

"I bet you were," she said as she moved back a bit. "I
mean, it had to have cost a fortune, and I know if I had a
pen like that I'd about die if I lost it."

He fingered the pen. "You came here to bring it back to
me?"

"Oh, no, of course not. I didn't even know who you
were, obviously. I mean, if I had, I certainly…it would have
been…" She shrugged. "Okay, let's just get this over with.

I'm sorry for saying what I said. I had no idea who you were, or I never would have said it. Can we forget it and start all over again?''

He doubted he'd forget that reproach in her voice, but starting over with her had its own appeal. "Okay. If you aren't up here to bring back the pen, why are you here?"

"I was told you were still here, you and..." She shrugged. "I had an appointment the other morning, when we met. And it was cancelled, so I came up now. I went to the other office and no one was there, and I thought I was too late. I'm so glad I found you."

She talked quickly and breathlessly, and he had to really listen to follow what she was saying. Being found by this woman wouldn't be all bad, he thought, but he didn't have a clue why she'd be looking for him if it wasn't for the pen. Unless she just wanted to tell him off even more. "If you're here to tell me more about the shortcomings of the company, I—"

"Oh, no, of course not. It's the child care," she said as she came closer, stirring the air again.

Child care? Oh, it couldn't be. She was a nanny? It seemed crazy, but in a way it made sense. She'd been coming for her interview with Rita when they ran into each other in the stairwell. Rita had cancelled.

He was stunned. She didn't look like any nanny he'd ever had. "Child care," he repeated as he watched her stop by the secretary's desk.

She exhaled softly, obviously calming herself, then spoke in a breathy voice. "Children are so important, aren't they."

Yes, he could see her as a nanny. Young enough to do the job and obviously interested enough to come back this late on a Friday evening for another interview. He looked

"Okay, quality time and care.

...ack that he seemed to be agreeing. ...ope. "Children are so precious, and ...at. I guess you could use that term ...m getting a bit sick of it. It's used as ...the child for the rest of the time. But ...tion and reassurance and—"

...r own words, when he unexpectedly ...oor to Zane Holden's office complex, the ...e'd left moments ago. "Let's go through ...as he pushed the door open and went inside. ...nt she thought Zane Holden might be around, ...d talk directly to him. But the offices were as ...y had been earlier. She followed this man, who ...human whirlwind, drawing everything in his path ...n him. Including her. She crossed the conspicu-...scale den-like area and followed him through a ...the far side.

...y were in a positively expansive room with walls of ...a desk that looked as if it floated over a huge chunk ...arble and metal, and pictures everywhere. But these ...e pictures of buildings, of partially completely blue-...nts. There were two solid walls, and she didn't have a ...ue how they could "go through" here and get anywhere. ...ut Terrel didn't stop. He tossed his jacket on a very messy desk, reached for some papers, put them in his briefcase. He slipped on the jacket and tugged at his cuffs as he looked at her.

"Is it time for questions?" he asked.

"Excuse me?"

He took the pen out of the briefcase, tucked it into an inner pocket of his jacket, then closed the case. "You stopped talking, so I assumed it was question time."

into those amber eyes and wondered if he'd literally run into the answer to his problems.

"Yes, very important." He glanced at his watch, regretting that he didn't have time to do the interview himself, and he just hoped that Rita was still around here somewhere. "It's getting late and I need to get going. Let me make a call and see who's still here."

Lindsey knew he was going to push her off onto someone else. He might have agreed to start all over again, but he didn't want to talk to her. The thing was, she wanted to talk to him. Matthew Terrel. Holden's partner. Equal to Holden. Co-C.E.O. This man in front of her looked the equal of anyone. His expensive, pale-blue shirt hugging broad shoulders, a darker tie perfectly knotted. His dark gray jacket off and over one arm. A watch on his wrist that she could probably pawn and use to buy a new car.

The man was power. He certainly would do, since she'd missed the man she'd come to see. Yes, he'd do very nicely. But he was trying to get away. He put the briefcase on the desk, laid the pen on top, then reached for the phone on the secretary's desk.

She spoke quickly. "Why don't *we* just talk?"

He held the receiver in one hand and cast her a slanted look. "I have an engagement, and it is getting late. I don't have the time."

"Since I'm here and you're here, and this is so important, why don't we both just take a few minutes and talk? This isn't something that can be put off much longer."

He studied her narrowly, bringing back that uneasiness she'd first experienced in the stairwell. Abruptly he turned, punched in some numbers, listened, then hung up and turned to her with an exasperated rush of breath. "I guess you're right. It's just you and me."

This wasn't a good beginning, him begrudgingly agreeing to talk to her. But at least he hadn't turned her away. "I think this is for the best. It actually saves time, instead of going through too many people. It gives everyone a clearer picture when it's not diluted by too many renditions of the facts, don't you think?"

He had the most annoying habit of pausing before he responded to her, and it made her nerves even more raw. The man would make a very effective bodyguard for Holden. He probably just made the people trying to get past him die from nervousness. She knew she was close to that herself. His eyes were narrowed, assessing, and for the first time she noticed a hint of gray at the temples of his rich brown hair.

She forced herself to move closer and hold out her hand to him. "I'm Lindsey," she said simply, not about to make this any more formal than necessary. She didn't need more barriers between them. "Just a few minutes, that's all we'll need. Not a lot of time. A brief meeting."

He put the jacket over his shoulder, looping his finger in the collar, then took her hand in his. She'd known there was strength in his hands. She'd felt it when they'd kept her from falling in the stairwell. But she wasn't prepared for a jolt of awareness when his hand closed over hers. Or the heat that radiated from him. Or the sudden dryness in her mouth at the contact.

"A few minutes," he murmured.

She barely kept a sigh of relief from escaping as she eased her hand back. She needed to think clearly to make these few minutes count. And if she had contact with him, she just couldn't think with any clarity. On some level she wouldn't explore, the man was damn sexy. That was dangerous. Diverting. She didn't need that. "Okay, let's get right to the point," she said, gripping her purse strap that was looped over her shoulder.

"We'll have...

"Sure, th... but hon... long... nee...

Fo... smile... thought s... breath, brac... to pass, the s...

"Well, I can... he said.

"Sure, of course... making her neck ache... strap. Her hand was a... leather. Nerves. And she on... she had to do. "Should I jus... questions you have?"

"Sounds like a plan to me," h... flipped open his briefcase, dropped... pocket, closed the case and gripped it i... ahead," he said as he turned and strode p... door.

She hurried after him, out into the corri... quickly to keep up with his long stride. It really... a miracle to make this man stop, even for a few... Somehow she knew that this man was seldom still... there was always an impatience to get on with things.

"As I see it—" she started quickly, double stepping to get closer to him "—it's all about doing right by a child, giving the security that child needs, and giving that child attention in good surroundings. Making that child feel safe."

She wasn't sure he was even listening to her, until he

Was he serious? The man was totally unreadable when he looked at her, so she said the truth. "I was just looking at this place. I mean, it's big enough to house a small nation and then some. It's huge."

He glanced at the room. "I guess it is. But it's just an office."

"Nice office," she murmured.

"Can I ask you something?"

She was wasting precious time. "I'm not finished. I didn't mean to give you the impression that that was all there was."

"It's not about child care. I wanted to know where you heard the things you repeated in the stairwell."

Obviously the man wasn't about to forget, so she had to watch every word. Being vague was her best bet. "Why?"

"Well, from where I sit, you're not a long-term employee around here. You don't own stock in the company, do you?"

"Of course not."

"Then, where did you get all that from?"

She could say *How stupid do you think people around here are?* but she caught herself. Vague. She had to be vague and unoffensive. "I just listened to some people around here talking. It seemed to be the main topic of conversation. I told you, I didn't mean to offend. I have this terrible habit of just saying what I think, and I'm working on changing that."

He shrugged, tugging at his cuffs again. "Maybe you should," he said.

She felt fire in her face. But thankfully he never saw it. He turned to get his briefcase, picked it up and said, "Go on. We don't have much time."

Chapter Four

"Okay." But she couldn't think of what she'd been saying. She took a stab at it. "I...I really think I need to make the point that being there for a child is only part of the equation in good child care. This isn't glorified baby-sitting, no matter what you might think."

"It's not?" he asked, one dark eyebrow lifting slightly. "Sounds like it is to me."

"Well, I guess it could be called baby-sitting on one level, but it's much more than that. There are so many layers to child care, so many nuances that people don't see. But the kids know."

"You sound as if you've had a lot of experience with children. Any of your own?"

"No, but I've been involved—" He was on the move again, and she went with him, trying to regroup as he crossed to the door and snapped off the lights. Only the low light of a moon rising in the sky over Houston lit the room. "I love children and I want what's best for them," she said, stopping by him in the dimness. "That's why I wanted—"

"What are your qualifications for all of this?" He cut her off as he walked away from the outer door, heading across to the side of the room and a set of closed, double doors.

She hurried after him. "I have a degree in Early Childhood Development. I'm working on my masters."

As she talked, she watched him push a single brass button on the wall by the doors. The doors opened, and light spilled into the darkened room from a single elevator car. He stepped inside, stirring the air around Lindsey, then turned with the light at his back. For a moment he was a dark shadow with brightness behind him, and her dream was there. An open escape to something, or someone. And the light. She bit her lip hard to bring herself back to reality. This wasn't a dream. It was reality—sharp, hard reality. All she had to do was step into the car with him, turn, face the doors, go down twenty floors and keep talking. She could do that.

He was talking, saying something about being impressed that she was going for her master's degree. He shrugged, his image becoming clearer as her eyes adjusted to the light.

"I barely got a law degree."

She stood very still, trying to get air in her lungs, but having no luck at all.

He motioned her into the car. "Come on. It's working. Don't worry about it. They were supposed to have the whole system in top shape by today. I've used the stairs too much lately. We can talk about your education on the way down and figure out how overqualified you are for what you do."

She went forward into the small space. She liked small spaces—always had. They meant safety. But she wasn't sure it would be that way with this man.

Lindsey hugged her purse to her middle and turned to face the doors as they slid shut. They were mirrored doors that bounced back a slightly distorted version of Lindsey

Atherton next to Matthew Terrel. But they gave an illusion of more space.

"How long have you been interested in child care?" he asked, and it startled her slightly to hear his deep voice confined by the small space.

She'd been interested in how kids were treated ever since she'd found out it wasn't normal for a six-year-old to have to hide in a closet to feel safe when they were left in a house alone. But he didn't want to hear that any more than she wanted to share it with a stranger, so she gave him facts.

"Four years...professionally."

"Where do you stand on discipline?" he asked as the elevator started smoothly downward.

She could feel him watching her in the reflective doors, but didn't look at him. "Discipline?" she asked, easing her hold on her upper arms and staring at the place where the two doors met. "I...I think a child needs limits." She exhaled. "They need rules and they need to be responsible for their own actions."

"Agreed," he murmured.

She looked up at the floor indicator, the floors slipping by so quickly that this would be over almost before it had begun. She girded herself and turned to look at him and not at a secondhand image in the mirrored doors.

"Listen, we need to talk about the money," she said, getting right to the point before she ran out of time. "Unless there's enough money, this *is* nothing more than glorified baby-sitting, and you can get that for a couple of dollars an hour from some thirteen-year-old who wants to buy makeup at the mall after school. This is much more than that."

"So, if you throw money at it, you end up with baby-sitters who are getting their master's degrees?" he asked.

crossed Indian-style. She laid her purse by her and looked up at him. "No, I don't put that on my resume. It's a given in this business. Why would anyone work with kids if they didn't care about them?"

"I don't know," he said, watching that passion he'd glimpsed building in her again. And it was fascinating.

"Well, I do know, and I wouldn't have anyone working for me that didn't care. Amy Blake doesn't have any degrees, but she's all heart when it comes to kids. Her own child is so lucky, even without a father. She's totally rearranged her life to be with her little girl." She spoke in a rush. "She loves her own child, and she loves the other kids that she helps care for."

"She works for you?" That didn't make sense. Unless the agency had gotten so fed up with their failure to find a nanny for him that the boss had come for the final interview.

"She's the coordinator and the heart behind the center."

"The center?"

He heard her take a breath, then she pressed her hands palm down on her knees. "Okay, Mr. Terrel, since we're stuck here and you've asked me to talk, I'm going out on a limb with you. I know that you and Mr. Holden are partners or associates or whatever you want to call it, and you must trust each other completely. You have equal input. You're both in charge, from what I hear, and even though he's the one who's been doing the work on this, I think you can help me. Either by agreeing to what I need, or by talking to him about it and getting his agreement."

She thought he was Matthew? "I don't know what you think, but—"

"Oh, I'm sorry if I misunderstood the arrangement. I thought you were co-C.E.O.'s or something like that. I thought you could probably take care of this. Or if you can't, maybe you could convince Mr. Holden that Just For Kids needs the funding badly. We need more programs, more people to help, so the child-worker ratio comes down. It's imperative that we have more supplies for the younger children."

He couldn't have cut in if he'd wanted to: she was talking quickly, and her hands were moving to emphasize her points. So he just watched, listened and took in the fact that he'd found L. Atherton in a stalled elevator.

"And a van," she went on. "A better van, for the after-school pickups. That would be great—nothing fancy, but one that keeps running and won't break down. And the oven in the kitchen, well, it just either burns or doesn't cook."

She assumed that he was Matthew, and he'd assumed that she was there as a nanny candidate. They'd both been wrong, dead wrong. "Just For Kids?"

"Mr. Lewis understood that it was the backbone of the company, that an employee who knew his or her child was safe and cared for and within arm's reach was an employee who could give more to the company than a worried parent." She spread her hands palms up. "He knew that having the center right here was a win-win situation. And sending back my requests for funding marked "Denied" just isn't right."

L. Atherton. The name scrawled on the bottom of every request that had crossed his desk. *Lindsey.* No wonder she'd said the things she'd said the first time they'd run into each other. He was the one cutting her job bit by bit. "You sent the requests, didn't you."

"Of course," she said with a slight frown. "I know they had to be annoying, but it's important." Then the frown was gone and she was talking quickly again. "If you could just talk to Mr. Holden and try to explain to him how very important the center is. He's got to have some semblance of a heart somewhere inside him, and if you could…'' Her voice trailed off and high color touched her cheeks, as she lifted one hand to touch her lips with the tips of her fingers. ''Oh, I'm sorry,'' she mumbled. ''I did it again. I shouldn't have said that.''

''You think Zane Holden is heartless?''

She bit her lip hard and tried to regroup, to do some damage control. ''I think he's not looking at the whole picture on this. Mr. Lewis saw it, and he—''

''Ran this company like it was a hobby, letting his heart get in the way of the business. That's why he's not at the helm of LynTech any longer, and why the company was on a downhill slide when it was acquired.''

''Then, why would anyone pay all that money for it if it wasn't worth it?''

''Some things are more valuable in pieces than they are as a whole.''

''I don't understand. Mr. Holden and you bought the company to break it up, and you both thought you could make money out of the rubble?''

He closed the space between them and crouched in front of her. ''It's called restructuring, and it works, especially in a high-tech company like this, where the original owner acquired and acquired and never cut his losses.''

''And the day care center is one of the casualties in this restructuring?''

For some reason the things he'd said to Matt about eventually closing the center seemed heartless when he thought about saying them to her. ''The idea of a business is to make money,'' he said bluntly. ''Not to give it away.''

''That's just it. It's not giving it away. It's making your employees happy, more secure—and that has to be a big plus.''

"More money in their paychecks would make them happy. But that's not going to happen, either, at the moment. Can't you understand that there isn't any money and there won't be any money for the center?"

She leaned toward him, and it brought waves of a subtle scent that he'd sensed the first time he'd been close to her. A light flowery scent that was barely there, yet seemed to permeate the air in the still elevator.

"I'm beginning to understand," she said with a frown that drew her finely arched eyebrows together.

"So the requests for funding increases are going to stop?"

Her frown deepened. "Not in this lifetime."

He'd been in wars before for business, but this woman was an unsettling adversary. She knew she didn't stand a chance, yet she wasn't backing down one bit. "It's a waste of time," he said tightly.

Her eyes narrowed. "Talking to you is a waste of time. That's obvious. I need to talk to Mr. Holden. Maybe he'll realize that what I'm saying is true. Maybe he'll start to think like Mr. Lewis, instead of thinking like…like an Ebenezer Scrooge."

"And I suppose that you're Tiny Tim who's going to show old Ebenezer the real meaning of humanity?"

His usual sarcasm, which worked so well in the business world, hit her and hit her hard. He could see it in the way her expression tightened and that color flooded back into her cheeks. Damn it, he hated the twinge of regret that came to him as he watched her. But what was there to regret in doing what he had to do? That was ridiculous.

"No, I'm not Tiny Tim, and I'm not about to try to make Mr. Holden human, I'm just trying to make sure that the kids get what they need. That's all."

"At the expense of the company?"

Chapter Five

"What was that all about?" Lindsey asked.

"They're working on it."

"And?"

Zane hated this, and wasn't in any mood for another "I told you so" from this woman. So he hedged a bit on the truth. "It's a computer thing, probably a programming error when they overhauled the system. The man who can do the analysis and reprogram isn't here, so they have to get him to come down to do it."

"It doesn't make sense that they don't have someone on duty who can deal with this. Why wouldn't they have it covered?"

It had made sense to him when he said it. "They're working on it."

"There's a maintenance man, John Olson—he's really handy with computers and the strangest things. He's repaired stuff in the center, worked miracles with things that by all rights shouldn't be fixable." Her eyes suddenly widened. "Oh, man. He was laid off last week, wasn't he." Her mouth formed an *O,* as her eyes widened on him. "Your Mr. Holden fired the only man who can get us out of here, didn't he."

She gave a deep, exasperated sigh. "What about the kids?"

"They're their parents' problem." It seemed so logical to him. "They can take care of them. They can make whatever arrangements are necessary."

"Day care in some other place, where they can drop them at six in the morning and pick them up at six at night? Where they don't see them for twelve hours? Or no day care, so the kids come home to an empty house and are terrified until their parents can get home from work?"

She was talking quickly, and he could see how passionate she was about the center. "Maybe you want the kids to lock themselves in a closet so they'll feel safe and so they don't feel vulnerable to the boogeymen out there."

She stopped abruptly, her breathing rapid and echoing in the small space. She was shaking slightly and clutching her hands together tightly in her lap. It made him uncomfortable. He stood, moving back from her before he did something stupid, like trying to make her stop looking so pained.

"No, of course not," he said as he straightened and put distance between them. "That's not going to happen."

Her tongue darted out to touch her pale lips, and she seemed to sink back against the wall. "But it *is* going to happen, and you don't have a clue what I'm talking about. You were probably born with a silver spoon in your mouth, and you probably had someone there all the time." She breathed unsteadily, but her words were slower now. "You had parents who never had to leave you alone so they could go out to earn money to keep a roof over your head and food on the table."

He'd had the roof and the food and the nannies, but as far as being alone...that was a matter of definition. "You don't know what you're talking about, either," he muttered.

"I know kids, and I know what they feel," she said

tightly as she stared up at him with no retreat in her. "And kids are forever."

He had a flashing thought that *passion* had been the wrong word to use to describe this woman. Her determination crackled around him. "If you care so much, why aren't you out in the projects and slums and low-income areas, fighting for day care?"

He'd thought that would stop her in her tracks, but he was as wrong about that as he'd been in thinking she was a nanny candidate.

"Maybe I should be," she conceded as she got to her feet and swiped at her jeans with both hands, brushing off imaginary dust or dirt. "But I don't have unlimited funds. I wasn't born to privilege. I was orphaned when I was six, then in foster care, then on my own. And I need to make a living."

She looked at him, only a foot of space separating them now, and there was an extra brightness to her eyes. Not tears, or self-pity, but something that added to his discomfort.

"Kids gets scared even in middle-class homes, and Mr. Lewis gave me a chance at LynTech to help those kids." Her voice dropped to a whisper. "I thought I could make a difference."

She could go from intense to vulnerable in a moment. "So, your bottom line is money, too, isn't it," he said with more bite than he'd intended.

"The bottom line is helping the kids."

That was enough for Zane. He didn't want to be in this closed space with a woman who could make him uneasy, who was starting to make him wonder if she'd been right— that he didn't have a heart. He turned from her and grabbed at the red emergency phone again. A kid was back on the line immediately. "Yes?"

"How long is this going to take?"

"I'm not sure, sir, but we're working on it."

"What's the problem?"

"That's just it, we aren't sure."

"What in the hell does that mean?"

"Sir, we thought the system was all in place. But the computer readout is all wrong. The thing is, we need someone to read it and figure out what to do. Where it went off track."

"Then, get someone to do it."

"Well, that's the problem. The only guy I know of who could do it isn't available."

"Offer overtime—whatever it takes," he said.

"That might not work."

He was tired of this runaround, and his frustration level was rising quickly. "Can you give me a straight answer on this? I don't have the time to play twenty questions."

"The guy who used to do it, well, he was let go last week. He was laid off, and his position was eliminated."

Zane had a vague memory of Matt agreeing to cut back on the maintenance staff, but this was ridiculous. "Do you know him?"

"Yes, sir, I do. John Olson."

"Then, call him and pay whatever he wants to have him come in and take care of this as quickly as possible."

"Sir, I don't think—"

"Just do it, and do it right now." He bit out the words.

"Yes, sir," the man said, and hung up.

Zane slowly put the receiver back on the hook and braced himself to face Lindsey.

If she smiled right then, he wasn't sure what he'd do. "He's on his way."

There was a touch of laughter, but no humor. "You're going to get them to call him in to rescue you, *after* he's been let go, after your Mr. Holden fired him to make the company more viable?"

Zane shrugged. "They'll get him here."

"He was fired."

"Laid off, with a severance package."

"Oh, that makes it better?" She came closer as she spoke; her hands moved in an abrupt arc and almost hit his arm. "So much for Mr. Holden's ability to make good decisions when it comes to business. This is just an example of how out of touch he is with what's really important. Now that you've been caught in one of his false economies, you have firsthand experience that tells you how wrong he can be. I think you can go to him and talk to him about the center, get him to listen and reconsider his decisions."

He would have laughed at her enthusiasm and the way her words got faster and faster as she built up steam with her argument, if only she hadn't been talking about him. He shook his head—the little misunderstanding about his identity had gone far enough for his tastes.

"No."

He could tell she was regrouping for another attack, and it came before he could fend it off. "You're afraid of him, aren't you."

This woman did something most people in business couldn't do to him…she kept him off balance. "Don't be ridiculous," he muttered.

"Ridiculous? It's ridiculous that you don't seem to be able to see what his decisions are costing this place. Even when you're stuck in this elevator, you aren't about to admit that he's out of line. *That's* being afraid."

Lindsey was in deep water, but she was past caring. This man pushed all her buttons and she was pushing his, too. She saw the anger flash in his eyes, the way his mouth thinned. She knew how angry she'd made him when he spoke through clenched teeth.

"Are you through?"

She caught herself in the face of his anger and started backpedaling again; she did it so often with him that she should have eyes in the back of her head. "I'm just trying to get across that the center is a terrific thing. I wasn't meaning to say that Mr. Holden is...well, I mean, I know he's a 'cut to the chase' sort, and, as you said, he can't think with his heart. So he needs to think with his head. Whether he has a heart or not just isn't important right now."

"It matters to him, I'd bet," he muttered.

She was at the end of her rope with this man. A cement wall couldn't have been more unmovable. "Okay, forget it. We aren't going to get anywhere with this. If you could just get me in to see Mr. Holden, I'll talk to him directly. That's all I need. Just to talk to him face-to-face."

"There's no reason for more talk on this subject."

"Talking to you isn't doing any good. And that's fair. You have your own ideas. But if I can get in to talk to him directly, I'll leave you alone. We can pretend that this never happened."

"How many times do you want to pretend we haven't talked?" he asked.

She was spared a response by the emergency phone ringing. He turned and snatched the receiver off the hook. "Yes?"

There was tense silence, then his voice, low and tight in the close quarters of the elevator car. "Listen, just do it."

More silence, then a sharp intake of breath. "Who am I? My name's Holden, Zane Holden."

Lindsey stared at him, praying that she'd heard wrong, that she hadn't been talking to Zane Holden all this time. But as he turned after putting the phone back on the hook with a cracking sound of plastic on metal, she knew her prayers were not going to answered.

She could only get one word past the tightness in her throat. "You?"

"Me. The man without a heart."

Lindsey backed up until she felt the cold wall behind her. She needed all the space she could get. *Zane Holden.* Why had she thought the man she'd heard about would be older, sharper and colder? Those gray-blue eyes were narrowed and shadowed by the overhead light.

The anger was hidden. His expression was unreadable. The man had total control, as much control as she lacked. And he had all the power. She tried to think what to do, but nothing except throwing herself on his mercy seemed appropriate. But then again, she wasn't at all sure the man ever showed mercy.

Maybe just telling him the truth was all that was left to do. It couldn't make things worse. "Okay, once again, I'm very sorry. I thought you were Mr. Terrel. You were in his offices, and you never said anything." She couldn't see that anything she was saying had an effect on him. But she plunged on. "It was my mistake, and I'm sorry for saying…well, that crack about your heart. Way out of line. Way, way out of line. None of my business. It has nothing to do with why I'm here."

"Doesn't it?"

She lifted her eyes to the ceiling in supplication. She dug one hole after another with this man. "All that matters is the center. That's the truth," she said, as much for her own benefit as for his. Looking at him again, she forced herself to maintain eye contact and not flinch. "It's the center. I want you to understand that we need the money, and it's a damn good investment in this company."

"Maybe I should put this all another way. I'm not building this company. I'm taking it apart to make each part more viable, then selling each off one at a time. Taking it apart and strengthening each part means cutting money spent to make the balance sheets look better. There is no extra money for anything."

Lindsey flinched at the finality in his tone and his words. She looked down at the floor, staring hard at the carpet. Sarcastic retorts flew through her mind and were rejected even as they formed. She had wished for time. The elevator wasn't going anywhere; Zane Holden wasn't going anywhere. But Zane Holden didn't want to talk anymore. Then it hit her that at first he'd been more than willing to talk.

"You were willing to discuss this at first," she said as she looked up at him.

"Sure, I thought you'd come to talk about the nanny situation."

"Nanny situation?"

"Just another problem I'm dealing with."

She'd joked with Amy about his having kids, but now that they'd met, she couldn't imagine that he had any children. "You need a nanny?"

He shook his head. "Yes. There's a situation that came up and we—"

A muffled ringing sound cut off his words, but it wasn't the emergency phone. He reached into an inside jacket pocket and took out a cell phone, then flipped it open. "Yes?"

Lindsey watched him turn a bit to exclude her from the conversation. But in this tiny space, there was no such thing as privacy. She sank back down on the floor, crossed her legs and leaned her head against the wall. There was no-place for her to go to avoid hearing what he was saying.

"I really don't have time for this. I'm stuck in an elevator." He moved one hand in a wide arc, but his voice dropped a bit, to a more intimate tone. "If I had my way, I'd be there, believe me. It's important to me, too."

A woman. Of course. Although Lindsey wondered where he fit a woman into a life that seemed to be all work, or how many children he had that needed a nanny.

"I know, I know," he was saying softly. "And I'll be there as soon as they get this elevator working."

He listened for a moment, then exhaled harshly. When he spoke again, a sudden coolness had crept into his tone. "If I could change this, I would. But the way things are going, I'm going to be late. So why don't you go ahead, and I'll catch up with you."

Lindsey closed her eyes.

"We'll talk when I get there," she heard him say. Then he said, "Is there someone you need to call about being late?" and she realized he was speaking to her.

She opened her eyes to see him holding his cell phone out to her. As she looked up into those blue eyes, something in her wouldn't let her say there was no one for her to call. No one to be worried, no one waiting. No one would be missing her except Joey, a huge orange tabby that she'd inherited when she'd rented her apartment. She'd never been a game player, not really caring what people thought of her, but right now, she didn't want this man to know how very alone she was in her life. Call it pride or call it craziness, she took the phone from him.

She ignored his heat still trapped in the plastic, and punched in her own phone number, then pressed the send button. It rang four times before her machine picked it up.

When her outgoing message stopped, she said, "Joey, it's me. I'm tied up for a while, but I'll be home as soon as I can get there. Dinner might be a bit late. See you soon and don't worry."

She pushed the end button, closed the cover, then handed it up to Zane. "Thanks," she said. "Now, can we talk some more about the center?"

"Don't you ever give up?"

"Not when something matters."

He pushed the cell phone back in his pocket. "Is your husband as driven as you are?"

"Husband?"

"Joe's not your husband?"

"No, he's not my husband," she said, fighting to control herself so she didn't laugh at the absurdity of what he'd just asked her. But she couldn't stop a smile. Maybe it was borderline hysteria, but it was there. "No, I'm not married."

"And that's funny?"

"Well, you'd have to know Joey," she said.

Zane knew it was more than time to get out of this place when a simple smile from her made him start to think things better left alone. Or when he found himself wondering how a man dealt with this woman and kept rational, and what sort of man it took to attract her.

"I'll pass," he said. He checked his watch, a bit surprised that they'd only been in the elevator car for fifteen minutes or so. It felt like forever.

"I know—places to go, people to meet," Lindsey said.

"Things to do," he said, tugging his cuff back over his watch.

"Like finding a nanny?"

"Exactly." He reached for the emergency phone again.

"Mr. Holden?" the voice asked.

"What's your name?"

"Andy."

"Okay, Andy, tell me what's happening."

"We found John Olson, and we had to offer him quite a bit of money for him to even come down at all. He'll be here as soon as he can. He says he can fix it just fine. It's simple. At least, for him it is. I couldn't understand what he was talking about."

"When will he be here?"

"He said he could get here in an hour."

"That's not acceptable."

"Well, sir, we can get you out."

"Then, do it."

"You'll have to use the escape door in the ceiling. You're only about six feet below floor level for the seventh floor, and we could get a man down there to help."

Zane heard Lindsey stir behind him, felt his body tense, and he spoke quickly. "Okay, let's do it."

"When the man gets there, he'll tap on the roof, then he'll tell you what to do."

"We're getting out?" she asked from behind him.

He hung up the phone, then turned. "I guess you're smart."

"How so?"

He pointed to the ceiling. "The only way out is through the escape door. It seems that Olson isn't going to get here for another hour, and I, for one, am not willing to wait that long."

"I was kidding about the trap door," she said, looking up at the ceiling.

"I'm not. It's either that, or Karen eats dinner alone at a very expensive restaurant and never forgives me, and your Joe goes hungry."

She shook her head. "Those aren't options, are they?"

"Not in my case."

She shrugged. "Okay, then, it's through the door."

Before her words faded away, there was a knock on the ceiling, and Zane looked up to see the trap door lift back and out of sight. A bald man with a flushed face looked down into the car.

"Sir, everyone okay in there?"

"Just get us out," he said.

"Yes, sir." The man disappeared, then came back and looked in again. "Here, grab this," he said as he lowered a metal step stool down through the trap door. "It's all I could find up here, but it'll get you high enough for me to help pull you up."

Zane grabbed the stool, opened it and set it on the floor. The man over them extended a hand through the door. "Okay, let's do it," he said.

Zane looked at Lindsey and motioned her ahead. "You first."

"Great, a trial run, and I'm the test subject," she said, but there was a suggestion of a smile on her lips as she spoke. One thing he'd say for her, she took things in stride. She picked herself up and did what she needed to do. He'd seen enough of that in the short time he'd known her, and he found that he liked it.

She looped her purse strap over her shoulder, then looked around and, without a word, put a hand on his shoulder to steady herself and climbed onto the stool. But even as she stretched up as far as she could, her hand didn't quite touch the man's hand over them.

"This isn't going to work," she muttered, and looked down at Zane. "How about a hand up? You know, like when you help someone into the saddle?"

He'd thought of picking her up and lifting her, but lacing his fingers together so she could get a foothold made a hell of a lot more sense to him. Until he did it. He positioned himself. Then she had both hands on his shoulders, fitting her one foot into his clasped hands, and for a second her face was inches from his. Her breath brushed his face; then it was gone.

She pushed, the man had her, and by the time Zane stood back, all he saw were her feet disappearing through the trap door. He grabbed his briefcase, got on the stool, then handed the case up to the man. Before the man could come back to offer a hand, Zane jumped, caught the edges of the opening and levered himself up and into the elevator shaft.

He scrambled to his feet on top of the elevator, in the middle of a mess of cables and wires and emergency lights. Lindsey was there with her face smudged with grease and her white shirt now less than white. Instead of seeing annoyance or anger in her expression, he saw that she was smiling at him.

The woman never reacted the way he expected her to. He brushed at his own clothes. "Don't even tell me you're enjoying this," he muttered.

"Well, maybe *enjoy* isn't the word, but I've never escaped from an elevator before. How about you?"

"I've never had the pleasure," he said, taking one last swipe at his jacket.

The workman motioned Lindsey to another stool sitting on the top of the elevator. A huge hammer blocked the doors from closing. "Let me get up there, then I'll help you out, okay?" He handed Zane his briefcase, then got on the stool, grabbed at the doorjamb and scrambled up and out.

He turned, laid on his stomach, and reached back in for Lindsey. She got on the box, stretching, and this time she was able to grab the man's hand, then half climb up the wall, pressing her boots against the metal partitions until she was out.

Zane followed, tossing his briefcase up and out. Then he grasped the doorjamb and lifted himself out of the shaft into the corridor. Lindsey was near him, and there was a dark smudge of soot or oil on the tip of her nose. He almost reached to brush at it, but stopped as sanity took over. At least, until she smiled again.

"What now?" he asked as he looked away from that smile to reach for his briefcase.

"Nothing. Sorry." When he looked back at her, her smile faded a bit.

The workman pulled the huge hammer out of the doors, and they slid shut with a dull *thud*. "Is there anything else I can do for the two of you?"

"My car's out in front," Zane said. He'd totally forgotten about Gordon until then. "My driver, he's been waiting forever. Let him know I'm coming down?"

"Yes, sir," the man said, and hurried off.

"The poor man," Lindsey said.

He looked at her. "What?"

"Your driver, just sitting there. You should have called him on your cell phone."

"He's used to waiting," he said, a bit annoyed to be given a lesson in manners.

"If he can wait a bit longer, you look as if you could use some soap and water before you leave."

"I could, but I'm not walking all the way up to the executive level."

"Tell you what, if you'll consider everything I said in there—I mean, the stuff about the center and our needs, just give it some thought—I'll get you some soap and water and a place to freshen up, and you won't need to climb any stairs."

He didn't believe it: she was actually negotiating with him. She never stopped surprising him. He bet Joe was never bored by her. And he'd take her up on her offer. He'd think about it. God knows, he'd be hard put not to think about what had just happened with her. He could honestly agree to that. It wouldn't make a bit of difference, but he'd do it.

"You've got a deal."

"You mean it?"

"Absolutely."

He felt a bit uneasy with his promise, when she grinned at him. "Follow me, then," she said, and turned to start down the hallway behind her. By the time he caught up with her, she had stopped at the stairwell.

"The deal was, I didn't have to climb stairs," he said.

"We aren't going up," she said as she pushed back the door. "We're going down."

He followed her into the stairwell—the second time they'd been in here together, but this time they were going in the same direction. He followed her as she almost ran downward, her hand skimming along the handrail as she went. She stopped at the landing for the sixth floor. "We're here," she said, pulling back the door and stepping out of the stairwell.

He followed, and she strode along the corridor to a set of double doors that had been painted blue with clear red trim. In the center of both doors was a heart logo, with a central collage of smiling children. Just For Kids was bannered over it in what looked like a child's printing done in crayon. Under it in simple type was LynTech Day Care Center. L. Atherton, Dir.

Lindsey reached into her purse for a ring of keys, then unlocked one side and pushed the door open. She motioned him to go inside. "I've seen your place, now you can see mine," she said.

He stepped past her into shadows; then the lights came on and he was in another world. He was in a place with clouds above, fairy tale characters on the walls, huge crayons used for screens, and tiny tables and chairs that looked like mushrooms and flowers, all painted in primary colors.

"This is my territory," she said from behind him as the door closed. "And I just happen to know where all the good cleaning-up places are."

He turned to her and that smile was there, an endearing expression that held something mischievous in its depths. She obviously thought she had him where she wanted him, but she was wrong. At least, about bringing him here. He wasn't so sure on a personal level. That smile was far too appealing to him—far too appealing.

"Good. That's the deal, isn't it?"

"Absolutely," she said as she crossed the room and went into a hallway. A light flashed on, and he followed her past a mural of Little Red Riding Hood to two doors, one painted blue with a Raggedy Andy doll on it, and one painted pink with a Raggedy Ann doll on it.

"Don't tell me," he murmured. "I'll take Raggedy Andy."

This time she really laughed, a soft husky sound, and he quickly moved out of its range and into the bathroom. He found a light switch by the door—and faced a room made for midgets. There was a row of sinks that couldn't have been more than two feet off the ground and mirrors that weren't much higher. He crouched down, laid his briefcase on the floor and looked in the mirror. He finally saw why Lindsey had been smiling out there. She wasn't the only one with grease on her face. He had one long smear across

't get out from behind the wheel when he saw him.
driver knew better than to waste time getting out and
~ing the door. Zane opened the door himself, but before
ot in, he glanced back, a bit curious to see where Lind-
had gone.

he hadn't gone anywhere. She was right by him, look-
for all the world as if she were going to follow him
~ the limo. And for an instant, he thought that might be
~resting, too. It would certainly guarantee that the drive
~uldn't be boring.

his nose, almost like war paint, and a large smudge on his
chin.

He almost smiled, but he couldn't. It wasn't funny that
he'd lost so much time, or that his dinner date and PR
conference was probably a thing of the past, or that he'd
have to tell Lindsey once and for all that he'd considered
her request for more funding and it wasn't going to happen.
They would eventually close this place down. But that was
on a "need to know" basis. And she didn't need to know
just yet.

He grabbed a handful of paper towels, turned on the
water and began to scrub at the mess on his face. When he
finally looked in the mirrors, he saw himself, not Scrooge
or the Grinch. Just a businessman. "A truly misunderstood
man, at that," he muttered at his expression, then straightened up.

He brushed at his suit, picked up his briefcase and
stepped out of the land of midgets into the hallway. When
he turned toward the main room, he saw Lindsey. She was
sitting on a mushroom bench at one of the tiny tables, her
arms around her legs and her chin resting on her knees,
just watching him. He walked toward her and realized that
she'd changed her shirt in favor of faded blue sweatshirt.

She sat up a bit, and he could see that mischievous twin-
kle in her amber eyes.

"Was there enough soap and water for you?" she asked
without getting up.

"After I got on my knees to use them, yes, thanks." He
stopped by her and looked down into those eyes that were
touched with humor. "Did I get all the dirt off?"

"Yes. Did I?"

"It looks that way."

She motioned to one of the toadstool chairs at her table.
"Have a seat."

"I'll pass. I need to get going."

"Places to go, money to save?" she asked, a smile softening her words as she stood.

"People to see," he answered.

"Of course, people," she said facing him with barely a foot separating them.

She'd washed her face, leaving slight dampness at her hair by her temples, and he'd bet she didn't have any makeup left at all. Odd, how she looked almost luminous in this light, even without the makeup. A trick of the lights? He wasn't hanging around to find out for himself.

"Then, there isn't time for a tour of the place?"

"No." He glanced at his watch. "Barely time for dinner, actually."

"Okay, it's getting late. Who knows, John Olson might have gotten here by now and fixed the elevators."

"I'll take the stairs."

"Good choice," she murmured as she turned from him to reach for her purse on the table. She stood and headed for the door. When he stepped out into the corridor, she locked up, then slipped her purse strap over her shoulder and walked with him to the stairwell.

If he'd thought the conversation about the center was over, he knew how wrong he was when Lindsey started to talk on the way down. "I wish you could see how we work at the center. Maybe you could come down and spend the day to see what we do and how important it is to the kids. Mr. Lewis used to come down and—"

Zane stopped her from reminiscing about the former head of LynTech. "Mr. Lewis did a lot of things I wouldn't do, and one of them is spending a day at the center." He glanced at her, but she wasn't looking at him. She was staring straight ahead. "I don't have a day to spend there," he said, vaguely annoyed that he was making excuses. He

hated people who made excuses, but that ⟨…⟩ from adding, "I don't even have ten minut⟨…⟩

"It wouldn't be a waste," she said, fall⟨…⟩ "Besides, how can you make an intelligent ⟨…⟩ out spending time there? It just makes sense ⟨…⟩ going to be fair and make a wise decision, y⟨…⟩ least get information firsthand."

He stopped abruptly and turned to find he⟨…⟩ above him. "What makes you think I haven't⟨…⟩ and fair decision?"

She blushed. He knew now that the blush⟨…⟩ her cheeks was a dead give-away that she kr⟨…⟩ pushing the envelope. But as before, she didn'⟨…⟩

"How could you have made a fair and w⟨…⟩ when the only contact you've had with the ⟨…⟩ sending you memo after memo asking for r⟨…⟩ or your washing your face in a child's sink?"⟨…⟩

He was at a loss, and he didn't like feeling⟨…⟩ had no comeback for her, so he did the eas⟨…⟩ turned to keep going down the stairs. He hear⟨…⟩ coming after him. But he only stopped whe⟨…⟩ main level, and only long enough to open ⟨…⟩ could walk out into the building's foyer.

He looked across the glass and mirrore⟨…⟩ the front doors, and saw his limousine at ⟨…⟩ headed toward the doors, Lindsey came ⟨…⟩ When he reached the doors, he gripped ⟨…⟩ and pulled the door open, standing back to ⟨…⟩

"It's been interesting," he said with a⟨…⟩ he joined her on the broad sidewalk out i⟨…⟩

"Absolutely," she said.

"Enjoy your dinner with Joe."

"You enjoy...whatever," she murmur⟨…⟩

He nodded, then turned to cross to ⟨…⟩

Chapter Six

"I'm sorry. Do you need a ride?" Zane asked.

Lindsey shook her head. "No, you have people to do...I mean, places to go, things to do—and I have my own transportation. But thanks." She hesitated. "I just wanted to say that I hope I gave you coherent reasons to support the center."

"You more than made your case," he conceded.

"I hope so," she said, then stunned him by adding, "Take the weekend to think things over, and I'll get back to you Monday."

Before he could say anything, she turned and walked away down the street. He watched her go—a single figure walking off under the glow of the street lamps. She never looked back. And he was left with the feeling that some spark in his world had gone with her.

He turned and got into the limo, then closed the door. "Gordon, I'm sorry to be so late coming down."

"The gentleman called, sir, and I informed the restaurant that we would be there soon."

Zane looked at his briefcase, but instead of opening it to do some work to make up for lost time, he tossed it onto the seat facing him, then sank back in the leather.

"She'll get back to me?" he murmured.

"Excuse me, sir?"

"Nothing, Gordon, nothing—" he said.

His cell phone rang. He took it out, answered it and heard Matt's voice.

"Zane, it's me."

"Give me good news. Tell me you and Rita found a nanny."

"As a matter of fact, we did. She's perfect. She passed all the tests."

Zane closed his eyes, and for a moment had an image of the woman he'd thought for a short time was the "perfect nanny." He pushed that aside as he opened his eyes again. "Thank goodness, that's settled."

He glanced out the window as the limo rounded the corner onto the main street, and she was there, under the glow of a Bus Stop sign. Lindsey was standing with two other people, waiting for the huge transit bus that was just pulling to the curb. She'd said she had transportation, but he hadn't thought of a bus.

"Well, it's a case of good news and bad news," Matt was saying in his ear.

He caught one glimpse of Lindsey getting onto the bus; then the doors shut and the limo went out around the slower moving bus. "Just tell me what's going on. After tonight, I can take anything."

"What happened tonight?"

He needed to concentrate on the problem at hand, not a potential problem that was embodied in a woman with passion who wasn't afraid to stand up to him. "I'll tell you later," he said. "Just give me the bad news."

"Okay, the nanny's perfect, but she's perfectly tied up until next week on another job. Then she's free."

"Offer her more money if she starts earlier."

"I tried that, but she said she couldn't just walk away

and leave the other people hanging. But she'll be glad to start a week from Monday. She's thrilled about a two-year-old, says that's the best age of all, and she's anxious to meet the boy."

"Okay, then, we need to get a temp to fill in for a few days," Zane said. "Get Rita on it. It shouldn't be too hard."

"Zane, I'm starting to think that taking over the world would be easier than this child-care mess."

It would probably be easier than taking on Lindsey and feeling as if he'd won. He was still thinking about her parting words. *I'll get back to you.*

"I'll talk to you later," he said to Matt, then closed the phone.

He had no doubt that he'd see Lindsey again. She wasn't about to give up. Actually, he knew that a part of him would be disappointed if she did.

Saturday

"YOU WERE TRAPPED in an elevator with that...that person?" Amy said. "It must have been like swimming with sharks."

The two women were in overalls, side by side in the main room of the center, each with a can of paint and brushes, touching up the murals on the wall. Little Bo Peep was looking as shabby as the Big Bad Wolf.

Lindsey stroked blue on Bo Peep's dress, but couldn't help smiling at the shock in Amy's voice. She hadn't felt much like laughing since walking away from Zane nearly twenty-four hours ago. It felt good to laugh.

"That pretty much sums it up. Although the shark was

dressed in a very expensive suit. It was nice—at least, until we had to climb out the escape hatch.''

It was Amy's turn to laugh. "I wish I'd been there to see that."

"No, you don't." Lindsey stared hard at the mural, then managed to find the words she'd pushed away for most of the day she'd spent with Amy. "Amy, he's pretty set about what he will and won't do for this place." She couldn't say that she had the feeling he was not only not going to give them extra money, but also probably cut some of their current funding. "I guess we'll just have to make do with what there is for now."

"He's no Mr. Lewis, is he," Amy said.

"He's no Mr. Lewis." Lindsey jabbed her brush at the wall, smearing brown on the tree trunk. "He thinks Mr. Lewis was way out of line in funding us to begin with."

"I don't know what I'd do without this place."

"You could get back into marketing," Lindsey said, trying to think of anything that offered hope. "I know Mr. Adams...was that his name?"

"Yeah, Jake Adams."

"He'd take you back."

Amy shrugged. "I don't want to go back. I want to be part of Taylor's life. And if I work eight hours a day in marketing, I'll have to wear grown-up clothes." She motioned to the overalls she was wearing and to Lindsey's jeans and paint-splattered T-shirt. "I'd be uncomfortable, and I'd never see her. This job is perfect. Well, maybe not perfect. I could use more money, but we manage. It works for us."

Lindsey looked at Amy, who turned to concentrate on touching up one of Bo Peep's sheep. She remembered when she'd first met Amy—a young woman, a young mother, a young widow. "Don't worry about any of this," she found herself saying. "If we can't get through to Zane Holden, we'll figure out something—maybe go to Mr. Terrel. Actually, it sounds as if Holden's selling the company soon, anyway, so maybe the next person in power will be another Mr. Lewis."

Amy glanced at her. "Or maybe another Zane Holden. Money and greed attracts that type, I think." She put her brush in the jar of cleaner on the floor between the two of them, and swiped her hands on her overalls. "I need to get going. Jenn asked to have Taylor for the day, and Taylor loves her doting aunt." She pushed the lid back on the paint she'd been using. "Since it's all the family we have, I wanted them to know each other, but now it's time I relieved her. And speaking of Jenn, she wanted me to ask you to come for Thanksgiving dinner."

Lindsey seldom "did" holidays, with each event being pretty much like the others. "Can I let you know? I've got so much work to do, and I—"

"It's an open invitation, and it isn't for another few weeks, so just let me know."

"Thanks for asking," Lindsey said.

"Sure. Should I put away the paint, or are you staying for a while?"

She glanced at the clock. "It's almost five," she said as she sank back with a sigh and frowned at Bo Peep's dress. "I think I made that look worse." Sort of the way she'd made things far worse with Zane Holden the night before. Good intentions, but bad execution. "Oh, well, at least the crayon marks are covered."

"It looks great," Amy said as she took some things across the room to a cupboard hiding behind a door painted to look like a giant box of crayons. "Besides, you've got an easy audience. The kids love the pictures. They aren't art critics."

Lindsey stood back, stretching her arms above her head. "Thank goodness. I told Zane Holden we needed a new stove."

Amy reached for the last of the paint. "And?"

"I don't think he heard me, but it's on the list he's got—that, and a van, and shelves in the storage room."

"How about a million dollars, and self-cleaning kids?"

"Not hardly," she said, but had an idea. "What about a facility on the bottom floor, in the back where all those huge conference rooms are? That would be perfect. We could have our own entrance, so the kids wouldn't have to go through the business area. And maybe we could figure out how to have some access to the outside and make a play yard."

"Lindsey, slow down," Amy said. "You're getting way ahead of yourself. Do you really think that a man who's balking at a stove and a used van is going to go for taking over conference rooms and erecting a jungle gym?"

"It's just a thought." She smiled. "Something to ask for next time, after we work all of this out."

"Sure," Amy said, "but I don't have time right now. I told Jenn I'd be there by five-thirty." She picked up the canvas backpack she took wherever she went. "You need a ride?"

"No, I'm fine. I need to do a bit here, anyway."

"When do you ever sleep?"

Sleep wasn't something she did very well lately. "When I'm tired," she said.

"See you Monday?"

"Right here, bright and early," she said.

When Amy had gone, Lindsey went back to her office to clean up; she slipped a navy sweatshirt with the center's logo over her T-shirt and overalls. After she cleaned most of the blue paint off her hands, she grabbed her canvas tote bag, turned off the lights and left.

She had until Monday to figure out some way to reach Zane Holden. ''A snap,'' she whispered as she headed to the elevators. ''No problem.'' As she pushed the button for the lobby, she grimaced. ''All it's going to take is a miracle.''

She just wished she believed in miracles.

ZANE AND MATT RODE down in the executive elevator, their talk about the futile search for a temporary baby-sitter almost lost on Zane. He kept having flashbacks to his ride with Lindsey the night before. Those amber eyes that could change from intense to mischievous to seductive in the beat of a heart. That intrigued him. Her spunk at not backing down even after she had to have known her plea was a lost cause—that fascinated him.

''And the Duke killed King Kong at high noon on the top of the Eiffel Tower.''

''What are you talking about?'' Zane asked Matt, as the elevator came to a stop at the lobby level.

''That's what I'm asking you. Did you hear a thing I said?''

''Sure, of course,'' he said, stepping out of the elevator as the doors opened. ''No baby-sitter so far.'' He headed for the entry doors, shaken for a moment when he thought he caught that scent—the flowery thing that seemed to cling to Lindsey. He shook his head, pushed open the doors and stepped out into the early evening.

''Okay, so you heard me. But I know you weren't really listening,'' Matt was saying as he fell in step by Zane on the way to the limo at the curb.

''I was thinking about something else.''

He opened the limo door, let Matt slip in, then he

climbed in, too. He settled in the back seat, and Matt sat facing him in the reverse seat. "Something I need to know about?"

He sank back and spoke to the driver. "Gordon, Mr. Terrel is going to The Regency, then I'm going home."

"Yes, sir," the chauffeur said.

Zane looked at Matt, who was patiently waiting for an answer. "I told you about meeting up with Miss Atherton last night?"

"A half-dozen times," Matt said. "The nanny escapade in the stuck elevator?"

"I wouldn't put it like that," Zane said.

"She got under your skin, didn't she."

"Matt, she's persistent. She won't give up, and has this incredible idea that she can get what she wants just by sheer will." He shook his head as the limo pulled away from the curb. "She can't, but she can't see that, either."

"Stubborn?"

"Stubborn as a mule."

Matt shrugged. "Tell her there aren't any options."

"I tried to, but she twisted everything I said, and she thinks there's hope."

"I'll tell her for you."

Zane glanced out the window of the limo—and it was déjà-vu. Last night Lindsey had been standing by the bus stop with two people. Tonight she was there, but she was alone. The slacks and sweater were gone, in favor of what looked like loose jeans and a sweatshirt.

"I'll tell her," he said, then spoke to the chauffeur. "Gordon, stop at the bus stop."

Matt looked back over his shoulder as the limo eased into the curb, and Zane put down the window by him. "Hello. Do you have a problem?"

Lindsey turned to him, and in the soft evening light she

looked incredibly young. Her short hair was slightly mussed. No makeup. Clothes a teenager could wear—although he doubted any teenager would look this good in them. Her initial surprise changed quickly to a smile, as potent to Zane as a jolt of electricity.

"Nothing that more money for the center wouldn't cure," she said as she came over to the curb.

"I can't do that, but I can spare you a ride on the bus."

She didn't hesitate. "Thanks, I'll take you up on that."

Without waiting for Gordon to get out and open the door for her, she opened it and slid into the limousine, bringing that hint of flowers with her. Then she was sitting beside him, a canvas bag pushed between them on the leather seat.

"Matt, this is Lindsey Atherton. Lindsey, the real Matthew Terrel."

If he'd thought she'd be embarrassed by the mistake she'd made last night, she surprised him again by offering Matt her hand and laughing softly. "The real Mr. Terrel. How lovely to finally meet the genuine article."

Matt grinned at her, shook her hand, then looked at Zane. "You failed to tell me that L. Atherton looked like this."

Surprisingly, that did seem to embarrass her. She drew back and wiped at her cheeks. "I've got paint on my face, don't I?"

"Not a bit," Matt said.

"Sir," Gordon asked, "a change in plans?"

"Where were you heading off to?" he asked Lindsey.

"Home," she said, and gave him her address.

"Do you know how to get there, Gordon?"

"Yes, sir, no problem," he said, and pulled away from the curb.

A phone rang, and Matt reached for the car phone set into the side wall. He said, "Terrel," then shook his head at Zane. "I'll take it."

While Matt talked in a low voice to whomever was on the other end of the line, Zane glanced at Lindsey. She was looking at him, and didn't look away when their gazes met.

"Thanks for the ride," she said. "I think I had the wrong schedule for Saturdays. Goodness knows when the bus would have shown up."

"Why were you taking the bus?"

"The truth?" she asked.

"Of course. Or is it a huge secret?"

She smiled again, and the expression was just as jarring to him as it had been from a distance. "No, it's no secret. I don't drive."

"You don't, or you can't?"

"No, I can drive okay," she said. "Well, it's not okay. I'm no good at it. I've got a license—not a Texas license, but it's valid. I don't own a car. It's just safer to take a bus or a cab or..." She motioned vaguely to the limousine interior. "A limousine. Although I hardly ever ride in one of these. Actually, never. How about you—do you drive or do you just get chauffeured around all the time?"

He'd almost forgotten how quickly she talked and how much energy she put into everything she said. He found himself smiling. "I drive. I like to drive, but it makes life simpler when I'm in a new city to take advantage of one of the company perks."

She looked around the interior of the luxury car. "Where did you get the money for it, if the company is so strapped?"

Something else he'd tried to forget. The way she asked direct, pointed questions. "It's part of my 'package' as C.E.O., so I can do my work without distractions," he said, wondering why he was justifying anything he did with the company to this woman. He was talking about distractions, and that's exactly what she was.

"Nice perk," she murmured.

Sarcasm with a smile. Very effective and hard to get too angry at. "Are you from around here?"

"No, I've only been in Houston for a little over a year. I came from Virginia."

"Your family's back there?"

"No, not really. I don't have family."

He was an only child, but there was family. If he cared to look for them, his family was just about everywhere. He just never looked. "Any brothers or sisters?"

"No, at least, I don't think so."

He started to smile at that, but could see that she wasn't making a joke. "I don't understand," he found himself saying.

Her shrug belied the tension in her words. "I went into foster homes when I was six. I don't remember exactly how that came about, except my parents were gone. Well, my mother died, and my father disappeared before I was born." She exhaled on a soft sigh. "He could have had any number of kids, and I wouldn't know."

He watched her eyes narrow as if she didn't want to look too closely at her past. And he couldn't blame her. "I'm sorry."

"Oh, you don't have to be. I survived, and things are okay. At least, they will be when the center gets the funding it needs."

He shook his head. "You never stop."

"Not as long as you're here listening to me," she said, and that smile came, such a welcome relief after the tension of moments earlier. "And you are listening, aren't you?"

He wouldn't admit that she had his full attention. Somehow he knew that if he admitted that, she'd just rev up even more for her attack. "I'm here," he said, and was thankful when Matt broke in on the conversation.

"Bad news again," he said. "We're up against a brick wall on this."

"The company?" Lindsey asked. "Something's wrong with the company?"

"No, it's personal," Zane admitted.

"Can I help?" she asked.

She almost startled him by offering. He hadn't expected that—not after the way things had been going between them. "No, not unless you know a good baby-sitter."

"Well, no, I don't, not really," she said, then sat a bit straighter. "But there's a great day care center at LynTech that could be a lot better with more funding. It's got adequate equipment and workers who really care. The only requirement is a child and a parent who's an employee at LynTech."

"The day care center?" Matt asked.

Zane shook his head quickly and cut Matt off. "No, we'll keep looking for a baby-sitter."

Lindsey couldn't believe how obstinate the man was. "And if you don't find a baby-sitter, I guess your wife's going to have to be a mother and stay home with the child?" she asked.

She spoke without thinking and was stunned by Zane's answer. "She's my ex-wife, and she was killed recently in an accident."

Zane's ex-wife? She was killed? That explained so much. "Oh, God, I'm so sorry. I had no idea. No one mentioned anything about it, and I just never—" He looked uncomfortable so she paused, but then couldn't help asking, "The child—a boy or a girl?"

"A boy, about two."

A son. "Maybe you should be the one to stay with him," she said, thinking it was a good idea. From his reaction, though, she knew she'd said something wrong again.

"Me? Hardly. That's what nannies are for."

There was a coldness in his voice that twisted something in her. "No, it's up to a parent to be there for a child."

"I'm not his parent," he said. "I'm his…" He looked at Matt. "What am I?"

"Someone who's taking care of the child his ex-wife had with her second husband?" Matt shrugged. "It's playing havoc with everything on this end. The boy's being flown in on Monday, and his situation has to be secured before he gets here."

Lindsey was sure she'd heard wrong. "Your ex-wife left her child with you?" she asked Zane, and couldn't resist adding, "Why?"

"That was my question." He shook his head. "Suzanne would never have left a child in my care if she'd thought it could ever happen."

"But she did?"

"By default. She forgot to change her will."

The man was taking in his ex-wife's child, and that idea touched Lindsey on some level. He had the ability to get beyond the horrendous situation with another man's child. Maybe she'd been wrong about him being heartless. "But you're willing to do it?"

"Don't look at me like that."

"Like what?"

"Like I'm doing something noble. I'm only doing what I have to, and only until an attorney in Florida finds a blood relative. The only other option was putting him in foster care in Florida."

No, he wasn't noble. He was practical, and the child was nothing more than a problem to solve. She felt something in her collapse. Maybe hope.

"At least you didn't do that," Lindsey said in a voice

that sounded vaguely flat in her own ears. "I guess a nanny is the next best thing."

"I was brought up by nannies, and I turned out just fine," Zane countered.

She'd debate that anytime. "Didn't you wish that your mother or father was there for you instead of someone they paid to be there?"

"I never thought about it."

"I don't buy that," she said.

"I'm not lying to you."

"Then, you're the only child in the world who didn't care who took care of them."

"And you're the expert on kids, aren't you," he said with more than a touch of sarcasm.

"No, but I was a kid," she murmured. "And I had people paid to take care of me. And believe me, if I'd had a choice, it wouldn't have been that way." She bit her lip, hating herself for exposing any of her personal life to a man like this. But something in her wouldn't give up on him.

"Zane tells me you've got a degree in Early Childhood Development," Matt said, cutting in.

She looked at the other man and realized she'd all but forgotten he was there. And now he was trying to distract her before she dug a deeper hole for herself with Zane. She found that she was grateful for the interruption. "Yes, I do. But having a degree and really knowing how to deal with children are two different things."

"Theory and reality?"

"Yes, exactly."

The car slowed, and Lindsey was thankful the ride was over. It had been a mistake to take it, but she'd thought she could talk to Zane more about the center. So much for intentions, she mused as she looked out. But what she saw wasn't her place. They were in an affluent section of the city and pulling up to the entrance of a very pricey restaurant.

"Ah, my stop," Matt said, then talked to Zane. "I'll be in touch tomorrow and let you know how this goes." Then he looked at Lindsey. "Very interesting drive," he said. "And nice to meet you."

"Thanks," she said.

With that, he got out, and as the door closed behind him, the limo seemed to grow smaller inside. It was the same sensation she'd had in the elevator. She moved closer to her door, and as the limo pulled away from the curb, she tried to think of something to say. But her mind went in circles.

A child. A dead ex-wife. The roller-coaster ride this man gave her emotions when she was around him. A striking man, whose possession of a heart was debatable. But he could touch *her* heart...or he would, if she let him. That thought almost left her breathless.

Chapter Seven

"Don't fight it," Zane said from out of the blue as they continued the drive to Lindsey's home.

"What?"

"I can see you stifling everything you're thinking of saying. That has to be exhausting."

Was he actually smiling at her? Was her chest tightening from being in the vicinity of that expression?

"It is," she admitted with a sigh. She'd been doing that all her life—trying to watch what she said, trying not to make waves or cause problems. But with Zane, things erupted in her, words came from nowhere, and she found herself speaking out in a way she never had with anyone else. But it was exhausting saying what she thought, too. "And it causes such trouble."

"Let's make things simple for you for a moment. I'll give you carte blanche for one statement. You can say anything you want to, and you get it for free."

"No negotiating?"

"Would you feel better if we did? How about you say what you're thinking, then I say what I'm thinking, and we call it even? How's that for a deal?"

She wasn't sure she wanted that. Maybe what he was thinking wasn't something she'd ever want to know. And goodness knows, half the things she had thought about him wouldn't be fit for saying out loud. And the other half were too personal ever to say out loud.

But she couldn't pass up the chance completely. So she took a breath and said, ''I was thinking that a child doesn't need a nanny, a person who will leave—a child needs forever. A child wants forever.''

''And that's a fantasy,'' he said without missing a beat. ''Forever just doesn't exist in this world—not for anyone. It's the moment that counts, period. And if anyone believes in forever, they're a fool. Besides, I'm a stranger to this kid.''

''But you're all he's got right now, so the right thing to do is to be there for him.''

''You're over your limit on saying what you think. But I'll cut you some slack. The right thing to do is to make sure he's taken care of—and he will be. Period. End of discussion.''

The limo slowed, and Lindsey looked out the window. They were at her place, the renovated warehouse in a light industrial area. She knew she should just get out and say ''thank you,'' and be thankful she'd been able to speak to Zane at all. She certainly didn't need to make any judgment on what he was doing with the little boy. He was right: it was the end of the discussion.

For once, she listened to reason and did the smart thing. When the chauffeur came around and opened the door, she said, ''Thanks for the ride, and good night,'' then got out and walked toward the entrance of her building.

She found her keys in her canvas tote and reached toward the heavy metal security door. But before she could put the key in the lock, she heard Zane's footsteps behind her.

''Lindsey?''

Zane had got out after Lindsey, a part of him thankful it

was over, and a part of him not willing to let it be over. "Lindsey?" he said again.

Her named echoed slightly on the all but deserted street, as she stopped and turned. "Yes?"

He didn't know what he wanted, but he'd had this same feeling, this spark, when she walked away last night. Some sort of excitement or challenge. God, he'd never looked at a woman as a challenge or a conquest, but Lindsey brought out the strangest feelings in him. Just once, he'd like to hear her say she agreed with him or thought he was doing the right thing.

Damn insanity, he thought as he stood near her. "You're giving up?" he asked.

"Giving up? How am I giving up?" she asked.

The harsh security lights only made her look more delicate. "I was certain you'd take one last shot, either at me, or to make a pitch for more things for that center of yours."

Her eyes were shadowed from the back light, but he could tell she was watching him intently. He could almost see her thinking, sorting through what she should say or not say. For a minute he was sure she was going to just say, "Good night," and go inside. But once again, he read her wrong.

"I was thinking today that you've got three or four massive—I mean, huge—conference rooms on the first level of the building at the back, and they're hardly ever used. You could have a full convention in them."

He'd been down there once or twice. "Or house a third world country?"

He knew she was probably blushing, but in this dim light he couldn't see much beyond her features. "They're big enough, and they're really nice and open, and I was thinking that it might be a good use of the space to move the center down there."

Zane had asked, and she was answering, with words that tumbled out. Her obvious enthusiasm for her ridiculous suggestion almost made it seem viable in some way. She came a bit closer, and he was captivated by the way shadows played at her cheeks and throat, at the way she used her hands to make a point, waving keys through the air with emphasis.

"Then the center could have a back entrance, and the kids wouldn't have to traipse through the lobby and go up very undependable elevators, and we could even get access to the back area and maybe have a playground of some sort. Someplace for the kids to play outside a bit. As it is we only have an indoor play area."

She took a breath, then said, "Well? What do you think? Is that a great idea or what?"

He stared at her. A great idea? He'd barely heard the words after the first part. He'd been so intensely aware of the passion in her that the rest had become a blur.

He was lost. The only great idea he had at that moment was kissing her. Just tasting her lips. He'd followed her for that. He knew that now. He admitted it to himself. He'd never been involved with an associate, and he'd sure as hell never chased after a woman in his life. But it seemed that with this woman, all of his rules for life were going out the window.

He heard her sigh. "Okay, what are *you* thinking?"

"Is it my turn to tell you what I'm thinking, with no recriminations?"

"Go ahead, I can take it."

She was inches from him, and even in the artificial light he saw the way her chin lifted just a bit. She was steeling herself for an attack. But that was the last thing in the world that he wanted—the very last thing. He moved closer.

"I was just thinking that you talk too much," he breathed, then reached to touch her.

She didn't move when he framed her face with his hands, touching the silky skin and feeling her tremble slightly. "You talk *way* too much," he whispered, just before he touched his lips to hers.

His need was overwhelming, that need to taste her lips and feel her warmth, to stop his words and her words. Yet the contact shocked him, almost as much as had the split-second realization that he'd wanted to do this from the moment he'd run into her on the stairs. That moment when he'd felt her body against his, her breasts against his chest, her scent surrounding him and mingling with her body heat.

As he tasted her, he knew something for certain that he'd never even thought about before. He could get lost in this woman, in her fire and her sense of passion. And he knew that if he touched her for one more second, there would be no turning back— But suddenly he realized it was all him. There was no response in her, no give and take. She was still...very still. And that cut through whatever lunacy he'd slipped into.

He moved back, letting her go with a very real sense of loss when he no longer felt her softness under his hands, or tasted her lips on his. She stared at him. The desire in him was raw. She was a dangerous woman, a woman who left him confused and off balance—two things he could never remember experiencing before with any woman.

"No recriminations," he said in a hoarse voice.

He didn't know what he expected, for her to laugh, or slap him, or tell him off. What he didn't expect was that she would just walk away. She turned from him, and, as he watched, she opened a heavy metal door, and without looking back, she went inside. The door clanged shut with a sound of finality.

"Bad call," Zane muttered. He was usually such a good judge of people. Of what they wanted. What they expected. But he'd blown it. Big time. So, forget it. Just let it be forgotten.

He went back to the car, got inside and said, "The hotel."

"Yes, sir," Gordon said.

As the car drove off into the night, Zane pushed his thoughts back as far away as he could. He'd never done regret well, and he wasn't going to start now. He wouldn't let the memory of her in this car, or the taste of her still on his lips, change that.

He wasn't spending time looking back and regretting his failed marriage, or the fact that Suzanne had found another man so quickly and had had a child. He sank back into the leather as he forced himself to shake off whatever strange mood Lindsey had brought with her.

He wasn't going to start playing the "what if" game, not now—and not with that woman.

Monday afternoon

LINDSEY DIDN'T WANT to be around Zane Holden again. Period. She'd start sending requests back up to him, but she wasn't going to plead her case in person. Zane was a man who did what he wanted. He used people. She wouldn't be used by him, no matter how inviting the man could be when he let down his guard.

When he'd kissed her, the shock had been so great that she'd frozen. And he'd let her go before she gave away any hint that when his mouth came down on hers, she was lost. She'd felt the world slipping away, the reality of who she was and who he was, dissolving into sensations and need and wanting and an ache that exploded in her. God, the man touched something in her, deep in her—and it scared her. She'd never let herself need or want anyone—not after having learned the pain of allowing that to happen. She couldn't let herself need this man.

Thank goodness he'd let her go, and she prayed that there hadn't been enough light for him to see her face clearly. If there had, he would have seen every raw emotion that was tangling in her, on her face. She'd never been good at hiding what she thought, much less what she felt. Thankfully she'd had enough strength to turn and walk away. She'd wanted to be alone to deal with the ache in her that his touch had caused.

After two long nights mixed up with the dreams and Zane and a loneliness that was almost unbearable, she'd been able to grab at sanity. By the time she went to work on Monday, she had control. She knew what she had to do. She was ready to stay away from Zane, to write another request and to forget about the kiss.

That lasted until just after four in the afternoon. Lindsey had spent a full hour in the kitchen, trying to coax the recalcitrant stove into making a batch of cookies that weren't burned. Then Amy burst into the small room with the cordless phone in one hand, her other hand over the mouthpiece.

"It's for you," she said in a forced whisper. "He said Zane Holden."

Lindsey waved her hand frantically. "No, no way. Tell him I'm not here, or tell him I disappeared. I don't care."

Amy frowned but put the phone to her ear. "I'm sorry, Miss Atherton isn't available." She listened, then said, "Just a minute," and put her hand over the mouthpiece again. "He says it's important, and he needs to talk to you. Maybe it's about your requests. What do I tell him?"

She reached for a towel and rubbed at the cookie dough sticking to her hands, hating the slight unsteadiness in them. She tossed the towel on the counter, clenched and un-clenched her fists to ease the tension in her, then forced herself to reach for the phone. Maybe Zane had thought about her suggestions. Maybe he was willing to negotiate on something.

"Okay, I'll talk to him," she said as she accepted the phone from Amy. Taking a deep breath, she pressed the receiver to her ear. "This is Lindsey Atherton."

"Miss Atherton," said a very formal-sounding man, and it certainly wasn't Zane. "Mr. Holden would like to speak to you."

"What's it concerning?" she asked.

"I'm not at liberty to say. He just requested that I contact you and ask you to meet with him."

The man sounded so businesslike that she felt a leap of hope. She might be right. Perhaps Zane had kept his word. He'd rethought her requests and maybe he'd changed his mind about the funding. If there was any chance of that happening, she'd walk on hot coals. She'd even break her vow never to be near Zane again. "Okay, I'll meet with him. When?"

"Right now, if you're free."

"Yes, of course. I'll come right up to his office."

"Oh, no, he's not in his offices. Could you come down to the main level?"

The main level? The conference rooms. Had he really been listening to her when she'd told him about her ideas for moving downstairs? She couldn't believe he had, but stranger things had happened in her life. "I'll be right down."

"I will meet you by the elevators in five minutes," the

man said, and before she could ask for his name or ask how she'd recognize him, he'd hung up.

She handed the phone back to Amy, who was watching her curiously. "Well, what's going on?"

"I don't have a clue who that man was, but he said that Zane wants a meeting. Downstairs in five minutes."

"Downstairs? Why down there?" Amy asked, as Lindsey tugged off an apron.

It hadn't completely protected the cotton of her short-sleeved sundress. A faint yellow stain from the colored candies she'd been using in the cookies marred the blue of her dress near the hem. She brushed at the stain.

"That's where the conference rooms are, and I talked to him about moving down there. I think he was listening." She frowned, then swiped at the stain one last time. "I look horrible."

"You look fine. You didn't tell me that you'd told him about that idea."

"I ran into him, and it seemed a good time to tell him to add it to the list."

Amy whistled. "I'm impressed."

"Don't be. Just hold down the fort here, and wish me luck. They've got two large kitchens off the conference rooms, and I bet the ovens work just fine."

"Good luck," Amy said.

Lindsey hurried out of the kitchen, past the reading circle to one side and the finger painting space to the other. She went into her office, got her purse and came back out. With a wave to Amy across the room, she left.

By the time she was heading down in the elevator, she had calmed a bit. She had to be very careful, had to put aside any feelings she had and make any compromises that wouldn't affect the center as a whole. She certainly couldn't allow her tongue to get away from her again.

The elevator stopped on the main level, the doors opened, and she was facing Zane's chauffeur.

The man smiled at her, nodded, then said, "Thank you for coming, miss."

"I don't understand," she said, hesitating.

"He's waiting for you." He motioned toward the exit. "If you'll come with me?"

"I thought he wanted to meet with me in the conference rooms."

"Oh, no, miss. I'm sorry if I gave you that impression. He's working from the hotel today and he needs to talk to you, to get some information, I gather."

Okay, she'd let her imagination run away with her. He just wanted clarification on figures, on her ideas. That was okay. That was a start. "It's my mistake."

"You'll come?"

"Yes, I'll come."

The chauffeur escorted her outside to the luxury car parked at the curb. He helped her in, then closed the door. She took several breaths to keep her nerves under control. As the car pulled away from the curb, she tried to settle back into the leather seat. But by the time the limousine pulled into an underground parking garage at one of the most luxurious hotels in the area, her stomach was in knots.

They parked in front of elevator doors, and the chauffeur was there right away, opening the door to let her out. He inclined his head to her. "Miss, he's waiting for you. You can take the last elevator to the top floor. He's in Penthouse A and I'll call to tell him you're on your way up."

"Okay," she said, and did as the man instructed.

In the hotel, she got into the elevator, and as she went up she rehearsed what she'd say. That she was grateful for his consideration. That she appreciated anything he could do for them. Maybe she'd reiterate some of her program ideas. One thing was for sure, she was going to let him do most of the talking. Every time she talked, she got in trouble. And anytime she let herself start to see him as a man— a devastatingly attractive man—she was in deep trouble. This time she'd leave as soon as she possibly could.

The elevator stopped and the doors opened to a large square area with only two sets of doors. She spotted Penthouse A right away. She crossed the thickly carpeted floor, knocked on the door and heard Zane call, "Come on in."

She pushed the door back and stepped into a place of total luxury. It wasn't a business suite but a personal suite, its rich decor compromised by the clutter that could only came from a child being there. Toys were strewn everywhere. A package of disposable diapers had been opened and spilled out onto an elegant brocade couch. And the smell of baby powder hung in the air.

In the middle of the clutter stood Zane, a man who dominated the space he occupied. Despite her nervousness and apprehension about talking to him again, something tugged at her when she took in his image. He'd probably started the day in an expensive suit, vest and tailored shirt. But now the jacket was gone, the tie was gone, the vest was laying on the coffee table, and the shirt was open at the neck, a dark spot on one shoulder. The in-control businessman, the man who with one look could make her heart pound, looked completely lost.

The tiny boy in his arms had pale blond hair cut in a Buster Brown style, huge blue eyes that were bright from recent tears and a trembling bottom lip. He was dressed in a disposable diaper, clutched a well-worn blue blanket to his cheek, and was arching away from Zane.

"Thank goodness," Zane said, struggling to keep the boy in his arms. "I thought you'd never get here."

She would have laughed at the awkwardness in the man

with the child, if she hadn't been so stunned. "The chauffeur said you wanted to talk to me, to get some information. I thought..." She shook her head. "Isn't this about the center?"

He was awkwardly patting the little boy's back, but having no success in easing the tension between them. "I need some expert advice."

"Excuse me?"

"You have a degree in Early Childhood Development, don't you?"

"Yes." Her spirits were sinking rapidly. She had let herself hope for so much, and obviously that had been a mistake. It was always a mistake to hope for too much. She thought she'd learned that long ago, but this man had made her hope. And for some reason, that hurt more than usual.

"Then, I need your advice about kids...this kid. His name's Walker," he said.

Her first impulse was to walk out the door and not look back, but a shuddering sigh from the little boy in Zane's arms stopped her.

"You could have called if that's all you wanted," she said as she drew closer, her voice tight. Her heart was being touched by the child and in some way by the man holding him. They were both lost.

"I would have called but I wouldn't have been able to hear you over the screaming."

Fighting the urge to smooth the remnants of tears off the child's flushed cheeks, she heard a soft hiccup. It made his tiny body tremble. "He's not crying now."

"Give him time."

She hesitantly reached to touch the child's hand, and was shocked when he wrenched toward her and almost out of Zane's hold. She caught him, drawing him close, and the blanket fluttered to the floor between them. His tiny arms wrapped around her neck in a tight hold, almost choking her. She could feel him shaking.

He was alone. He was terrified and didn't understand any of this. She knew how he felt, and it almost broke her heart. She looked at Zane and could tell that he wasn't too stable at the moment, either. She should have enjoyed the sight of confusion on his face, but it was so genuine, so human.

A man who could buy and sell conglomerates without blinking an eye, but he couldn't deal with a tiny child. She fought the urge to touch him, too, to reassure him that a baby couldn't destroy his world. But that impulse died when she saw the way he brushed his hands together, and the way he frowned at the child. Just holding the boy made her heart ache, but for Zane it was an inconvenience, something almost distasteful. She held more tightly to the frightened child in her arms.

Lindsey spoke, automatically lowering her voice to keep from startling the boy. "Where's the wonderful nanny?"

Zane turned, pushing at the toys and diapers on the brocade couch to clear a space, and he sank down onto the cushions. He reached for a full baby bottle amid the toys and set it on a side table before he leaned forward. With his elbows on his knees, he raked both hands through his hair, then he looked up at her. "I told you before, she isn't available until next week."

"The baby-sitter?"

"The hotel has a service, and they're contacting someone even as we speak. Meanwhile, I'm stuck. I don't know what he wants, and I thought someone with your background could figure it out. Rita brought him here from the airport an hour ago, but she had to leave to get her own kids. He's been crying ever since she left."

There was a knock at the door, and Lindsey turned to see Matt Terrel striding into the suite. He hesitated for just a fraction of a second when he saw her there, then came across the room.

"Everything under control?"

"They're better," Zane said, motioning to Lindsey and the boy.

She softly patted the child's bare back, and could literally feel him relaxing. She ignored Matt and spoke to Zane in a low voice. "You asked me to come all this way to figure out why a child's crying?"

"I need ideas, input, facts, something."

"You make it sound like a business problem."

"It is a problem, and there's a logical solution. I just don't have the data to implement it."

She could feel anger rising in her and tried to keep it under control. It wouldn't do anyone any good for her to get angry, least of all the child. "He's not a problem to be solved and fixed. And as to data, with children that's called 'instinct.'"

She thought she'd been reasonable and controlled in her response, but some of the reprimand she'd felt must have filtered into her voice.

"I don't need a lecture. What I do need is—"

"Input?"

"Suggestions."

"None of this is in my job description," she said in a tense whisper as she slowly rocked back and forth with the boy.

"Are we going to be able to get to work?" Matt asked.

He was as annoying as Zane, Lindsey thought. "I don't know," Zane said. "I don't know what's holding up that baby-sitter, either. The concierge said it wouldn't be more than an hour, and it's going on two hours."

"Okay, if it means we can get to that contract, I'll go down personally and check at the office to see when she'll be here,'' Matt said, then dropped his briefcase on an end table and headed for the door. ''Anything to get this in motion.''

The door clicked shut, and Lindsey looked at Zane. ''What's so important to the two of you?''

He shrugged. ''Work. It's piling up. For now, do you have any ideas what to do with him?'' He frowned at the boy and spread his hands palms up in a form of surrender. ''No matter what I do or try to give him, he screams.''

''He's scared,'' she said, pointing out what she considered totally obvious. ''Lots of kids that come to the center are scared at first, afraid to be away from their parents. That's why it's so important that the parents are close by. It makes them feel some sense of security. And if we could afford a Mommy And Me program, where each parent could take a few hours a week to spend with their child at the play area, I think—''

He cut off her words by standing abruptly and coming toward her, getting so close that she could see a flare of gold at the irises of his eyes. ''Please, I don't want a PR presentation about the center at the moment.''

She bit her lip hard to keep from saying what she wanted to at that moment. Instead, she tried to speak evenly and softly. ''Then, I guess I don't have any reason to be here. I need to get back to the center and the work *I* need to do.''

The boy stirred when Zane started to talk, and Lindsey shifted to gently bounce a bit to comfort him. ''You work for LynTech, and I need your services here for a little while. With all your education, I felt you'd have some answers.'' He nodded at the child. ''And it seems you're good at this. It's the first time he's been quiet since Rita left.''

The baby snuggled even closer, and she didn't want to

Chapter Eight

"Damn, you're a tough negotiator," Zane murmured. "Throwing that in just when you knew you had me. You have a real instinct for bargaining when you know your opponent is vulnerable."

The smile touched his eyes and the transformation was stunning, but short-lived when Lindsey asked, "And you're vulnerable?"

His eyes narrowed; the humor slipped away. "I'm in a receptive position at the moment," he said.

"So, you'll reconsider the funding?"

"All I can promise is to take another look at it. Take it or leave it."

She shifted the child in her hold, and knew that Zane was wrong. She wasn't any good at negotiating. She never could have followed through on any threat to leave. She knew she didn't have the heart—not when the boy's hold on her tightened and he sighed softly. She wasn't going anywhere—at least, not for a little bit. But Zane didn't have to know that.

"And the stove?" she prodded.

"Yes, the stove, too. First thing tomorrow, fixed or replaced."

"Okay, I'll get him settled and that's it, right?"

feel overwhelmingly protective of the tiny life. "He's disturbing your work, isn't he?"

"He was," he said, his voice a whisper now, but rough and tense. "I have tons of work. If I can't get him to settle down, my schedule is shot to hell."

"Welcome to the real world of children," she murmured.

"What would it take for you to help me out for a while, just until he settles or the baby-sitter gets here?"

"Now, that's a loaded question," she replied.

"Okay, keep it simple."

She jumped in with both feet and didn't flinch. "A new stove for the center. I just burned three batches of cookies in the old one."

"I'll have someone look at it and fix it."

"And if it's not fixable, a new one?"

He blew out an exasperated breath. "Okay, okay, a new one."

Walker stirred slightly, but kept snuggled tightly against her. "*And* you have to reconsider the requests for funding for the center," she added in a whisper.

His eyes narrowed for a moment. Then he suddenly smiled, an expression that came out of nowhere, the way the sun did on a cloudy day. And it brought just as much heat with it.

"You make that sound so simple," Zane said, then turned and pushed more things off the couch so she could sit down.

She sank into the fine material with the child. "When was he changed last?"

He glanced at his watch. "Rita changed him just before she left."

"And food?"

"I was trying to give him a banana, but he spit it out at me. And a bottle is a dangerous weapon in his hands." He stooped to pick up the bottle and hand it to her. "Maybe he'll take it from you. Rita brought a bag full of groceries with her—said there's stuff in there that the baby-sitter in Florida said he liked. But I only got as far as the banana, and if that was any sort of indication, the sitter didn't know a thing about what he liked."

She eased the baby around until she was cradling him, then offered him the bottle. "It's okay, sweetie," she whispered to him, holding the bottle so he could see it. He looked at her, his eyes huge and bright, then at the bottle. He reached for it with both hands. "Good boy," she said, when he started to drink.

She could feel him getting heavier as he relaxed more, and his eyes began to flutter as he drank. "He's exhausted," she whispered.

"He's not the only one," Zane said on a low sigh.

She looked up at the man standing over her, his fingertips tucked into the pockets of his slacks and the huge damp spot on his obviously expensive dress shirt. An attractive man, even when he was disheveled. "Well, you're not the one who flew all this way to be with a stranger."

"Touché," he muttered.

"Sorry," she said, and looked down at the child in her

arms. "You're tired," she said softly. He shifted, turning more into her embrace at the sound of her voice.

She looked back at Zane who was still standing over her and staring at her intently. "What did you say his name was?" she asked.

"Walker."

He stirred slightly at the sound of his name, but as she made a hushing sound, he settled again, and his eyes finally closed. "What's he been saying?"

"Saying?" He looked puzzled.

"He's a toddler. He talks."

"Rita said he was talking all the way here, but once he got here, all he did was scream. I think he's been saying, 'Mama,' and definitely 'No.'"

"Most kids can say 'no' quite well," she murmured, and when Walker frowned, scrunching his eyes tightly shut, she glanced back at Zane. "Could you turn down the lights?"

He moved out of her line of sight, and the lights soon went out; the only illumination was the glow of the setting sun that filtered in through opaque draperies.

"I'm going to clean up," he said in a low voice from somewhere behind her. "I'll be right back."

She simply nodded and settled more into the cushions with the child. She didn't have to turn to know Zane was gone. She could literally sense the emptiness of the room behind her. Shifting again to get more comfortable, she rested her head on the high back of the couch. Closing her eyes, she started to hum "Rock-a-bye, Baby," keeping time with soft pats on his bottom as she held him.

No conference room. No talks. No offers. Just a negotiation for a stove in return for helping a child. She smiled slightly, thinking of the new stove and of getting the best of the man...at least for a few moments. A lovely thought, very satisfying, she thought with a sigh.

The next thing Lindsey knew, Zane was saying her name softly through the darkness, a gentle, low, seductive sound—until the reality of the situation came to her. She must have drifted off herself for a few minutes. Despite the one kiss, this wasn't seduction; he was waking her, trying to get her attention without waking Walker.

Slowly she opened her eyes and he was there, in the soft shadows of the room. He'd changed his shirt and was bending over her and the child, close enough for her to inhale the scent of soap and freshness that clung to him. Now *that* was seductive, and something she would have moved away from, if she could have moved. But the boy was heavy in her arms.

"How is he?" he whispered.

"Sound asleep."

"It's a miracle," he said, and he smiled at her in the dim light. That was seductive, too, almost as seductive as his soft "Thanks to you."

She had to get out of here. She was off balance and wasn't at all sure how to regain her balance with Zane. She really needed space. She'd been here long enough. "Where can I put him down?" she asked.

"I've got a crib set up in the second bedroom."

She shifted to the edge of the couch, then stood with the baby in her arms. Zane led the way through the shadows. They crossed the room to an open door that spilled low light into the living area. She followed him into a bedroom that had obviously been rearranged in a hurry.

A double bed had been pushed to one side against the wall, and a brand-new wood crib stood against the opposite wall. A changing table, an adult rocking chair and a toy box were neatly arranged by the crib. Everything was new, and except for mussed blankets in the crib, the room looked undisturbed.

Lindsey went to the crib, then carefully maneuvered Walker until he was in the bed. He whimpered, but when she stroked his back and whispered, "It's okay, love," he sighed, shifted onto his tummy, then pushed his diapered bottom into the air. His eyes closed and the only sound in the room was faint sucking as he found his mouth with his thumb.

She carefully put a blue lamb blanket over him, waiting to make sure he wasn't going to stir, then turned to go back into the other room. But Zane was right behind her, and the collision was instantaneous. She felt the strength of his body, then his hands on her arms. She had always been so coordinated, but she seemed doomed to stumble into this man every time he was around.

She was inches from him, looking up into his shadowed face. Every instinct in her came painfully alive, and it was all she could do to turn away from him, mumble a "sorry," and get out of the room. She headed for her purse, and Zane was behind her. This time she was careful when she turned.

"I need to go."

"You earned that stove," Zane said.

She was unnerved when he came closer, and she tried to keep her distance. "And the reconsideration for funding," she said to try to get this back on a business footing.

"Right to the point, as always," he said.

"Sorry, but I didn't want you to forget."

"A deal's a deal. I won't forget." Unexpectedly he touched her chin with the tip of his finger. "But, I like the way you think." Heat was at the point of contact, and she trembled when he whispered, "It's damn attractive, actually."

He was damn attractive. And she was damn weak for just standing here. He moved closer, and she ducked away from him. The idea of another kiss was as frightening as it was exciting. There was no way she was going down that road again. No way. She was shaken just thinking about it—shaken by the realization of how much she wanted him to kiss her. A man who had the power to destroy every dream she had for the center.

And that realization kept her from doing something even more stupid, like moving closer to him. Whatever spell he could weave with his touch was gone, and she ignored the hammering of her heart, the unsteadiness in her body.

She crossed to the door, but before she could open it, it was pushed back and Matt was there. "We're in luck, people." He paused and reached to his right. "What's with the lights in here?" Then there was light, and it was almost blinding.

"That's better," he said, then moved aside to let a woman who was behind him step into the suite. "Audrey Linguist. Mr. Holden, Miss Atherton. We have a baby-sitter."

Lindsey looked at the tall, thin woman, probably somewhere in her mid-twenties, wearing black leggings with a baggy sweater knit from bulky yellow yarn. She was carrying a large tote bag, and acknowledged them with a vague nod of her head. For some reason, Lindsey didn't like her on sight, but wasn't going to let that matter. It wasn't her concern, and no one was asking for her opinion.

"Where is he?" Matt asked as he came in and closed the door.

"Asleep in the bedroom," Zane said.

Matt looked at Lindsey and lifted one eyebrow. "Nice work. I'm impressed."

"He was really tired," she murmured, holding her purse against her middle.

"Now we can get to work?"

"Of course, but could you show Miss Linguist where the boy is, Matt? Then come back out, and we'll get down to business."

He didn't argue, obviously willing to do whatever he needed to. "Sure." He motioned to the baby-sitter. "This way," he said, and the two of them crossed to the second bedroom and went inside.

"The limo should be out front. Just tell Gordon where you want to go," Zane said to Lindsey.

She nodded, then turned and reached for the door. But before she could leave, Zane spoke to her again. "Lindsey?"

She turned, and he was still standing by the couch. "Yes?"

"Thanks for everything."

He looked genuinely thankful, and it stirred something in her. "I got a stove out of it. That's fair."

Suddenly he switched back to the cut-to-the-chase businessman, and that man—the one she kept thinking she caught glimpses of—was gone again. "For future reference, always ask higher than you can get, then you have a lot of negotiating room."

He was so smug, so sure of himself now, that she couldn't resist a parting shot. "For future reference, Mr. Holden, you should know that I would have done this just to have you reconsider my requests for the center. I can always make cookies at home."

He shook his head and on a low chuckle said, "Well, damn, I'm slipping."

"I guess you are," she said, then went out into the hallway with his rough chuckle following her.

"What's so funny?" Zane heard Matt say as the door clicked shut behind Lindsey.

He shook his head. "Nothing." He turned to Matt. "Things settled in there?"

"For now." Matt retrieved his briefcase and headed to the dining alcove. Zane followed and flipped on a light over a table littered with paperwork that should have been done hours ago. Two laptop computers were amid the clutter, and three phones and a fax machine sat on a side table.

Zane reached for one of the top folders and took a seat, as Matt settled across from him. He pushed the laptop back to make space, then flipped open the folder. "I just hope we can bring this under control. Lewis was way off base the past couple of years." He scanned several financial readouts. "Way off base."

He stopped at a page that held figures on resources—charts that showed the decline of viability for certain departments. As a whole, LynTech was dangerously close to collapse, but with each individual part standing alone, there could be strength—real strength—if the right cuts were made. Serious cuts.

He skimmed the columns and stared hard at the bottom section headed Day Care Program. Right beside it was the financial chart. Zane stared at it as he took out his gold pen. There was no way to keep it open, no way at all. He had promised Lindsey he'd reconsider it, but there was nothing to reconsider. In four months there wouldn't be a day care program.

He should have just told Lindsey. He'd surely never had trouble telling anyone bad news in business before. But something had kept him from telling Lindsey. And he'd promised her a stove that worked. That frustrated him, and angered him.

"What was that about a stove?"

He looked up at Matt. "What?"

"I thought I heard her thanking you for a stove."

Zane sat back and laid the pen on the papers. "I agreed to get the stove fixed in the day care center in exchange for her helping me here tonight."

Matt looked down at the papers, then back at Zane. "What are you talking about? Aren't we closing that place down by March?" he asked. "Has there been a change of plans that I don't know about?"

"No. It's still going to be eliminated. The stove is a stove. It'll work until it closes down. Their stove apparently doesn't work. Maintenance would have fixed it eventually. I'll just speed it up. Make things easier all the way around—and then we've got peace and quiet. It was a deal at twice the price. It's done. And things are still on track for the downsizing."

"That's a relief. I thought the way things were, maybe you were going soft."

"The way what things are?"

"With the two of you. Your bringing Lindsey here."

"There is no 'two of us'—and she wants funding. She's not going to get it, but she's not going to quit until it's dead and gone."

"And she doesn't know that it's a done deal that it's going to close, does she."

"There hasn't been an announcement and there won't be. That's a sure way to kill interest in the project if they know you've got trouble. Keep a lid on it. When it happens, it happens, but we'll choose the time. I've told her the truth—that there won't be new funding. But she's got a one-track mind. She needs to get a life outside of work."

Matt actually laughed at that. "Boy, that's the pot calling the kettle black, isn't it? You only date when you want free PR advice. And to go any farther than dating? Forget it."

"I did that once, and I didn't do it well. I might do foolish things, but I learn." He wanted to change the direction of their conversation. "You're the one that needs to get out."

Matt's smile disappeared. "I get out when I want to, and when it won't distract me from something this important. Speaking of which, why did you ask her up here, when you could have called her?"

Matt was as bad as Lindsey for using logic against him. "I wanted someone to take him off my hands for a few minutes, and you weren't volunteering." He'd been going crazy, and when Lindsey had arrived things had shifted. He'd enjoyed their sparring. Whenever they met, it was never boring. Damn, she was a good diversion. Part of him knew that she'd be more than a "good" diversion for any man. "She got things under control."

Although, he'd almost lost control for a second or two. The kiss had been a given on his part. It was she who had killed it before it could begin. That had jarred him—and the feeling still lingered.

"So, when will Lindsey know about the closure?" Matt asked.

Zane shrugged. "When we announce it. When the time's right."

Matt frowned, but only said, "Whatever."

Zane knew one thing about Lindsey. She was a survivor. From what little she'd said about her past, and the way she kept up a steady assault on him about the center, he figured she'd be okay. And maybe that was part of what drew him to her, beyond her looks and subtle sexiness.

"She'll land on her feet," he murmured.

"And your conscience will be clear?"

"What does my conscience have to do with anything?" he asked. "It's business and it's not personal."

Matt leaned forward, hunching his shoulders slightly as

he placed his hands on the papers in front of him. "Zane, we don't need this."

"What?"

"She's getting to you."

She'd gone beyond simply "getting" to him, but he wasn't going to go into that with Matt. "And that's personal, not business, my friend."

Matt held up both hands, palms out. "Okay, okay, I get the message." Then he sat back. "You know, I think we're going to pull out at LynTech, and I just don't want any surprises. There's too much at stake. The kid is enough of a surprise, enough of a complication. We don't need another complication thrown into the mix."

"She's not a complication," Zane said, but could have sworn that was a lie. It shouldn't be, but somehow, on some level, he knew it wasn't the absolute truth.

"Okay. I've always admired your ability to separate business and pleasure."

Pleasure? That word fit Lindsey. It was a pleasure to look at her, to inhale whatever fragrance clung to her, to watch her expressions, to spar with her. He pushed all that aside.

"Speaking of business," he said, pushing his file toward the center of the table. "While we have peace, let's take advantage of it."

For over an hour, no sounds came from the extra bedroom, but Zane still couldn't totally concentrate on what he was doing. Time after time, Matt read off figures, then had to read them again before Zane got them. "Damn it," he muttered, pushing back from the table. "Do you want a drink, some coffee, something?"

Matt waved the offer aside. "No, thanks."

Zane got up and went to the bar built in the wall by the kitchen area, looked at the line of bottles and opted for a bottle of water. He'd thought he could do this; take in Suzanne's child, look after him until a relative was found. And he would. But that didn't mean he could do it without paying a price. He drank a long swallow of the cold water, then went back to the table.

"Here," Matt said, as Zane sank back down in his chair. "These are the best I can do on the revisions."

He read the figures. "These are great. At least one of us is thinking straight."

"Do you want to call it quits for a while?" Matt asked, sitting back and clasping his hands behind his head as he stretched out his shoulders and neck.

"You've got plans?"

He sat forward and started stacking his papers. "Plans to get a bit of dinner, then start on this again. You want to come along, or are you seeing what's her name again? The PR wonder?"

"Karen—and no, I'm not." He wasn't about to go into detail about the miserable dinner he'd had with her after showing up late. Nothing he'd said placated her, and by the time he sent her home in the limo while he stayed at the bar, he knew he wouldn't be seeing her again. If he wanted PR advice for the company, he'd pay for a consultation or go to the company's marketing department.

A loud crying, only slightly muffled by the closed door to the second bedroom, seemed to explode around him. "Dinner sounds good," he said.

"Should we just get something sent up?" Matt asked.

He shook his head. "No." He motioned to the closed door. "Not with that going on."

As he moved around the suite getting his jacket and tie, the crying didn't let up. He was at the door, ready to leave, his hand on the knob, but something stopped him.

He hesitated, then glanced at Matt. "I'll be right back."

He headed for the bedroom, opened the door and looked inside. The baby-sitter was curled up in a chair by the bed, wearing huge earphones that were connected to a silent television. Walker was in the crib, standing at the rail, gripping it with both hands and screaming at the top of his lungs.

Zane crossed to the baby-sitter and tapped her on the shoulder. The woman almost jumped at the contact, then saw it was him and sank back in the chair.

"What's going on?" Zane asked, raising his voice to be heard above the baby's screams.

The woman shook her head, then pulled the earphones back. "What's the matter?"

"What's going on in here?"

She glanced at Walker, then back at him. "I'm watching television."

"What about him?" he said, motioning to the crying baby.

"He's crying. If you pick them up every time they cry, you'll never get them to stop. They get spoiled real easy."

"Stop him," Zane said tightly, trying very hard not to scream at her.

"He's okay," she said, and seemed about to put her earphones back on and continue watching the television.

"I'm not okay," Zane said. He pulled her earphones off completely, barely missing pulling her hair with them. "Stop him now," he ground out.

She stood, grabbing at the earphones and shaking her head. "You don't need to get nasty with me," she muttered. "You're paying me to baby-sit and I am, so what's the problem?"

If he had to tell her there was a problem here, he knew he wasn't going anywhere and leaving her with the child. "It's time for you to go."

"They said you wanted me for a few days."

"*They* were wrong," he muttered. "Just get out of here."

"You have to pay me for one day, minimum," she said.

"You've got it."

"Okay," she muttered. Stuffing her earphones into her tote and leaving the TV on, but blaring now, she strode out of the room.

Zane hit the off button on the TV, then crossed to the crib and picked up the boy. About the only thing the woman had done was to dress the child in blue flannel sleepers. But under the softness of the fabric, Zane felt the rigidity of the child. Walker didn't cuddle in as he had with Lindsey, and he didn't stop crying, either, or screaming, "Go way, go way!"

"I wish I *could* go away, buddy," he muttered. He called, "Matt, find that bottle for me near the couch!"

By the time he got out into the other room, Matt was coming toward him with the bottle. But before Zane could take it from Matt, Walker grabbed it and flung it away, barely missing Matt's head.

"No!" he yelled, then the crying started again.

"What happened with the baby-sitter?" Matt asked over the din.

"She wasn't any good," Zane said, jiggling and patting the baby awkwardly. "She was unsuitable. I just wish I had a clue what he wanted."

"Whatever it is, you're not it," Matt said from a safe distance now.

"Thanks."

"What now?"

"Either you hold him while I call the concierge to get a replacement up here, or you call."

There was no choice there. Matt didn't hesitate to grab

the phone. While he made the call, Zane walked around the room, jiggling the boy and talking to him. "Come on, give me a break. What do you want?"

"They'll get another sitter," Matt said. "But it might take an hour or more."

"Great," Zane muttered.

"You shouldn't have driven off the first one before you had a replacement."

He grimaced. "Live and learn."

"Do you want me to call Lindsey?"

The idea was tempting, far too tempting. "No."

"She worked magic on him before. I just thought—"

"Just figure out something to make him stop crying." He looked around the room. "That stuff Rita brought with her—the bag's on the other side of the table. I think I put it on the floor someplace. See what's in it."

Matt crossed to the table, crouched down behind it, then held up a bag of cookies. "How about these?"

"Try them."

He brought the bag over, tore it open and took out a chocolate sandwich cookie. He'd barely held it out before Walker made a grab for it; and the crying stopped abruptly when the child had the treat in his hand.

"Cookie, me want cookie," he said on a sob, then reached for another one Matt held out. "More cookie."

It startled Zane for a minute when he spoke without screaming or throwing something. He was a real little person. That seemed odd somehow. "Give him more," he told Matt. "He wants cookies."

"He likes them," Matt said.

Zane crossed to the couch, put Walker down on the off-white carpet right in front of him and helped Matt pile cookies in front of the boy. Finally the world was quiet. Blessedly quiet.

Zane breathed deeply. "Well, that was easy."

"Sure, and what happens when you run out of cookies?"

"Hopefully, by then the new baby-sitter will be here."

"Okay, I'm out of here. I need food. What are you going to do?"

"I guess I'll order up," he said.

"Tell you what, I'll take the papers with me and go back to my place to work. I'll go over them with you tomorrow."

"I'll be in at eight, okay?"

"Sure, and good luck."

Zane grimaced. "I think I'm going to need it."

Matt's laughter as he closed the door didn't help at all. Zane looked at Walker, chocolate covering his hands and face, crumbs on the off-white carpeting. Those blue eyes turned on him, bright with recent tears. Suddenly he smiled and held out to Zane the remnants of the cookie he'd been eating. "Wan some?"

"No, thanks, guy," he said. "I don't want some. You eat it."

Walker grinned, stuffed the rest of the cookie in his mouth and reached for another one.

Zane leaned back on the couch and tried to figure out when he had lost control of his life. Was it when the attorney came into his office with the news of Suzanne's death and his temporary custody of Walker? Was it when he got stuck in the elevator with Lindsey? Was it when Walker got here and took over the hotel suite? Or was it when he kissed Lindsey the first time, and wanted desperately to do it again just a few hours ago? He ran a hand roughly over his face, sank lower in the couch and grimaced as Walker rubbed a gooey chocolate hand over the stomach of his blue sleepers.

"All of the above," he muttered in an answer to all of his questions. "All of the above."

Chapter Nine

Tuesday

"Your stove is fine, just needed some adjusting and a new thermostat. You shouldn't have any more problems."

Lindsey turned from stacking boxes of paper towels in the tiny cupboard in the center's kitchen. The repairman in navy coveralls had shown up first thing that morning, saying he was there to fix the stove. Now he was closing his toolbox and speaking for the first time in two hours.

"Thanks for coming so quickly," she said.

He glanced at her, then gripped his toolbox as he readied to leave. "They put a rush on it. Otherwise, you would've been lucky to get it done at all. Staff's so short." He went to the door, then stopped and frowned at her. "You heard about John Olson, didn't you?"

She remembered John Olson's name very well. "Yes, I heard about him."

"Get this. He was fired, and he'd been here for years. But he got his revenge."

"Revenge?"

"Listen to this, the High and Mighty upstairs fire John, then a week later one of them gets stuck in the elevator.

Not only does he get stuck, but it's with some woman. Probably trying to impress her—and the elevator gets stuck between floors. John's gone. Andy, the fill-in guy, who doesn't know beans about the lifts, can't figure it out. The guy and the woman end up having to crawl out the hole in the top and up the shaft.'' He laughed at that. ''Damn, wouldn't ya have liked to have been there to see that? The guy explaining to his date why they had to shimmy up cables.''

She smiled at the memory. ''It must have been something.''

''Know what the best part was?''

She had her own view of that, but she let him talk. ''No.''

''John comes in, flips a switch and bingo, bango, done! *And* they pay John a ton of bucks to do it.'' He laughed again. ''Served them right, I'd say.''

She knew her smile deepened. ''I'd say so, too.''

''Damn right.'' He motioned to the stove. ''I hope that works for a while.''

''They said we could get a new one if it doesn't.''

''I wouldn't hold my breath on that one. They'd sooner nail this place shut than put money in it.'' He shrugged. ''Probably will, anyway. They're cutting everything. Just ask John Olson, eh?'' He touched his beaked cap with one hand. ''See you later,'' he said, then left.

Lindsey took off the apron she'd been wearing over beige slacks and a teal shirt, and headed for her office. The man's last words had taken away any of the humor she'd felt. There was no way they could just shut down the center. Cutting was one thing, but closing it… She tiptoed through the main room, past the kids napping on their mats and Amy sitting in the rocking chair with Taylor in her lap, her eyes closed, too.

She went through into her office, closed the door and leaned back against it. No, Zane wouldn't be closing the center if he fixed the stove. That didn't make any sense. But then, he was responsible for John Olson losing his job. She tried to think. No, he'd agreed to reconsider the funding. She shook her head.

But even as she sat at her desk, she couldn't shake an uneasiness. She hesitated, then picked up the phone and called Zane's office. She'd just thank him for the stove repair and ask him if he'd had a chance to rethink the funding. That couldn't hurt. She wouldn't have to see him, or be alone with him, or be at the penthouse with the child there. A simple phone call.

"Mr. Holden's office."

"This is Lindsey Atherton down on six at Just For Kids. Can I speak to Mr. Holden?"

"I'm sorry. He's not available. Do you need to reschedule your appointment?"

She'd totally forgotten about that. "Oh, no, thank you. I just needed to speak to him."

"I'll let him know," the secretary said, and the line went dead.

"Thank you, too," Lindsey muttered as she hung up.

By the time Lindsey was ready to leave, Zane had not returned her call. He'd stayed "unavailable" all day, and the last time she'd called up to his office, she'd gotten his voice mail. No call, no contact. She got her things and headed down to the bus stop, thinking that he probably hadn't called because he was busy. That had been obvious every time she'd been around him. Work was his focal point in life. Correction—the *bottom line* was his focal point, not people or the child, and definitely not her and what she needed.

That niggling uneasiness about everything was growing,

and she hated it. She had to believe he was as good as his word. She didn't have to like what he did in other areas of the company. Or the way he saw Walker as a nuisance and a problem. She didn't have to like anything about him, as long as she got the funding out of him and the center stayed intact. That was her bottom line.

No limo pulled up to the bus stop today as she waited for her ride. No blue-eyed man asked her if she wanted a lift home. And when she got to the loft, there was only Joey waiting for her. The huge orange tabby cat meandered out of the bedroom area into the main space, as she came in the front door. His meows echoed faintly off the polished hardwood floors, white plastered walls and high ceilings with their exposed piping painted black to blend with the roof area.

"Okay, okay," she murmured as she stepped out of her shoes and padded barefoot through the living space, past scattered pillows, and two low couches done in navy linen, facing each other and framed by bleached wood tables holding wrought-iron lamps. The former tenant had furnished the place, but decorating had been beyond him. And all she'd done since being here was add plants everywhere she could. Everything else was the way he'd leased it to her.

She entered what passed as a kitchen; an alcove with doorless cupboards, granite counters, a stainless-steel sink and an old-fashioned restaurant refrigerator pushed against the wall under high, transom windows.

She fed the cat, put on coffee, then headed for the bedroom space on the opposite wall. Potted palms framed the doorless entry in the six-foot partitions that defined the space. A huge metal-framed, king-size bed stood under the transom windows and faced an armoire and a dresser. She'd replaced a navy spread with her own white down comforter and matching pillows.

The bathroom to the right was done in granite—cold and sterile-looking except for the ferns and more palms. She stripped off her clothes, stepped into the freestanding shower and turned on the hot water. When she finally emerged from the steamy bathroom with her damp hair in a towel and wearing a short, white terry-cloth robe, she felt better.

She meandered back into the living space, which was filled with shadows now from the early evening through the bank of windows that looked down over the business area of the city. She flipped on two side lights, then crossed to one of the couches that faced a television built into a side niche. With the news turned on, she sat and tucked her bare feet under her.

Before she could figure out what the newscaster was saying about the Middle East, Joey had joined her. He jumped onto the couch and into her lap, and curled up to settle there. She tickled his ears and felt his motor start. She'd never had a pet before, but he was fitting in just fine— independent but affectionate.

"You're spoiled," she said. "Spoiled rotten." And all the company she needed.

She stared at the television, at depressing news—pictures of storms on the east coast, then terrorism—but even that couldn't distract her enough to forget about the center and Zane. She fought a sinking feeling that he wasn't going to do anything for her. He'd got what he wanted from her— and almost more than he knew with his kiss—but his payment had been a stove repair. That was probably going to be it.

She didn't know why she felt so deflated. He did what he wanted to do. Took what he wanted to take. He used people. That was why he had gotten to where he had in business. He was a user. A man who attracted people, obviously attracted women, and got what he wanted. And he got rich along the way.

She touched her mouth with the tips of her fingers, almost afraid to put her tongue to her lips in case she could still taste him there. That was foolish, she thought, but that didn't stop her from wiping her hand across her lips. The man took life on his terms, and she wasn't going to let him use her. She wasn't going to let herself believe that she caught glimpses of something deep in the man, something that touched her own soul. Foolishness in its highest form.

She wasn't going to let herself fall into a trap of trying to please him, either, or trying to get his attention in any way but with words and logic. If she could just keep a distance from him, and from whatever web he seemed to weave when she was around him, she'd be okay. All she wanted was to help the center survive and thrive. To somehow take a tiny bit of fear out of a child's world.

The phone rang on the end table near her left elbow, and she shifted, put the television on mute and reached for the receiver. "Hello?" she asked, expecting Amy on the other end of the line.

But it wasn't Amy. "Lindsey, it's Zane."

She sat up straighter. He was returning her calls finally, she thought as hope leapt in her. "Yes."

"I'm not interrupting anything, am I?" he asked.

"No, not at all. I just…I thought your secretary had gone to the school that trains them to say you're 'unavailable' no matter what's going on. I must have called ten times today."

"She's well trained, but she was telling you the truth. I haven't been available all day. I haven't even been in the office most of the day."

"But she let you know I'd been calling?"

"No, actually, I didn't know. Matt's been taking care of the office end of things today."

She sank back in the couch, struggling to keep hope afloat and to try to block a mental image she had of him from her mind. The blue eyes narrowed on her. That considering look. She pushed that away.

"If you aren't returning my calls, are you calling because you've reconsidered the funding requests?"

"No, I haven't had the time or opportunity."

He said it quickly, decisively, and her hope sank even farther. "Then, what is it?" She didn't mean to sound abrupt, but she had to fight not to hang up on him. She just wanted to get this over with and get off the phone.

"The last time, you suggested I should have called for advice instead of having Gordon bring you to the penthouse. Remember?"

More free advice? She sat a bit straighter. No, nothing was free, and her advice for him wouldn't be. "I remember."

"I thought I'd take you up on it."

"That wasn't an offer, it was a suggestion," she pointed out.

"I'm taking the *suggestion.*"

Damn, she didn't want him to be this conciliatory. She didn't want to feel there was any humanity in the man. "You've got the baby-sitter. Why do you need to ask me for advice?"

"No, I don't."

"Don't what?"

"Have the baby-sitter."

"What happened to 'Miss Sunshine'?"

That brought an unsettling sound from Zane, the softness of laughter tinged with ruefulness. "Miss Sunshine? She's gone, and so is the backup sitter the hotel's concierge found for me.''

"Well, you've got the money to buy the best help there is, obviously, so what's the problem?"

"Finding that help. I've just got to fill this week with a baby-sitter, until the nanny's available, and you'd think I was asking for world peace and a trip to Mars."

"And you can't buy either one, I take it?"

He sidestepped her barely veiled sarcasm. "Walker's making it impossible. When he's not racing all over the place, he's getting into anything that isn't locked or higher than two feet off the ground, or screaming at the top of his lungs." He took a deep breath. "Listen, the last sitter was here for the morning, then pleaded a headache and took off running."

"Powerful little guy, isn't he," she said, finding herself smiling at the frustration in Zane's voice. She wasn't usually vindictive, but he was bringing out a lot of things in her that she'd never known were there.

"This isn't funny," he muttered.

"Of course not," she lied.

"The last sitter said something about a car ride calming down kids, but she didn't volunteer, so we borrowed a safety seat from the hotel and Gordon is driving us around. But Walker's nowhere near going to sleep."

"He's not crying—at least, I can't hear him."

"Right now he's not. But he's not looking as if he's going to sleep anytime soon, and if he's awake he never slows down. Sort of perpetual motion."

"You're in the limousine?"

"Yes, with a two-year-old who's gone through two packages of cookies already."

"No wonder he's not sleeping. He's on a sugar high."

"And?"

"Just don't give him any more cookies, and wait it out."

"For how long?"

"I hope you've got a full tank of gas."

"Oh, great," he said. "Any other suggestions?"

"Keep driving," she said, taking perverse pleasure in his ineptitude.

"With all your education, that's the best you can come up with?" he muttered.

"Sorry."

There was an ear-shattering scream, then muffled voices, before Zane was back on the line with the baby crying in the background. "How much do you want?"

"What?"

"How much do you want to help me out on this?"

Oddly, even though she'd thought of trying to negotiate something else for the center by helping him further, it angered her that that had been his first thought. Pay for it. She knew right then that if he'd just asked her to help because a little boy was in desperate need of love and attention, she would have melted. But his approach—she didn't like at all.

"What are you offering?" she asked bluntly.

"Name your figure."

She wanted the Mommy and Me program to be funded, but was wary of asking too much. She knew better than to push that hard or that fast with someone like Zane. But there was something else she wanted very much. "I need more money for salary increases."

"I'll look at any ideas you have," he said quickly, as the baby continued screaming.

"You've seen enough of my proposals...and that request has been in there every time."

"It's *your* salary you want increased?"

"No, Mr. Lewis was generous with my salary. I want to

be able to increase the salary of my coordinator, Amy Blake…by fifty percent.''

''You had twenty percent in your proposal.''

He *had* read her figures. She'd thought he had just passed them on. The knowledge strengthened her resolve. ''It's fifty percent, now.''

''I can manage ten percent.''

There was nothing to lose, and everything to gain for Amy. ''Fifty.''

Walker screamed louder in the background, and Zane raised his voice to be heard. ''Twenty percent.''

''Forty,'' she said, and Walker let out another bloodcurdling scream.

''Thirty.''

''Thirty-five, but retroactive to September.''

There were muffled sounds coming from Zane, then he finally said, ''Okay, okay, agreed.''

The idea that a tiny child was bringing Zane Holden to his knees was thoroughly appealing to her. And the fact that she'd got a full fifteen percent more money for Amy than she'd first requested was a bonus, indeed. All because of a little boy. How appropriate, she thought. How the mighty have fallen. She'd just bet there hadn't been many people in this world who had ever come close to bringing down Zane Holden.

''Agreed,'' she said.

''You're a killer negotiator,'' he muttered. ''Just don't tell me you would have settled for less.''

''I won't tell you that,'' she said, smiling on her end of the line. Her taste of victory was sweet. Better than sweet, it was fantastic. He'd given in, and this was just a first step. ''Where do you want me to go?'' she asked, standing. She was anxious to get dressed and leave before he changed his mind.

"You don't have to 'go' anywhere."

"What?"

"Just ring us up. We're outside your building."

She stood very still, one hand pressed to her middle, the other gripping the phone tightly. "Here?"

"Downstairs. We'll be right up, as soon as we get past this metal door."

She didn't want this at all. But she couldn't back out—not now that she had the agreement for Amy's raise. Damn it, whether he knew it or not, he'd got the last laugh this time.

"Okay," she said, sounding braver than she felt. "I'll ring you in. Take the service elevator to the top floor. I'll meet you by the gate."

Zane heard the buzzer and a click. When he turned the latch on the security door, the barrier opened with a low squeaking sound. Whoever had redesigned the warehouse into apartments hadn't spent much money on the amenities in the entrance. The floors were scuffed wood and brick, the walls scarred planks with a door on either side. The whole place was worn-looking, except for fairly new-looking brass name plaques on each door.

Overhead lighting was stark and made the area look even more barren. And the "elevator" was really little more than a huge wire cage on cables, fronted by a chain-link safety gate.

While Zane struggled to get the gate up and keep his hold on the boy, Walker calmed down, seemingly struck by some sort of fascination with Zane's struggles and the huge cage they finally stepped into.

Zane had had no intention of going anywhere near Lindsey's place when he got in the limousine an hour ago. But after driving all over the city with a crazed two-year-old throwing cookies, spitting milk and screaming at will, he'd acted impulsively by telling Gordon to drive here.

He'd always liked lots of options in his life, but he'd almost run out of them with the child. The only option seemed to be getting to Lindsey. At that moment when he'd picked up the phone, he'd been willing to do whatever it took to have some peace again. He just hadn't planned on having to negotiate with her. He just wanted to get her help, get peace restored, then get the hell out of town.

"Go up, way up?" Walker asked.

"That's the plan, kiddo," Zane said as he tugged to get the gate back down, then push the button for the next level. The lift lurched once, then slid at a snail's pace upward.

Walker grabbed at Zane, his tiny arm around the man's neck in a tight grip. "Up, way up," he whispered.

Lindsey had done hard negotiating on the phone, and a part of Zane admired her taking advantage of the situation. He would have, too, if it had been him. He almost laughed at the memory of her pinning him down, but it wasn't any laughing matter now. He'd just agreed to something that would last less than a few months, just to get her help. He'd approve the raise, retroactive and all...for now. It's what he needed to do.

The thing was, doing whatever it took had never before bothered him in business, but in this case it didn't sit right. He knew it was well worth whatever he'd had to promise her, to get help with Walker, but that didn't stop the bad taste in his mouth: she didn't have any idea that this was short term. A part of him wanted to tell her the truth. But he stopped himself. Soon—he'd tell her soon. At least he'd give her a heads-up before he did the actual deed.

They reached Lindsey's floor, and she was there—first just a glimpse of bare feet followed by shapely legs exposed under the hem of a white terry-cloth robe. The robe was wrapped around a slender figure, barely suggesting first the swell of hips, then high breasts. Finally, he met her amber gaze.

He felt like smiling, just seeing her there—but she wasn't smiling. Her hair was damp and skimmed back from her makeup-free face. There was nothing added to her, no attempt to be anything other than what she was. And he'd bet she had no idea that she was more stunning that he'd ever seen her before. Beautiful—definitely not happy, but beautiful.

She looked…resigned, and that bothered him too much to even look at his reaction right now. He didn't want to deal with anything on that level at the moment. Or to deal with his feeling when the minute those eyes went to Walker, the smile came.

Walker started to bounce in his arms, and the peace was broken. "Me go! Me go!" he yelled, way too near Zane's ear for comfort.

Lindsey came closer, a smile teasing the corners of her full lips. She gripped the bottom of the wire mesh gate when the elevator stopped, then tugged it up and out of the way. With nothing between them, Zane faced her, and as their eyes met, he sensed a tension in her that almost made him blink.

Why hadn't he thought of it before? She was in a robe, looking for all the world as if she had just gotten out of a shower—and maybe bed before that? He hadn't stopped to think about what she might have been doing, or who she might have been doing it with. She was a woman made for more than polite conversation—a hell of a lot more.

And there was Joe. Zane didn't move from the elevator, even though his instincts were to get as close to her as he could.

Chapter Ten

"Me go play," Walker was saying in Zane's arms, but in a blessedly lower voice.

"Listen, this might be a bad idea," Zane said quickly as he stepped off the lift and onto her floor. "Just say so, and we'll go. No harm, no foul."

He watched Lindsey carefully, the color that touched her cheeks setting off her freckles. "You want to back out on our deal?"

That hadn't entered his mind. Not with her in front of him in a bathrobe, and perhaps nothing else. "Forget the deal. If you're busy—"

"No, we won't forget it. You agreed to give Amy that raise...retroactively." She came closer, bringing a stirring of air and a mingling of heat and soap and sexiness. "You're coming inside and you're keeping your word. Or we all go down to the car and drive around. Okay?"

Zane looked down at her, at the way her chin lifted, at the freckles on her nose, at the way her eyes seemed to dare him to leave. But he found that the idea of seeing her with Joe, was almost distasteful to him. The car might be a good option.

"Are you alone in there?"

Color flushed her cheeks again as she said in that low, breathless voice of hers, "Very alone."

If she was alone, Joe was stupid. What man wouldn't be with a woman like this? But Joe's loss was his gain. "Okay, we're coming inside, then."

She turned her full attention on Walker. "Want to come play, Walker?"

"Huh, me play," he said, starting to bounce from excitement.

"Let's do that, champ," she said, turned to head back through the open door to her apartment. "Coming?" she tossed over her shoulder to Zane.

Zane followed her into a huge loft with beams and pipes overhead and broken up into various areas by partial walls that rose about six feet and were topped by heavy, molded shelves. Plants seemed to be everywhere, and packing boxes were placed off to the left side of the space.

As he swung the door shut behind them, he glanced ahead and saw Lindsey by one of two navy couches. A television was on, tuned to the news, but with no sound.

"You must have been desperate to come here," she said, eyeing Walker, who wore denim overalls and a white T-shirt that even Zane knew were so cookie-smeared that they were beyond help.

Desperate didn't begin to describe what he'd been a few minutes ago. "The ride in the elevator made him stop crying."

Walker was wiggling frantically. "Me get down. Me play. Peeze, peeze?"

"Is it safe to put him down?" he asked Lindsey.

"He's curious. New places, new things. Let him down, and we'll keep an eye on him."

"Down, down now," the boy said loudly.

"Okay, for a bit." Zane put him down, and was surprised when he didn't run off. He felt the boy grasp his pant leg. "Why didn't *I* think of sensory overload to stop him?"

"Distraction is the name of the game—anything to give him something to figure out. It breaks the routine they get into with crying."

She came closer as she spoke, and the minute she was within range, Walker reached for her and grabbed at her hand. "Play, me play, car, car, car."

"He wants to ride again?" Zane asked.

"No, he probably wants a car or truck to play with."

"Huh, truck, me want truck," Walker said, nodding vigorously, his silky hair dancing around his face.

"You're a translator, too," he said. "I'm impressed."

"No, I've just been around kids long enough to know their shorthand."

"Play now, peeze." Walker tugged hard on her hand.

"Okay, okay," she said, and led him over to a side table. She picked up something and turned to offer it to Walker. It looked like a white ball, but Zane realized it was a ball of yarn.

"Look at this," she said to the boy, crouching in front of him. "Soft." She brushed it against her cheek, then against his. "Soft, isn't it? It feels good."

"Huh, soft," Walker said, and let go of her hand to take the yarn from her.

She looked over his head at Zane. "Did you get any background on him?"

"He didn't come with directions or a way to turn him off."

Her smile came again as she looked back at Walker. "You little stinker—you're driving everyone nuts, aren't you." He paid her no attention as he started to tangle the yarn around his cookie-stained hands.

"The yarn's yesterday's news," Zane said, as the traces of chocolate caught in the yarn.

"It's disposable," she said easily as she stood. "Have you tried television with him?"

"I never thought about it."

She scooped Walker up in her arms and crossed to the television. "How about cartoons, Walker?" she asked him. "Funny pictures, crazy animals?"

"How much does a two-year-old really know?" Zane asked.

"Lots—" she said as she touched the buttons.

Cartoons appeared on the screen, along with the sound of frantic music as a mouse ran after a cat ten times its size. The noise irritated Zane, but Walker was instantly enthralled.

"They're like little sponges," Lindsey said as she lowered the sound slightly. "They just soak up everything, and sort it out and file it away for later."

She put Walker on the floor where he could see the screen, then took the loose cushions and pillows off the couch closest to her, banking them behind him. "But as to understanding? I don't know. They understand sadness and separation and hurt and happiness and joy and fun." She eased Walker back a bit until the cushions supported him. "They love noise and color and shapes and sounds," she said, smoothing his blond hair before she stood.

She sighed softly as she looked down at Walker, who let the yarn ball roll away as he became more intrigued by the images on the television. "Cartoons. They fit the bill." She cast Zane a slanted look. "Aren't you going to take notes?"

"I'm tired, but I'll remember what you're saying," he said. A night of working late and a day without a baby-sitter while he ran after Walker and deluding himself into thinking he could work at the penthouse—it had taken its toll. He sank down on the softness of the other couch and looked up at Lindsey. "I'll remember, hopefully."

She dropped down on the opposite end of the couch from him. "Then, ask questions. That's why you're here."

He stared at her—a softness surrounded her that made her look almost ethereal. Good heavens, he was losing it. "No, I just wanted…" He ran a hand roughly over his face. "I needed help."

She curled back into the arm of the couch, tucking her bare feet under her. She motioned to Walker, who was staring at the television, rocking from side to side, transfixed. "Don't you have a television at the hotel?"

"I don't know. I never looked."

She laughed at that, and the soft sound that seemed to echo around him.

"You never *looked?*"

"I never watch it, so I never noticed. But I definitely will check when we get back." He settled back a bit, the softness of the cushions and the slight smile on her face making a potent combination.

"My suggestion is to find it and use it when you need it. Or maybe just get a real house."

"I'm at the office too often to feel the need for a house. But I'll buy a dozen TV's if they work this well for him."

Her laughter bubbled up again, filling the world around him. "You're in over your head, aren't you," she said.

"It seems so," he responded. Just watching the lingering humor deep in her eyes, he admitted to himself that he could get in way over his head with her, too. The idea appealed to him right then, very much. But he remembered the way she had avoided the kiss. And he remembered Joe. Zane glanced around at a place that looked masculine, except for the plants everywhere, and the woman so close to

him. He didn't want to see or meet anyone else here tonight.

"What else can I do to maintain the peace?" he asked
her in an attempt to get back to the problem at hand.
"Should I make a list?"

"Maybe so. A short one. He won't be here that long, but
I'm going to need some tips."

He didn't know if he imagined it or if the distance between them suddenly grew. Odd. The smile was completely
gone now—no lingering gleam in her amber eyes. He could
almost mourn its passing, and he wished he knew why it
had died.

"You didn't bring up his bottle or diapers, did you?"
she asked.

"No, but I can call Gordon to bring them up."

"I'd suggest you do that. Maybe with a bottle and a dry
diaper, he'll get tired and sleep."

He took out his cell phone and called down to the limo.
After asking Gordon to bring up the baby bag, he slipped
the phone back in his pocket and looked at Lindsey. She'd
gone over to Walker, and was sitting down by him on the
floor, apparently watching him while he watched the cartoons.

"Gordon's on his way up," he said.

Without looking at him, she nodded. "Buzz him up. The
button's right by the door."

He got up, crossed, buzzed Gordon up, then went out
into the hallway. When he came back in with the diaper
bag, he handed the bag to Lindsey, then returned to the
couch. He watched in silence as she changed the boy,
dressed him in a blue blanket sleeper that she found in the
bag, settled him back into the cushions. Then she started
him on his bottle.

The whole scene was so damn domestic that it jolted

him: Lindsey, the child, the giggling when she tickled him, the way she stroked his cheek as he settled down again, the way she held the bottle for him, smiled down at him. Zane closed his eyes for a moment. He really was losing it.

Suddenly Walker squealed, and Zane opened his eyes in time to see the little boy shoot upright and toss his bottle into the air. It barely missed hitting the television screen. "Kitty, kitty, kitty cat," the child shrieked as he scrambled to his feet and took off across the room.

Zane had an impression of Lindsey reaching out for Walker, but the boy evaded her hands and ran toward a huge orange cat that had appeared from some other part of the loft. The cat saw the boy and his back went up, but the animal obviously decided that discretion was the better part of valor: he ran in the other direction. He took a flying leap at a potted tree near a half wall, got tangled in the branches, then somehow ended up on the top edge of the six-foot divider.

Lindsey got to Walker at the same time the boy got to the tree and grabbed the lowest branch. She reached for him, caught him and tumbled backward with him in her arms to the hardwood floor.

Zane jumped to his feet and ran across to Lindsey and Walker, but by the time he got there, Lindsey was already scrambling to sit up. She had Walker on her lap, preventing him from going after the cat. The tree rolled to one side, scattering leaves and something mossy on the wooden floor.

Zane righted the tree, then hunkered down in front of Walker and Lindsey. She had a firm hold on the boy and was laughing out loud.

"He's fast, isn't he," she said as she handed the child to Zane.

"The cat was faster," Zane said, glancing at the animal that was safely out of the way on the ledge and looking down at them. He let Walker stand, said, "Take it easy," then let him go. He turned to Lindsey, noticing that her robe had fallen open partly in the melee and that her legs were exposed to her thighs. Thankfully, she was shifting around to get up, so he didn't have to apologize for staring at silky skin and legs that seemed to go on forever.

He moved back and held out his hand. "Are you okay?"

She took his hand, her fingers delicate as they gripped his to help her get to her feet.

"I'm just fine," she said as she faced him.

Her hand slipped out of his as she turned to look at Walker. The boy was at the bottom of the wall, beyond the tree, reaching up as far as he could to try to get the cat. "Play, kitty cat! Me play kitty."

The cat coolly cleaned himself, now that he had at least four feet between himself and the tiny human tornado that had gone after him. Lindsey straightened the tree some more, then nudged the spilled moss toward the pot with her bare toes.

Even her toes were attractive. Zane looked away. "Where's your broom?" he asked.

"In the kitchen by the stove. I'll keep an eye on the cat-hunter in here, if you'll get it."

He went to find the broom and a dustpan, then brought them both back and swept up the soil and leaves. He took it all back to the other room, got rid of the trash and returned.

He didn't know how Lindsey had done it, but Walker was back by the pillows, the cartoons diverting his interest from the cat. She looked up at the tabby, then stood and came back to the sofa. Walker stayed put, and the cat stayed on the wall.

"Sorry about the cat," he said, sinking down by her on the couch.

"Don't worry. Joey's survived worse than an excited toddler."

Joey? A cat? He would have burst out laughing if he hadn't felt the oddest emotion: he was *relieved* that the Joey she'd left the message for was a huge cat. "He's the one you were going to cook for?" he asked. "He listens to messages?"

"He's very intelligent." Lindsey cast him a shadowed look. "He's picky. He doesn't like canned food— Don't look at me like that."

He hoped to hell that she couldn't read his thoughts. Not when they were all jumbled up with soft terry cloth, slender legs, and a woman who moved with a subtle sexiness that she didn't even appear to be aware she possessed. Not when he was ridiculously relieved that Joey was a cat. He rerouted his thoughts when he found his eyes lingering on the way her hands were smoothing the robe that covered her thighs.

"You cook for a cat?"

"I told you, he's picky—"

Her fingers pressed on the white cloth—pale pink oval nails.

"He likes fresh food."

Zane shook his head. "And he takes messages off the answering machine?"

The color came to her cheeks again. She was so easy to read when she was embarrassed.

"He can hear when I talk, and it calms him down."

He believed that, after seeing how her voice had calmed Walker so easily. "He's got it easy, I'd say."

"He's had a rough life, and he deserves some care."

"Cats have nine lives."

"No, they have one—and Joey's had it rough. He was abandoned here when the man who owns the loft moved out. The guy just took off and left the poor cat. And from what my neighbor, George, says, even when my landlord was here he didn't bother much about the cat. George— he's an artist, he lives next door, and he doesn't remember to feed himself half the time. He tried to help out with Joey, but it was touch and go. He's better now, though. He's a survivor.''

''And you like that in him, don't you.''

She glanced at Walker. ''Everyone deserves to win at least once in their lives.''

As she spoke, he heard a tinge of sadness in her voice, and it bothered him. ''I'd say Joey hit the jackpot.''

''He earns his keep.'' She looked back at him. ''You won't find a mouse in the house.''

He smiled at that, a bit taken aback by how easily smiles came around her. It seemed an eternity since he'd had any reason to smile—until Lindsey. He looked around at the stack of boxes along one wall. ''So, you haven't been here too long?''

''About a year or so. I just haven't really had time to unpack. The place came furnished, so there wasn't any rush. Just some plants and stuff. That's about all I've contributed to it so far.''

''What about a roommate, besides Joey? Anyone going to burst in here at any minute and wonder what you're doing with a kid and a frazzled man on your couch?'' He didn't realize he was going to ask the next part of the question until it was out, but he'd wanted to ask it from the start. ''Is there a man in your life?''

Lindsey curled her legs under her, hugging her arms around her chest. Talking with Zane was like riding a roller coaster. This man—in dark slacks and a collarless, long-sleeved gray shirt—went from small talk to unnerving questions without batting an eye. She wasn't sure she liked that. ''Lots of them, but they all tend to be between a year and five years of age,'' she said, trying to joke—anything to fight the tension between them that seemed to come from nowhere.

''Okay, is there anyone in your life who doesn't use crayons to write notes?'' he asked in a low voice that only increased the tension. ''Any pen users?''

She couldn't play this game—not when she thought about the gold pen and was sitting so close to its user, with little between the two of them but fragile space and thin terry cloth. ''No, no one.'' The last thing she wanted to do was keep this going, so she grabbed at anything to change the subject. ''You never went in to work today?''

''I was there for two hours, then had to go back to the penthouse. I thought I could work from there.'' He shrugged and barely contained a yawn. ''I never thought this would all end up to be so complicated.''

''You thought you'd have your nanny, tuck him away somewhere so he wouldn't be in the way, and your life would go on as if nothing had happened?''

''I guess that was the general idea.''

''The best-laid plans of mice and men?'' she said, just as Walker shot up and scooted over to where they sat. He climbed into her lap, and bounced up and down. Despite the fact that his eyes were heavy, he wasn't giving up and going to sleep.

''Me play, peeze, play?''

She touched his cheek. ''No sleeping, huh?'' She glanced at Zane. ''Maybe the car would work now.''

He held up both hands. ''I'm not getting in any car with him if he's going to scream again. I can't take it.''

She looked back at Walker. ''How about we go for a ride?'' she asked. ''Go in the car?''

He scrambled off her, to the floor, and ran for the door. "Go, yets go!"

She stood. "I'll go for a short ride with you. Maybe it'll put him to sleep."

Zane hesitated, then stood to face her. "And?"

"I need to get dressed, then we can—"

"What's it going to cost me?"

His eyes narrowed, but that didn't minimize the impact his gaze had on her. An impact that only seemed to increase the longer she knew him. "It's a bonus. No charge."

"You got a deal," he murmured.

She turned, hurrying toward the bedroom space and speaking without looking back. "Give me a minute."

She dressed quickly in jeans, a blue sweater and leather sandals, then hurried back into the living room. Zane was holding Walker, and both of them were looking up at Joey, who was still on the wall. For a stunning moment, their profiles echoed each other—the man and the child. Then they both turned, and the thought was gone.

"Ready?" Zane asked.

She grabbed her keys and the diaper bag, and met them both at the door. "Ready."

She stepped out, let Zane and Walker out, then locked up and crossed to the elevator. As they got to the cage, the other door off the hallway opened and George came out of his loft. He stopped when he saw the three of them.

"Hi, George," Lindsey said, knowing that in all the time she'd been there he'd never seen anyone coming from her loft except Amy.

He approached them and reached for the cage front. "Here, let me get that," he said.

Lindsey watched the middle-aged man—his gray hair caught in a ponytail, six earrings in his right ear, and wearing his usual attire of well-worn, paint-stained sweats—lift the barrier.

He turned to Zane, looked at Walker and lowered his voice. "Looks ready to sleep," he murmured.

"Let's hope so," Zane said.

"Cute little guy," George said with a grin as he tapped Walker's knee. "Sleeping is when I get along with kids the best."

"George Armstrong, Zane Holden," Lindsey said. "George is my neighbor."

George nodded. "Nice to meet you, and don't worry about shaking hands. You've got your arms full." He glanced at Lindsey. "I'm heading out to meet the group for some brainstorming," he said as he stepped into the cage. He looked at Zane. "Artists getting together to figure out new ideas."

"A think tank?"

George laughed as he got inside, motioning them to get in after him. "Good heavens, no. Nothing corporate. Just creative." When the others got in, George closed the gate, then hit the down button. "No offense," he said to Zane as they rode down.

"None taken," Zane murmured.

Walker stared hard at the strange man beside them. Lindsey saw him spot George's earrings, the silver hoops probably looking like a toy to him, and she was thankful that they got down to the bottom level without the child making a grab for the jewelry. Unfortunately, she hadn't figured on George opening the gate and moving closer to them to let them out first. The boy took his opportunity and lunged for George's ear.

Lindsey moved quickly, caught Walker's hand, and in the process hit Zane in the chest with her elbow. She heard him exhale sharply, and she looked up at him as her hand caught Walker's. Zane was inches from her—so close that all she'd have to do to touch him was to sway a few inches toward him. She didn't understand why she would have loved to be free to touch him, just to make that contact. She didn't understand that at all.

"Nice interception," George said on a laugh, breaking through her crazy thoughts. He quickly got a safe distance away from Walker. "The kid's fast, I'll give him that."

Lindsey pulled back, letting go of Walker so she could put some space between herself and Zane. How could he get to her so easily? Make her angry, make her laugh, and make her want to touch him? She backed away from that thought immediately. "He went after Joey first thing, and almost caught him," she said in a slightly breathless voice.

George laughed again. "Good thing a cat has nine lives," George said as he crossed to the outer door.

"My thoughts exactly," Zane said in a low voice.

Lindsey fought the urge to look at him. She didn't want to see if he was laughing or if he was just intense. So she followed George and stepped out into the night.

George stopped on the sidewalk and motioned to the limousine by the curb. "Your ride, I take it?"

"Yes. Can we give you a lift?" Zane asked.

George shook his head and motioned to his old VW behind the limo. "Thanks, but I've got my own ride," he said. "See you later." And he headed toward the old car.

"Let's go," Zane said. His arm brushed Lindsey's as he crossed toward the limousine.

Gordon was there, opening the door for them. Lindsey got in and moved to the far side beyond a car seat strapped in the center of the back seat, and Zane climbed in with Walker. With amazing dexterity, the man got the boy in the car seat and fastened the belts. Then he sat back, as Gordon got behind the wheel and spoke to them.

"Where to, sir?"

"Just drive. I'll let you know in a bit."

Walker squirmed, then reached toward a partially empty box of cookies left on the seat facing them. "Cookie, cookie!" he squealed, the sharp sound echoing painfully in the closed car.

Zane started to reach for them, but Lindsey stopped him. "Not if you ever want him to sleep."

He drew back, casting her a sheepish look. "I don't want him screaming, either."

She looked away from Zane, and opened and closed side compartments in the limo, trying to find something distracting. The last one she opened turned out to be hiding the perfect solution. A small TV-VCR combination. She pulled it up to eye level by the other seat.

She heard a soft "I'll be damned" from Zane, as she flipped through channels and found a movie about a whale. Walker had quieted, forgetting about the cookies; he leaned back in the seat, staring in fascination at the screen.

She glanced past the boy at Zane, and she was thankful that the car seat was firmly between them.

"Live and learn," he whispered.

She looked at Walker, saw his eyes flutter slightly, his lids grow heavy. She touched his hand that rested on the side of the seat, and slowly caressed the silky skin. "Sleepy boy," she breathed.

He sighed deeply, settled back even more and closed his eyes. She kept touching him, maintaining that contact, and said in a low voice, "He's exhausted, but he fights it."

"He was driving me nuts. This turned out to be more than I figured on."

She drew back from Walker, clasping her hands in her lap. "Well, it's hard, but you did the right thing."

He frowned at her. "I did what I had to do."

She sensed him shift, but she kept her eyes straight ahead. ''I never would have thought you'd put yourself out for a child, let alone the child your ex-wife had with another—'' She put her hand over her mouth, swallowing the rest of the words.

Chapter Eleven

"Oh, shoot," Lindsey mumbled behind her hand. "I'm sorry."

Zane reached out past the sleeping child and touched her hand with his—an amazingly gentle touch, thought Lindsey.

"Don't." He eased her hand down, holding it in his for a moment. "I can take anything you say about me." He drew back, breaking the contact. "I survived when you told me I didn't have a heart, didn't I?"

She pressed her hand to her thigh, unnerved that she could still feel his hand on hers, even though he was no longer touching her. "I should never have said that, either," she whispered. "Besides, I had to be wrong. You're giving Amy a much-needed raise. It's going to help her a lot. And you're looking after Walker. There's definitely a heart in there somewhere."

"You think so?"

Her throat tightened, as his eyes narrowed. For a moment, the man whose expression was hard to read was plainly touched by something she'd call pain. But it was gone in a flash, and she had to glance away. "Yes," she said softly, concentrating on her hands pressed against her jeans. "And Amy is going to be so grateful. And Walker...he's lucky you were there for him."

"I'll be lucky when they find this elusive relative."

The bottom line was getting rid of the boy. He never veered from that. "And if they don't?"

"Something will be worked out." He looked toward the driver. "Gordon? Is there someplace around here that we can get some coffee and a bite to eat?"

"Nothing fancy."

"I just want food."

"Okay, I know a place with great food."

"Sounds good." He sat back and glanced at Lindsey. "I'm starving. I haven't eaten. Do you have time?"

She should have said no, that he could get something to eat on his own, but she didn't. Something in her didn't want to end this evening, even though part of her knew she should. She wasn't terribly sensible right now, nodding and saying, "Yes, of course," and listening to her heart instead of her head.

"Great." He sighed.

"What about Walker?"

"I said, they're looking for relatives and—"

"No, while we eat."

She almost laughed at his expression of sudden understanding as he looked at the sleeping boy.

"Oh, sure, Gordon can watch him."

She looked at him, at the shadow of a new beard at his jaw. Words that she never even knew were there came out in a rush. "Have you thought about keeping Walker yourself?"

"Me?" He shook his head. "You're way off the mark on that one. There's no way that would work out."

"But how do you know it wouldn't?"

"Trust me, it wouldn't. The relative they find—"

"What if that attorney finds a relative, and they only take him in to care for him to get their hands on any money that goes with him?"

"That's not my problem, as long as he gets the care."

The car stopped before she could say anything, but that didn't stop a certain anger in her at his words.

Zane leaned forward and spoke to Gordon. "Drive around, and I'll call when we're done."

"Yes, sir. Ask for Steve inside, and he'll take care of you. It's not fancy, but the food's excellent, and they're open."

"A good combination," he said, then opened the door and stepped out.

Short of refusing to get out, Lindsey had no choice but to follow him. She eased past Walker and out into the night then hesitated. They were in front of what looked like a false-front diner, sort of western looking and hardly the sort of place where a man like Zane would eat.

"The Swing Inn?" she said.

Zane shrugged. "Food's food, and Gordon seems to think it's good." He touched her arm. "Come on, we might not have much time if Walker starts screaming again."

His touch made her heart race, and she bit her lip hard as she went with him up two wooden steps and through the swinging entry door. There was country music playing, the smell of fried food in the air, and only two other customers in the red vinyl and wood space.

A man who was wiping the counter along the back wall looked up. "Evening."

"Steve?" Zane asked.

"That'd be me," the man said with a grin that was shy a few teeth.

"We need something to eat."

Steve motioned expansively. "Take your choice of seats."

Zane turned and led the way to a table by the front windows that overlooked the street. He held out a chair for Lindsey, then took the one opposite her at the Formica table.

Steve was there, holding out plastic menus to them. "Drinks?"

"Coffee," Zane said, then glanced at Lindsey.

"Coffee," she echoed.

When Steve left to get the drinks, Lindsey looked at Zane. "You weren't serious about what you said out there, were you?"

He frowned. "I'm hungry. I'm serious."

"No, about the relatives and Walker."

"The deal was, I keep him until they find a relative. I'm doing that."

She sat forward, keeping her voice down. "But you have to care, to be putting yourself out like this."

"Don't do that to me." He stopped her dead with his words. "I'm doing this because I had no choice."

"Of course, you had a choice. You could have refused, and you didn't. He's here, and maybe—"

"Don't even go down that road."

Steve was there with the coffee, and motioned to the menus. "What'll you have?"

Zane looked at Lindsey. "What would you like?"

She hadn't even opened the menu, and food was starting to sound less than appetizing at the moment. "A grilled cheese sandwich," she said, off the top of her head.

Zane ordered the same. As Steve left again, he lowered his voice. "Stop looking at me like that. I don't have room for anything in my life that I don't plan on, and I never planned on kids. I was a rotten husband, and he's Suzanne's child. That's the bottom line.''

She saw something in his eyes. Was it regret, or was that just her wishful thinking, her attempt to humanize him to justify her feelings. She wanted him to care. Period. But maybe he was feeling anger. Anger that he was admitting any sort of defeat in his life or... That brought another disturbing idea that she was surprised she hadn't had earlier. ''It's because he's the 'other man's' child, isn't it.''

He looked genuinely shocked. ''How can I resent a child she had with another man, when I never wanted a child?''

''Never?''

''Our last fight was about how selfish I was—self-centered, egocentric. I probably forgot a few of the adjectives she used to describe me that night. She'd finally figured out that I wasn't built for marriage, let alone kids, and she went out and found someone, apparently right away. Maybe he was there all along, I don't know. But it's past, done, over, and these past two days have only reinforced that fact. A child doesn't fit into my life at all.''

He was so unemotional about it that it shook Lindsey. The most important things in this life, to her, were marriage and children. The ''forever connection'' she used to dream about as a child.

Suddenly Steve was there, setting the sandwiches in front of them, but she ignored hers.

''Are you serious?'' she asked Zane.

''I told you, marriage didn't fit into my life. I made a mistake that I won't repeat. And a child certainly wouldn't fit in. It's that simple.''

She bit her lip against a surge of overwhelming sadness. The one thing he wanted and actually structured into his life was being alone. The one thing she would have given anything for, was to not be alone.

She looked away from him, down at her food. "Aren't you terribly lonely?" she asked in a low, slightly unsteady voice.

"No."

One word. *No.* It was so simple for him. She looked back at him, as he started eating his sandwich. The man had to have been lonely; he had to have felt that emptiness. It couldn't be a condition that only she'd felt. Then again, maybe he was the exception. Maybe he was a person who didn't need anyone. She just wished that she were like that. Despite the fact she'd made her life alone, it wasn't the life she wanted.

She fingered the sandwich, tearing off pieces, not trusting herself to talk for a moment. Then she sipped some coffee and looked at Zane over the cup in her hands. "Good sandwich?" she asked in a tight voice. Safe, mundane words masked what she was really thinking.

"Food," he said as he reached for his cup.

She looked away and out the window, at the same time as Gordon drove the limo past the restaurant. "He's still going," she murmured.

"Good. Hopefully, Walker's going to stay asleep."

"He should." She pushed her food away and sipped more coffee before looking back at Zane. He was intent on eating, and as she cradled her mug in both hands, a sadness touched her. Maybe it was more for her than for him. He chose his state of aloneness. He deliberately set about making it happen. But she had never chosen it. It had been thrust on her by life. First, both her parents worked and left her on her own; then their deaths pushed her into another realm of aloneness.

She swallowed hard, hating the burning at her eyes. She seldom let herself dwell on "what ifs" in this life, but Zane was bringing that out in her. And she could almost hate him for that.

"A penny for your thoughts?" he murmured as his gaze met hers.

She was startled, almost spilling her coffee. She carefully set the cup down before speaking. "What?"

"Should I up my price for what you're thinking?"

She bit her lip hard, took a breath to steady herself. "No, it's free. I was thinking about how perverse life gets at times, how people act in the strangest ways."

"How so?"

"Most people would do anything to not be alone in this life. But you…you deliberately choose to cut yourself off from people."

"I told you, I'm not lonely. I like company," he said softly, smiling faintly.

"On your own terms."

The smile lingered, little more than a crinkling near his eyes and a lift of the corners of his mouth. "If I can get it on my terms."

"Do you negotiate everything in life?"

He slowly sat up and turned to her. "I negotiated with you, didn't I? Anything in life is negotiable."

"No, that's not true." She looked away from him, down into the coffee cup she gripped tightly in both hands. "No child gets to negotiate their life. No child gets to negotiate their way out of being left alone, or being scared and hurt."

"Life's not perfect," Zane murmured. "Kids are resilient, from what I've been told. They learn to cope."

Her image shimmered back at her from the surface of the steaming liquid, and she bit her lip hard when she realized she was seeing the little girl she'd been. "Sure, they cope by locking themselves in a closet rather than face the boogeyman. They cope by crying themselves to sleep, going from place to place, never connecting, never feeling as if they belong.''

She didn't realize that Zane had moved until his hand was touching hers where it gripped the mug. ''Who are we talking about, here?''

There was aching gentleness in his voice, something that touched her heart in a profound way. ''Kids.''

''You?''

She drew back, the connection so intense that she could barely breathe. ''I guess so.''

He pressed his hand to the tabletop, a strong hand that she wanted nothing more than to hold on to. But the man wasn't an anchor; he wasn't for Walker and he certainly wouldn't be for her.

''Do you want to talk about it?'' he asked.

She hated the idea that tears were getting too close to the surface, and mostly because of this man across from her. If she was given to fantasy, she would have let herself pretend that Zane really cared, that whatever it was he touched inside her was real, and that she could tell him the things hidden deep in her soul. But that person didn't exist, and the words didn't come.

''No, it's over and done.''

She spotted the limo cruising past again, then looked at Zane's nearly empty plate. ''I need to get back, if you're ready to leave.''

He stared at her so intently that she almost flinched, before he looked away and motioned to Steve. ''The bill?''

The man hurried over and laid a piece of paper on the table. Zane took out his phone and called Gordon to come to the front, then took some money out of his wallet and laid it on the bill. He looked at Lindsey. ''Ready?''

She was more than ready, hardly able to absorb the feelings in her at the moment. She moved quickly, keeping a distance from Zane, and leaving, sensing him behind her, hearing him say good-night to Steve. The limo was waiting, and they got in.

Walker was sound asleep, the TV flickering with blue light, the movie over and the station dead. Zane hit the off button, then sank back as the limo pulled away from the curb.

Neither of them spoke on the way back, and when the limo pulled up in front of the warehouse, Lindsey realized she wished that it had a door on her side for her to get out. The last thing she wanted was to have to crawl over Zane to make her escape. But as the car stopped, he opened his door and got out first. She looked at the sleeping Walker, touched his cheek lightly, whispered, "Good night," then got out into the night.

She stopped, looked at Zane and said, "You won't forget Amy's raise?"

"No, I'll get on it first thing in the morning," he said.

"Thanks," she said, and started for her home, but he was with her, falling in step with her, not leaving her. She got to the outer door, unlocked it, went inside, and Zane was still there. She stopped. "You don't have to see me up."

"Yes, I do," he said, and she didn't have it in her to argue.

They went up in the lift, got out and crossed to her door, which she unlocked, as Zane leaned around her to push it open. She moved quickly to avoid touching him, stepping into her place. When she would have turned to try to say good-night to him again, again he was right there.

He looked past her and grinned, an endearingly boyish expression. "He's still there."

She turned and spotted Joey still up on the wall. "He's probably scared to death," she murmured.

"Should I get him down for you?"

She shook her head. "He'll come down when he wants to or when he gets hungry."

"Stubborn, huh?"

"Smart," she countered.

He looked down at her, close enough for her to hear him exhale softly. "Lindsey, I can admit that maybe I don't understand what it is to have a rough childhood."

Why did he have to be so touchingly human right now? "No, you don't."

His breath brushed her cold skin with heat. "I'm sorry you do, that you went through it."

"I don't want pity," she managed to say, hating the way her lips were quivering.

He was motionless for a moment, then slowly came even closer and reached out, framing her face with the heat of his hands. Somewhere in the background she heard the door swing shut, enclosing them in the loft, but her whole attention was riveted on Zane.

"Hey, it's okay. It's okay," he breathed roughly. Then, with a familiarity that should have come only after years of intimacy, he leaned down and found her lips with his.

In one shattering moment, Lindsey connected with him in the most basic way possible. She had never felt it before in her life, had never had that sense of being linked, feeling of wanting to be closer than was humanly possible to another person. She was being absorbed by him, surrounded by him—and she wasn't alone.

Lindsey had heard stories of finding a missing part of yourself in another person, of feeling in some way that you're whole because of that person. But she'd never felt anything near that in her life. She'd always felt unconnected—until that moment with Zane. Until his mouth claimed hers, and his tongue invaded her, bringing heat and pleasure everywhere. Making her heart pound, and the world slip away.

His touch was on her as they moved backward, making it to the couch; then they sank down into the linen, tangled together, a raw urgency between them. His hands were at her throat, then slipped down, finding the hem of her top and slipping under it. Skin against skin made her gasp, bringing searing heat, drawing at something in her that coiled tighter and tighter. He found her breasts, and even through the fine lace of her bra his touch caught at her, building an ache in her, drawing a sob from her lips.

She arched toward the caress, low moans escaping from her, pleasure climbing to an ecstasy that glowed white hot through her. They were falling backward together, onto the soft cushions, Zane over her, his lips and hands exploring her body. Her eyes were closed, her breathing deafening in her own ears. The slight bristle of his new beard brushed her naked skin, fiery paths skimming over her, sensations running riot over her nerves, making her feel more alive than she'd ever been in her life.

She yearned toward it, to the source of the pleasure, to Zane. She clasped him to her, holding onto him for dear life. All she wanted was to never have it end, to never have it stop. To have this go on forever and ever. To never be separate, to never be lost again. His touch was on her breast, and she gasped softly, the intensity of sensations almost beyond bearing.

Lindsey just wanted to feel Zane, to feel his skin, and she tugged at his shirt, trying to remove that barrier. Somehow she managed to get her hands under his shirt, against the hot slickness of his skin, his stomach, then his chest. And she felt his heart against her palm. That sense of connection intensified, his heart against hers, as if she could feel the essence of the man.

"Oh, my," she breathed, the need for him, and to be here with him forever, a living thing. That need was everywhere, filling her, touching her soul. Forever, and forever. The chant was building, surging through her, filling the world for her and Zane. Someone was there for her, someone was touching her. The man she now knew she'd wanted from the first moment she'd run into him, was there for her.

Pure fantasy, pure need— A sharp knock sounded on the door.

Zane shifted, muttering, "Who?" as he twisted back to look over his shoulder at the door.

He shirt was open and untucked, and when he looked down at her, she could see the same need in his eyes as must have been in hers. But before she could pull him back to her, George called through the door, "Lindsey, are you home?"

And at the sound of his voice, everything shattered. All she wanted was to fall back into her fantasy, into a world of just her and Zane, but the truth exploded all around her. This was no "forever connection," and it never would be. It didn't matter that she knew if she let herself go one more inch, she could love him. She wouldn't, she couldn't, no matter how much she wanted forever. This man didn't think about forever. He'd told her that. He'd been honest. She'd been fooling herself, deluding herself, but she wasn't going to let it continue.

"Tell him to go away," Zane whispered, reaching for her again.

Heat fled from her, draining away at breathtaking speed, and she pushed back when he reached for her. "No, no," she whispered, awkwardly twisting to get away. He shifted back, and she was free of him, turning away, tugging at her top to cover herself.

''What's going on?''

His voice was low and rough, and she had to force herself to look away from his bare chest. Tanned skin, a faint *T* of dark hair disappearing into the waistband of his pants. She jerked her eyes up, back to his face, and the sight of the evidence of his desire was almost her undoing.

''I can't,'' she whispered. ''George…''

His frown grew intense. ''You and George.''

''No, no, we…he and I, we're friends, neighbors.''

''Then, what?''

''This is wrong,'' she breathed past the ache in her throat.

He didn't move back any farther, but a distance was growing between them, a buffer of sorts, and she desperately needed to keep from doing something incredibly stupid.

''Wrong? Did I misunderstand? I thought…'' He raked both hands through his hair, spiking it slightly, then sank back in the cushions. ''I was wrong?''

She wished he'd been wrong. But she knew that saying she hadn't wanted him to touch her was a lie she couldn't maintain for a single moment. It was almost as monumental as the lie she'd be telling herself if she said she could do this and not regret it. He was close, yet not touching her, and with that broken contact came a soul-deep chill.

''This…it's wrong,'' she managed to say. ''I can't do it.'' She tugged at her top, but her hands were shaking so hard that she couldn't even to do that. ''Damn it,'' she muttered.

''Here,'' he said. ''Let me do that—''

Then Zane touched her, brushing her hands as he reached to tug at her top, smoothing it. She held her breath until he moved back from her.

''Now, answer the door.''

She moved away from him, her legs rubbery but doing her bidding, and she crossed to the entrance. She opened it, and George was there. "George?"

He hesitated, looking behind her, then back at her. "Oh, boy, I'm sorry. I was just…" He held up one hand. "Good night. Have fun. I'll talk to you later."

She sensed Zane behind her. "Don't go," she said, afraid to be alone with Zane again.

"Good night," Zane said.

George nodded. "Good night to you, too."

"You don't have to go," she said quickly.

He hesitated, looking at her. "Yes, I do," he said, and headed down the hallway.

She turned, and Zane was right there, but there was no way she was going to close the door again. She was an adult now, not a little kid, and adults could control to whom they gave the power to hurt them. She wasn't about to give it to a man who admitted he didn't want or need anyone in his life. Love didn't just happen—a person let it happen. And she wouldn't settle for anything less. Or anything less than forever.

She wrapped her arms around herself to stop a trembling deep in her being. She'd been alone all her life, and that wasn't going to change just because Zane had touched her. "Good night," she whispered, and looked down, staring hard at the floor where his shoes were just inches from hers.

She heard him exhale, a rough rush of air, but his shoes didn't move. Nothing happened. Finally, she had to look up, and he was staring at her. His face was all but unreadable. His eyes were narrowed, his mouth set and his hands pushed into the pockets of his slacks.

"Why?"

"I don't—"

"Yes, you do. Why?"

She tried to find words, anything to make him understand. "I shouldn't have let that happen," she said with aching honesty. "It's wrong. I can't deal with your idea of what life is. I won't. I need..." She bit her lip. "It's just not that simple for me. I can't just take whatever there is, then walk away." She took a shuddering breath. "I won't."

"All or nothing?"

She nodded, her face on fire now. "Yes."

He stared down at her, then slowly rebuttoned his shirt and tucked the shirttail into his pants with quick strokes. He didn't look away from her. Finally, he murmured, "That's too bad."

At the door, he stopped right in front of her. He didn't come any closer, but he stared, his eyes trailing to her lips and bringing heat to her cheeks before meeting her gaze again.

"It's a shame," he said softly, and she didn't ask what he meant. She knew.

She hated the tension that was knotting her up inside. "Remember where the center is, if you need it. Walker's welcome there."

"I don't think I'll forget," he said, then hesitated, his gaze again dropping to her lips.

She cursed the fire in her face, as he turned and left.

Chapter Twelve

As Lindsey quickly closed the door, she heard the sound of the gate outside being lifted. Then she was alone, eyes closed, her heart hammering in her chest. She took a breath, crossed the room, and turned off the television. As she reached for the lamp by the couch, the phone rang, startling her.

She hesitated, certain it was Zane calling from the limo, and very certain she didn't want to talk to him. She stared at the phone until it went to the answering machine. After the *beep,* she literally held her breath until she heard a woman's voice.

"Hey, Lindsey, it's me, Amy. I was just calling to see if—"

She grabbed the receiver and said, "Amy?" Relief made her legs slightly weak. She sank down on the couch. "It's you."

"You sound relieved."

"I thought...I was talking to Zane Holden, and I halfway—"

"Zane Holden? You were talking to him? Wow, I'm impressed. First the elevator, then he calls you?"

"We talked," she hedged, not sure why she didn't just tell Amy that he'd been there.

"Lindsey, is it bad news?"

She rested her head against the cushions. "No, good news, actually. He agreed to give you a thirty-five percent raise, retroactive to September."

The line was dead silent, then Amy said, "Are you serious?"

"Very serious."

"Lindsey, this is the same man who said there wasn't any money for anything for the center, and now you're saying he not only got the stove fixed, but he's giving me a raise—a big raise? What happened?"

Lindsey closed her eyes. "I negotiated with him."

"What did you have to negotiate with? I mean, to point out the obvious, you aren't exactly dealing from strength with the man. He's got all the power."

That was more true than she even wanted to think about. "He's got a two-year-old that's driving him nuts, and he wanted help. So, I offered help...for a price."

"My raise?"

"For starters."

"What does that mean?"

"That means I'll get him to agree to funding more than just a salary raise."

"I hope so."

"So, why were you calling?"

"Oh, I almost forgot. As I mentioned before, I would really love you to come for Thanksgiving dinner. It's going to be just me and Jenn and Taylor. And Jenn is wanting to make a huge turkey dinner. Besides, you shouldn't be alone on a holiday."

She almost refused, but then she opened her eyes to the space around her. It felt even emptier now. "Thanks. I think I will."

"That's great. I'll let her know. We can talk about it in a few days, and I can give you directions and stuff, okay?"

"Thanks for asking me," she said, then hung up.

Alone. She hugged herself. Yes, she was alone, and Zane Holden had ripped away any protection she had against feeling the ache that had always been such a part of her life. Joey jumped into her lap, stropping her arm, settling on her thighs. She wasn't *completely* alone.

She scooped him up and headed for the bedroom area. "I guess it's just you and me, kiddo," she said, and her voice seemed to echo.

LINDSEY HAD THE DREAM that night, about being locked in the blackness, alone. No sound, no feelings, just her. Then the thumping of someone coming, the sound of a lock being released, brilliant light. Every other time she'd had the dream, she'd been jerked awake by the light, but this time the dream kept going for a split second longer.

Light flooded around her, and a shadow came out of the light, a huge shadow. A man. She started toward the light and the person, and she could almost make out who it was coming for her. She wanted desperately to see who was there, but the answer was snatched away from her in a flash. She woke with a start that made her heart pound.

She heard her rapid breathing, found herself sitting bolt upright in the bed, in the dark, alone. Nothing. No one. Just Joey, heavy across her legs. She fell back into the pillows, rolled onto her side, and the cat moved away from her.

"Damn it, damn it, damn it," she sighed.

Joey walked across her thighs, then up her side to her shoulder, before he lay down on her. She felt his rough tongue on her cheek. "Okay, okay, I know you're there," she said, reaching out to cuddle him to her chest. But even when she managed to fall into a light sleep, she couldn't shake that sense of loneliness.

Wednesday

BY MORNING, Lindsey was exhausted. She'd ended up having to take an over-the-counter sleeping pill, then almost slept through the sound of her alarm. By the time she stepped off the elevator on the sixth floor and headed for the center, she was awake but her mind felt fuzzy.

She approached the entrance, then hesitated when she saw a familiar face outside the doors. She'd met Rita Donovan, secretary on the executive level, many times, because Rita's two sons used the center. But they were in the after-school pickup program, giving Rita no reason to be at the center first thing in the morning.

And Simon and Anthony were seven and nine, not small enough to be the child she had in her arms, or to require the diaper bag she had slung over one shoulder. They were dark like their mother, not towheaded, or...

She got closer and realized who Rita was holding in her arms. *Walker.* "Rita?" she said.

The woman stopped just before opening the door and turned, at the same time Walker spotted her. "Linny, Linny, me go play," he said, shocking her by saying her name almost as much as he had by being there in the first place.

He'd been dressed in denim overalls and a cotton T-shirt, and his feet were bare. She smiled at him, held out a hand to take his in hers, but spoke to Rita. "What's going on?"

"Good, I was hoping you'd be here," she said, as Walker lunged toward Lindsey.

"Me go play, kitty?" Walker asked, as she caught him in her arms.

"Joey isn't here," she said, then looked past him at Rita. "What's he doing here?"

"It's a long story, but briefly, Mr. Holden called me into his office ten minutes ago, handed me the boy and asked me to bring him down and give him to you. He wants him to stay here for the day." She pushed the door open as they spoke, and the two of them went into the center.

The place was already alive with children. Amy was there with two helpers, and children from toddlers up to preschoolers were playing in various areas of the room. Amy looked over at her, then handed a storybook to one of the helpers and came over to the door area. She saw Rita, then Walker, and looked as confused as Lindsey felt.

Lindsey stepped in. "Rita brought Walker down."

Amy looked at the boy. "So, this is Walker, the baby-sitter eradicator?"

Lindsey shifted him to her hip and nodded. "None other. Seems Mr. Holden wants him to stay here with us for the day."

Amy grinned at Lindsey. "I'd say things are looking up."

"I'm glad they are for you," Rita said, putting the diaper bag on a side table by the door. "Mr. Holden looked as if he hasn't slept all night, and work's piling up."

So he hadn't slept, either? Neither had she, but she knew his lack of sleep wasn't in any way similar to the sleeplessness she'd suffered from for so long. "Tell Mr. Holden we'll be glad to have Walker here for the day. The center closes at six, so I'll expect him here by then."

"I'll let him know," Rita said, and started for the door, but stopped and turned. "Oh, Lindsey, he said something about telling you he'd expect to negotiate for it. Does that make sense?''

"Yes, it does," she said, not sure what she'd ask for this time, but she knew she was going to make it count. He'd admitted needing the center just by sending Walker here, and the center needed his approval for the funding. This was definitely a step in the right direction.

She shifted Walker around when he started to squirm, then set him down on the floor and crouched in front of him as he gripped her arm with both hands. "Want to play?" she asked.

He looked around with wide eyes, but never let go of her hand. When Amy reached for him, he drew back, holding onto Lindsey. "Huh, me play. Tuck?" he said softly.

Lindsey looked at the boy, then hugged him to her. "Sure, sweetie, we'll find a truck for you," she said, and went with him over to the play group. She eased him over to a knot of toddlers playing with blocks on a foam mat, kneeled down, found a dump truck and showed it to him.

He looked at her with a serious frown, then down at the bright red truck. Suddenly, from nowhere, a smile came, a smile that was startling. It stunned her that she'd seen that same combination of expressions before at the oddest moments. The boy had only been around Zane a few days and already he was picking up some of the man's mannerisms and expressions.

She gave the truck to Walker, started to stack blocks in the back of it, then sat back and let the boy take over. Within minutes, he was lost in play, first alone and then with the other children. Eventually, she found she could move back and that he was okay. But if she tried to leave completely, he came after her. His courage was growing, but he needed the security of someone he knew around at all times. And she was all he had right now.

"Don't worry," she told him. "I'm here." She bit her lip. That's what Zane had told her last night, but it had been a lie. No, a truth, but only for that moment. She tried to push that thought away and concentrate on the fact that she had an opening to ask for more from Zane for the center. The man had nothing to give personally, but he had everything to give financially.

ZANE SIGNED THE PAPERS in front of him, stacked them, then handed them to the man across the desk. "Here you go," he said, sitting back. "That's the last counteroffer. It's fair and it's reasonable. It's up to you what we do with it."

Ron Simmons, a man of about fifty with a shock of prematurely white hair and dressed in an Armani suit, sorted through the papers. Then he looked at Zane with eyes as unreadable as anybody's Zane had dealt with in this business.

"Personally, I think you've got one hell of a counteroffer here. Good for both sides. Lots of potential."

"So, you'll go with it?"

"Not so fast. You haven't convinced Sol Alberts. And without Sol, there's no deal."

"So get him," Zane said, loosening the dark gray tie he was wearing with a pale linen shirt. "I'll talk to him."

"He's leaving late tonight for his place in Aspen for a long holiday. He might be gone until after Thanksgiving."

"I'm not waiting till then for an answer, and I can't go to Aspen."

"Listen, I think this is a good deal. I'm going out on a limb here, but if I can arrange something for tonight, are you available?"

The only good news Zane had had all day was the new baby-sitter. She'd had to be gone for the day, but she'd be back by six and she seemed good with Walker. He glanced at the clock. It was six-fifteen. "Anytime after seven."

Simmons motioned to the phone on the desk. "If I can use your phone, I'll find out."

Zane pushed the phone closer to the man, then crossed to the bar to get some bottled water. He'd barely twisted the cap, when a knock sounded on the door. Before he could say or do anything, it was opened, and Walker came running into the office, hesitated just long enough to spot Zane, then ran full tilt at him. He hit Zane in the legs and grabbed him in a bear hug.

Lindsey hurried in after him, stopping when she saw Zane. "Oh, I'm sorry, he's fast. Really fast."

Zane looked across at Lindsey, as Walker let him go. She was just inside the door wearing a pair of brown slacks and loose white shirt. She looked as if she was going to say something, but her eyes shifted to a place behind him, and she gasped, "No, Walker, no."

He turned just in time to see the boy reaching for a vase on one of the low tables grouped with leather easy chairs, to one side of the windows. Zane lunged for the vase and managed to grab it, right before Walker got to it. He drew it back and set it on a higher ledge. Then Lindsey was there, so close that the scent of her was everywhere around him. It went with her as she passed him to scoop up Walker, just as he lifted a small book off the table.

She had the book before he could throw it across the room to where Simmons was just finishing up his conversation. She glanced at Simmons and whispered to Zane, "Sorry. When no one came down to get him, I tried to call, but got your voice mail." She slipped the book out of Walker's hand, put it down by the rescued vase and kept talking in a low voice. "I didn't know if you were even still here."

He had tried not to think about her all day, had tried to focus on his work, and he'd done a decent job of it...until now. Now, he was staring at her, and he knew it but couldn't help it. He watched her full bottom lip, the sweep of her neck, the pulse beating quickly at the base of her throat.

God, he could almost taste her in his mouth. Feel that silkiness that he'd experienced the night before. He tried to refocus, watching her lift Walker, shift him to her hip and fumble in her pocket to pull out a set of keys.

Dangling them in front of Walker, she distracted the little boy, and Zane wished he could be as easily distracted from the memory of what had almost happened last night.

He'd tasted frustration then, and seeing her again only brought that back full force. He had meant it. It was a shame that things couldn't be different. It was a shame that she wanted something he couldn't give.

Zane made himself focus on what she was saying to him, and not on the memory of her lips against his, the swell of her breast in his hand, that pulse beating wildly at her throat. He shifted to get more distance.

"Good," he said, hoping he wasn't agreeing to a mass murder or something. But he'd obviously said the right thing: the shadow of a smile came to haunt her lips.

"I thought the baby-sitter must have bit the dust, when Walker showed up downstairs."

"Oh, no, she's fine. In fact, she's good. Walker likes her, I think. But she had to do something today—a prior engagement—but she'll be back when we get there."

She shifted Walker to her other hip, let him take the keys. Zane watched her watching the boy, incredibly long lashes shadowing her eyes.

"I'm glad you found someone who's good with him—"

"Holden?"

Zane was startled, Simmons totally forgotten until right then. This deal was vital to LynTech, and he'd forgotten about it while he'd been watching this woman. He turned to Simmons, who had hung up the phone.

"What's the word?"

"I didn't realize your family was here."

Zane didn't have a chance to say anything to correct him, before he came toward them and said, "Sorry if I made him late. I'm Ron Simmons, a business associate, and you are…"

"Lindsey, and this is Walker," she said.

Walker eyed the man, then smiled and held the keys up for him to see. "Me got keys," he said proudly.

"And they're great keys," Simmons said with a smile. He turned to Zane. "How about eight o'clock at La Bonnet near the airport? He and his wife will stop there before their flight, and he's agreed to meet with you."

"Okay, eight tonight."

Simmons went back to the desk and pushed the papers in his briefcase before he turned to Zane. "Good luck with the negotiations." He smiled at Lindsey and the boy. "Good to meet you."

Zane crossed to shake his hand, then showed him to the door. "I appreciate your support on this."

Simmons paused. "It's good for both companies. Hopefully it'll go through." He glanced at Lindsey and Walker. "You know, it might not be a bad idea to take your wife with you. Mrs. Alberts is going to be there, and a pretty face never hurt."

Zane didn't have time to say anything to correct the misimpression before Simmons strode out of the office. And he didn't bother going after him. He *had* been mistaken, but he'd given Zane an idea that was taking root. He'd thought about something all day, even when he hadn't been directly considering what had happened with Lindsey the night before.

But it had never gone away. Nor had the feeling that he wanted more. She fascinated him and intrigued him, and despite the knowledge that she wanted all or nothing, he couldn't just walk away. Not yet.

He closed the office door, then crossed to where Lindsey had set Walker down and provided him with coasters from the table. She was intent on the little boy, her slender fingers spreading the coasters in front of Walker and her voice low.

"See, colors and shapes. Pretty?"

"Piddy," Walker echoed as he reached for the nearest coaster. "Real piddy."

"Why didn't you explain to him about Walker…and me?" she asked without preamble.

"It didn't matter. I got what I wanted—a meeting with a man who's been avoiding me for the past two weeks."

She lifted her chin a bit, the action exposing her slender throat and softly parted lips. "Of course, the bottom line, I forgot," she said, and straightened up to face him. "Glad it worked out for you, that you got what you wanted."

If he had what he wanted, he never would have left her loft last night. "For now. I still have to get through the dinner and convince the other man that we have a good deal for him."

"Speaking of deals, Rita mentioned you'd negotiate about Walker being down there all day."

She wasn't going to say a thing about last night, and that was okay. He went a bit closer, until he could catch a hint of the perfume she wore. "Okay, what's on the table for this negotiation?"

"I anted up a full day of caring for Walker, and I was thinking that the center really needs good transportation."

"What on earth for?"

"If we can't pick up the school-age children when school lets out and can't bring them to the center to meet their parents, they'll probably be going home alone to empty houses. Latch-key kids." She frowned and wrapped her arms around herself. "The van we have now is a piece of scrap metal held together by goodwill and bailing wire."

He smiled at that description. "Okay, so what do you think a fair exchange for the care today would be? More bailing wire?"

"No, we need two vans. Mr. Lewis had said that he'd take care of it, but he was gone before he could get it done."

She was good. She asked for more than she knew she'd get, so she could settle for less and still win. He'd seen her requests: "A dependable van." But he liked her overreaching like that. "How about one slightly used van? Totally safety tested, with company insurance and dependable? It was used in the car pool program."

"The car pool program that you canceled?"

"It wasn't—" He cut off his own words, not about to go into an explanation about cost-effective programs. Not here, and certainly not with her. Not when the center was due for the same fate. That caused a twinge—the idea of letting her think she was in this for the long haul. He appeased his conscience, though, with the thought that they'd have dependable transportation for a few months. "It's a van and it's dependable and it comes with maintenance from the company garage."

She narrowed her eyes. "I'll take a used one, *if* you give us two."

Damn, he'd told her he didn't play games, but he was right. He'd managed to draw her right into range for his next offer, the one he really wanted to work. "Okay, two, *but* you have to put something else on the line to get that."

She hesitated, then asked with obvious caution, "What?"

He'd never manipulated a woman before to go out with him, but he found himself on new ground with Lindsey every time he turned around. "The man who just left, Simmons, he's set up a meeting for me with an important associate, Sol Alberts. It's a fly-by thing, meeting up before he and the wife take off for Aspen for a few weeks.

"I heard that much before he left." She turned, stooped down over Walker and took a piece of the coaster holder out of his mouth. She must have eyes in the back of her head, he thought.

"No, no, that's not for eating," she said, giving the child the keys he'd discarded earlier. She stood up and looked at Zane. "What do you want from me?"

He should just tell her he wanted to spend time with her, to talk and watch her, to figure out what was going on with him when she was around. He should tell her how a man could do things that surprised even himself. But he couldn't. She'd run like hell if he did. She'd made that clear enough last night. But if she thought something was at stake for the center, he knew, she'd have to consider it.

"It's important, very important—the opening I've been waiting for. And Simmons suggested something that makes sense."

"What's that?"

"He thinks that if you came with me, you could distract Mrs. Alberts and give me time to get to her husband."

Her face colored. "What?"

Whatever conscience he might have had wasn't taking this lightly, and he had to figure out what to say that wasn't a total lie—but still got him time with her. "You cannot only carry on an intelligent conversation with the wife, you can cover my back. Your negotiating skills are very effective.'' She'd gotten more out of him that way than anyone he'd faced before. ''I could use you to keep track of me, too, to let me know if you see that I'm fumbling it or acting like Ebenezer Scrooge.''

''What about Matt? He can charm the wife and watch your back.''

''He's busy.''

''Isn't there anyone else that can go with you?''

''Busy, all busy or unavailable or out of town or uninterested or unsuitable. Will you bail me out on this?''

She studied him for a moment, then asked, ''I don't have to do anything else but talk to the wife and make sure you don't shoot yourself in the foot?''

He looked at her, into eyes narrowed by dark lashes, and a real truth slipped past the facade he was trying to build. ''I'd like you to be there.''

''It's going to cost you,'' she said without missing a beat, and he could have sworn he saw a smile in the depths of her amber eyes. ''Two *new* vans *and* drivers,'' she said.

He couldn't help the burst of laughter that came of its own accord. ''Okay, okay, two vans—but the used one, and drivers. Now, will you go with me?''

There was no hint of a smile now. ''Just the dinner?''

He wanted so much more from her, but he couldn't rush it. ''That's it.''

She did smile then. ''You've got a deal, Mr. Holden.''

Chapter Thirteen

Lindsey heard the buzzer about the same time she finished putting on the fifth dress she'd tried on since Zane dropped her at her place an hour earlier and took Walker back to the penthouse. She fought the urge to take off the ivory sheath and put on the simple black dress she'd tried first. The buzzer sounded again, and she knew she was stuck wearing the ivory silk with thin straps, a straight neckline and slim skirt. Simple, understated and the most expensive dress she'd ever owned. Five years old, and it had only been worn twice.

She slipped on matching strap sandals with medium heels, took a breath and headed toward the door. She hit the intercom. "Yes?"

"Zane."

"I'll be right down," she said, not about to have him up here again. That was too dangerous. She hurried back to the bedroom area to get her purse and a black lace shawl, and to take the time to put on simple pearl earrings. The best jewelry she had, too. As she crossed the loft to leave, she stifled the logic in her. This wasn't smart. Not at all. But so much was at stake. The two vans and two drivers. She was pleased by that, very pleased. She was also afraid of being alone with Zane again. But she could do it.

She left the loft, rode down on the lift and got out. As she stepped out the entry door, Zane was there. The man never looked bad, but right now he looking achingly handsome. The dark suit was well cut and expensive—but it was the way he wore it, that sense of not caring what he wore but knowing it worked for him.

His gaze flicked over her, and even in the low lights by the entrance she didn't miss the way he glanced at her lips before meeting her gaze.

"You look terrific," he said.

"Is it suitable?" She nervously smoothed the silk at her hips. "I could change. I've got a black dress, with sleeves and—"

Unexpectedly, he came closer and touched her lips with his forefinger. A jolting connection. "It's perfect."

She turned from the contact, an instinctive act of self-preservation, and would have gone to the limousine, but there was no limo. Just a dark car, low and sporty—a convertible with the top up, sleek and sensuous. "Where's the limo?"

"I told you before that I can drive, and this seemed like the time to do it." Zane started for the car. "I left the limo at the hotel in case Mrs. Greenleaf needs it."

She went after him. "The new baby-sitter?"

"A real grandma type, and Walker likes her. If I didn't need a nanny full time, I'd think of asking her to fill in part time." He opened the passenger door and stood back for Lindsey to get in. "This is just like grown-ups."

She glanced at him, finding him so close that all she'd have to do to touch him was move a few inches to her right. She made very sure she didn't do that. "Excuse me?"

"A car, you and me, no cookies, no whale movie, no screaming." He grinned at her suddenly, delivering a jolt to her, and he probably had no idea that he'd done it.

She slipped into the two-seat interior, and Zane closed the door, shutting in the scent of leather and newness. He got in beside her, started the engine, a low, rumbling throb, and put the car in gear.

Business, business, business, she told herself, pushing aside the memory of the night before. It seemed a lifetime away now. "So, give me the rundown," she said, focusing past Zane on something, anything else. "Why is he so important to LynTech and to you?"

He shifted through the gears smoothly, and despite the fact that Lindsey could literally feel the power of the car around her, Zane drove at a safe speed through the night. "Sol Alberts is the head of a group of investors who are very interested in buying a subsidiary of LynTech in the Pittsburgh area, a small tech support company. I want to make him realize that it's the best deal he ever got in his life. He's the last of the group involved that has to agree to the purchase. He's also the majority stockholder."

"Why are you selling if the subsidiary is so terrific?"

"It's liquid assets if it's sold. It's an albatross unsold. Mr. Lewis should have done this five years ago and solidified what he had here. We need liquid assets now."

"Money. Lots of money," she said, wondering if he ever did anything that didn't come down to dollars. "You want Sol Alberts money because..."

He glanced at her, a fleeting look, but she felt as if he saw what he wanted to see.

"It can be used to build up the rest of the corporate structure."

"And that will..."

"Make LynTech, in part and in whole, more solid and stable."

"And more enticing to future buyers when you turn it over?"

"Exactly." He slowed for a light and looked at her again, but this time his gaze lingered. "You catch on very quickly."

"What's so hard to understand about you taking things apart so you can get what you want to get? Walker does that, too. He stacks blocks, higher and higher, then very carefully knocks them off one at a time. When he gets down to the last block he starts all over again."

"Is that bad?" he asked as he drove on.

"You're making lots of money at what you do, so you must be very good at it." She meant that. "But don't you ever want to build something just to build it and keep it?"

He shrugged, the car's speed building a bit. "Why?"

"Mr. Lewis had a real pride in LynTech. When he first talked to me about the center, he was as enthusiastic as I was. He loved to build and enhance things. It excited him to nurture things. To have pride in what he did."

"And he ended up dumping it all."

"No, he got old and he's got his hands full with that daughter of his, so he retired to spend time with his family."

"Ah, yes, Brittany Lewis, the daughter who gets engaged like other people change their hair color."

"I think she's been *almost* married four times. This one's a French businessman, or maybe he's a politician—I don't remember what I heard."

"Whatever, he's off with some spoiled brat, and now it's up to me to make this company work. The only way to make it work is to section it off, to funnel money into the parts that are left, until they are all sold for the most money possible."

"Then you just walk away? You destroy whatever you need to, to get what you want. Then you leave, right?"

She hadn't meant to say that, because she actually could

admire the brains behind what Zane did, the dedication, the talent. But she couldn't get away from a feeling that he could leave anything without a backward glance. He had let his wife go without a flinch. Lindsey knew he wouldn't hesitate to take what he wanted from her, then leave. And he was going to leave Walker.

He slowed the car and glanced at her, an intense look that made her tense. "You aren't going to do something noble at dinner and try to stop this sale, are you?"

"Could I?"

He slowed and pulled up to the valet parking at a building that had to be a restaurant, although it looked more like a medieval castle—towering, turreted and imposing. He stopped the car and turned to her before he got out, gripping the back of her seat with his right hand, the steering wheel with his left. "I'm going to tell you something that can't go any farther. Agreed?"

She nodded.

"Only Matt knows this because we're in this together. LynTech is crumbling. We knew when we went into it that we'd have to make some tough decisions to salvage the company. But we also knew that we could pull LynTech out and make it viable again. We need the liquid assets from this sale. If we don't get them, we could lose everything."

"You mean, LynTech would fold?"

"I don't know if it would be that dramatic, but it would be devastating on many levels. So, if it's a problem for you to be in on this, let me know now."

She looked at him, at the way the shadows played at his throat and eyes. Imposing. Very imposing. The only problem she had was the fact that he drew her like a moth to a flame. And she had the most awful feeling that he would burn anything or anyone that got too close. She'd already been too close and had felt his fire. And for some reason, she cared. She was experiencing a need to help him. It would help her and the others, but it was also important to him.

"I'll let you out of our deal," he said, when she didn't respond right away.

She understood that they both needed this. "No," she said.

"I need to know if that's true, because it's the bottom line for LynTech. If LynTech falls, I'll move on, poorer but smarter. The others won't have that option."

Leaving. That's all he spoke about. "You've got my word, there won't be a problem."

He exhaled, then softly touched her shoulder with the tips of his fingers. Fire. Pure fire, even through her lace shawl.

"Thank you."

She turned away and stepped out into the night. Zane was there, touching her elbow and motioning toward the open entrance doors as he allowed the valet to park his car. Silently they went up worn stone steps into an entry with stone walls displaying hanging tapestries on either side. There were cobbled floors underfoot and high beams overhead. A gentleman in a cutaway coat who had been by a massive reception desk, greeted them.

"Good evening and welcome to La Bonnet."

"My name's Holden, meeting Mr. Alberts."

"Ah, yes. Mr. Alberts is here and asked me to see you in." He motioned them toward a stone archway ahead of them. "This way, please."

Zane touched Lindsey on her elbow again, and she wished that she could feel that touch and still keep whatever composure she had from crumbling. Short of jerking away from him, she couldn't get free, so she walked with him into a cavernous room dominated by stone and wood and greenery. Partial walls of stone separated a series of tables and defined a space of polished wood for dancing in the middle. A tuxedo-clad man sitting at a spectacular grand piano provided music.

The host lead the way to the right, into an area that probably was in one of the turrets she'd seen from the outside. The whole scene was overwhelming to her, something she couldn't have made up even in her wildest dreams. A fantasy. And she felt like Cinderella, going to the ball but knowing that at midnight it would all be gone.

"Sol?" Zane said as they approached a table by a bank of windows near the back. A short, bulky man in a less-than-formal suit stood to face them. Sol Alberts had the sort of face that had more lines and creases than most, but with lively eyes that were as expressive as his bellowing voice.

"Glad you could make it," he said, gripping Zane's outstretched hand and pumping it vigorously before looking at Lindsey. "Oh, and look who you brought with you—the second most beautiful woman in the world."

Lindsey moved closer, held out a hand, and had it pumped just as enthusiastically. "Thank you. I'm Lindsey."

"Lovely, lovely," he said, then motioned to a lady at the table, as slender as he was stocky and smiling as broadly as her husband. "This is my Emma. Emma, Zane and Lindsey Holden."

"Oh, no," Lindsey said quickly. "We're not married."

Emma smiled. "Oh, you're engaged? That's lovely."

Zane touched Lindsey on the small of her back, effectively silencing her. As she slipped onto the high-backed leather chair that a waiter was holding out for her, she looked at Zane. He hadn't said a thing. He was settling in the chair beside hers, and saying with real deference to the man, "Thank you for this meeting." He could be charming, and he was charming the man and woman across from them every bit as much as he could charm her. "I really appreciate it. I know Simmons gave you the overview, but I thought—"

"Zane," Sol said, sitting forward. "This place has fantastic food and the best piano player in the world. Our flight doesn't leave until eleven. We're ten minutes from the airport, so we have two-and-a-half hours. Why don't we talk, enjoy the food, maybe dance, for two hours. Then I promise you an uninterrupted half-hour before we leave for you to try to convince me why we should do business."

The man might have been charmed, but he had just taken total control. What surprised Lindsey was the way Zane simply nodded in agreement.

"You've got a deal."

He motioned to the waiter and ordered expensive champagne, then turned to Sol and Emma. "You're going to Aspen?"

"We've got a place there to get away from things, and the holidays seem like a great time to do that very thing." He glanced at Lindsey, then Zane. "What are you two doing for the holidays?"

"Nothing much," Zane murmured. He looked at Lindsey, the hint of a smile deep in his eyes. "Are we?"

"Oh, no, not really," she said, flustered at the way he could shift gears and fall into the other man's plans.

"I've got a great idea," Sol said. "You're not doing anything, we've got plenty of room, and our plane's waiting at the hangar. Come with us. Then we can really talk."

Lindsey darted a look at Zane and was unnerved to find him staring at her. She had the strangest feeling he was going to say yes to Aspen.

"Aspen?" he said to her. "Sounds good, doesn't it?"

It sounded terrifying to her. Aspen. Zane. These two people thinking that they were together. Terrifying. Then she saw something in Zane's expression. He was waiting for her to do what he'd brought her here to do.

She looked at Sol and Emma, made herself smile and sound very grateful. "Oh, thank you, that's a lovely idea, but Walker...he can't travel, and we really can't leave him."

"Walker?" Sol echoed.

"He's two, a little boy."

Sol frowned. "You two have a child?"

"Oh, no, no we... I don't have any children, but Zane...well, Walker, he's with Zane. It's a custody thing, and he just got here. He's trying to settle in. There's been too much upheaval for him lately."

Emma spoke up. "Dear, of course you can't leave a two-year-old if there's a custody fight."

Lindsey let her think what she wanted to think. She went with the truth as much as she could. "He's very delicate right now and needs Zane to just be there for him."

"What about bringing him with you?" Emma asked.

"He can't leave the city right now," she said.

"Oh, of course, the custody thing. That's too bad. But maybe later, when things even out for all of you?"

"Maybe sometime," she said, and was very thankful when the waiter approached the table.

As the man poured the champagne and Sol tasted the sample, Zane slipped an arm around her chair and leaned toward her, his breath brushing her skin as he whispered, "Thank you, Tiny Tim."

She closed her eyes for a moment, fighting the feelings that his whispered voice sent through her. She opened her eyes as Sol spoke up.

"A toast? To new friends, and old business."

She found a flute in front of her and lifted it with the others in a toast, took a sip and welcomed the coolness that slipped down her throat. She sat back while the food was ordered, letting Sol and Zane decide what to get. True to Sol's promise, no business was done. They talked about Sol and Emma's four children, the grandchildren, the dog they had who hated to fly—and by the time dessert came, Lindsey was feeling oddly comfortable with the couple. Emma was a quiet lady, but obviously the woman behind the man. And Sol could admit that.

"If it wasn't for my Em, I don't know where I'd be today," he said, as the dishes were discreetly cleared and after-dinner brandy brought to the table. He touched his wife affectionately on the arm. "She stuck with me, even when *I* wouldn't stick with me!" he said on a laugh. "Zane, your half-hour's going to be here in ten minutes, so take advantage of the music and the ten minutes. I'm going to."

Sol stood and led his wife to the dance floor in the adjoining room. Zane looked at Lindsey. "Do you dance?"

"Sometimes."

"How about now?"

She stood. "Let's dance, and we can go over a battle plan before you head off to war."

"One last pleasure before the fight?" he asked as he stood and took her hand in his.

Pleasure. That's what she felt when he brushed her arm as they headed for the dance floor. "Yes, I guess so." Cinderella was alive and well.

On the dance floor he turned to her, and she was in his arms before she could brace herself for the contact. She meant to keep a distance between them, to keep his heat and his essence away from her with a safe buffer of space between them. But that never happened. The pianist started to play a slow, sensuous version of an old Beatle's song, and she felt Zane's hand slip to the small of her back.

He drew her even closer, until she was moving with the man as if they'd danced together all their lives. Without a thing in her to fight it, she rested her head on his shoulder, closed her eyes and let Cinderella come out again. A fancy ball, prince charming…glitter and beauty. And a sense of fitting against another person as if you'd been made for that moment.

She was lost right now, letting herself drift in the fantasy, and she didn't do a thing when she felt Zane kiss the top of her head. Or when his hand slipped a bit lower, an almost intimate touch. She even loved his scent, subtle, seeping into her. She floated with the fantasy, feeling like a princess, wondering just how soon midnight would come for her. Because it would come. She knew that. But she wasn't going to think about it for just a bit longer. Just a few more minutes.

"You're a good dancer," he murmured, his breath ruffling her hair.

Right when he spoke, she took a misstep and had to right herself to keep going with the rhythm. "Sorry," she mumbled.

"You can't take a compliment, can you?" he asked, his voice a low rumble against her cheek.

Not when he made her so totally aware of everything wrong with her. Of the fact that she had no business dancing with him, of holding onto him. The man wanted nothing but the moment, and that's just what she was holding onto. This moment.

She stumbled again at the thought of how fleeting the moments in life truly were. A flash, then gone. And love came in a flash, too. Love. Just like that. She loved him.

She couldn't. She missed her step again. But this time she didn't try to fall back into rhythm with him. She needed that space right now, and needed it badly.

"I...I'm sorry," she said, and turned out of his hold, moving away from him to head back to the table.

He was at her side before she made it to her seat, pulling out the chair for her, but he didn't touch her again. She sat, picked up the brandy snifter and took a sip of the mellow liquid. She took another drink, and considered draining the glass.

"It's made to be savored and appreciated," Zane said, making her hand jerk slightly.

She deliberately took another drink of the brandy before putting the almost empty snifter on the table. "It's good."

"So are you."

She didn't think she'd heard him right. Instinctively she turned to Zane, and wished she hadn't. He was studying her from under partially lowered lids, but that didn't minimize the fire that his look stirred in her. "I'm what?"

"Good. You've charmed Sol and Emma, and Walker worships you. You might not be able to drive, but you can dance. And I told you, you can't take a compliment. You need to practice saying a simple thank you."

"Thank you," she said in a small voice. "How's that?"

"Good. I'll get back to you with more compliments," he said, as Sol and Emma returned to the table.

Lindsey drank the last of her brandy, then stood as Sol and Emma took their seats again. "Excuse me, I'm going to the powder room. I'll be right back." She motioned vaguely to Zane and Sol. "And it's business time."

Zane didn't turn to watch Lindsey leave. He could literally feel the emptiness beside him and behind him. Odd. He couldn't quite figure that out, but didn't have a chance to think any more about it; Sol got right down to business as he'd promised. By the time Lindsey came back, Zane knew he was a winner. Sol was going to take his offer. And all they had to do was shake on it.

And when he looked at Lindsey slipping into the chair beside him, he knew he was a winner in that area, too. The moment she'd gone into his arms on the dance floor, he'd known that bringing her here was one of the smartest things he'd done lately. Or maybe getting stuck in the elevator had been the start of it, and he'd just had the common sense to keep it going. Whatever it was, no matter how she objected, she was as deeply involved in whatever was going on between them as he was.

He looked away from her as the thought of being alone with her later started other ideas that he didn't want to entertain just now. He looked at Sol, a bit surprised that he was looking at Lindsey, too.

"What about you, Lindsey? Do you think this is a good idea, us buying out the subsidiary? If you're anything like Emma, you're as involved in this business as Zane and I are, so I'd like your gut feeling on this."

She bit her lip, and Zane knew she measured her words. "I always think that it's better to build something than to take it apart. It's harder, but more important in the overall scheme of things. Sometimes making a hard decision to take a part out, to make the whole stronger, is necessary. What I know for sure is that anything Mr. Lewis built is worthwhile. The man invested a lot of himself in everything he did. So, if you go ahead with your investment, you'll get a good company that was built with purpose and care."

Zane heard the words coming from her that he'd said earlier, yet she'd changed them to the point that he had to think about them to absorb them. He was so intent on Lindsey that it startled him when Sol clapped his hands together.

"Excellent. Excellent." Sol looked at Zane. "If I were

you, I'd keep her around. She's brilliant. Gives it heart.'' He touched his chest. ''Not something we find in this business very often, eh?'' He looked at his watch. ''And on that lovely note, we need to get to the airport.''

Keep her around? God, he wanted to, for as long as she'd stay. It was simple, so simple. She gave everything heart, maybe even him. He stood, as Sol and Emma got up. ''So, is it a go, or pass?'' he asked.

Sol held out his hand. ''From everything I've seen, and—'' he nodded toward Lindsey ''—heard, it's a go. We'll iron out the details next week, but you can get the paperwork started.''

The men shook hands and they all said their goodbyes, then Emma and Sol were gone, and it was just him and Lindsey. He glanced at her, and wondered why he didn't feel that rush of victory he usually did at times like this.

Damn it, he didn't want this. He didn't want to let himself care, or feel. He didn't want emotions that felt so raw that he could almost sense each breath Lindsey took. ''Do you really think that you can do this business on emotions and feelings and caring like that?''

''How can you do it *without* feeling something?'' she whispered, then stood and picked up her purse and shawl. Without taking the time to put her shawl around her shoulders, she started walking away from the table, and from Zane.

Zane felt his world move. A few words from Lindsey, and he had to grasp at logic to keep his footing. He got up and went after her, across the restaurant, up to the exit and out into the night. She was there by the valet parking curb, fumbling with the shawl at her shoulders, and he went toward her.

''Damn it,'' she muttered as the shawl tangled, and he moved closer.

"Here, let me help," he said, giving his ticket to the valet, then touching the soft lace of her wrap.

She stood very still as he smoothed it over her shoulders, and he fought the urge to surround her with his arms and ease her back against him. Something in him wanted to feel her body pressed up against his again, the way it had been when they were dancing. He craved that sense of closeness, that blurring of the lines between two people. He drew back. It also scared the hell out of him to be that needy with another person.

Chapter Fourteen

The car was there. Lindsey was being helped in, and Zane circled it to get behind the wheel. He'd take her home, go back to his penthouse and have a good stiff drink. Maybe two or three good stiff drinks. He drove out onto the main street and headed in the direction of her loft.

"I know how hard it was for you to do that, and I appreciate it," he finally said.

"I told the truth."

"Yes, you do do that, don't you," he said.

"Now what are you going to do?"

He fingered the leather steering wheel, and wondered why his instant response would have been "Celebrate with you," but it never came out. Instead, he spoke rationally. "Figure out how to make LynTech as viable as possible."

He turned toward the city center and heard her sigh softly. But she didn't speak again. By the time he slowed and stopped in front of her loft, he felt tension in the car.

He was going to let her get out of the car and go inside, and then he'd go home. The tension in him was easily explained. But he didn't understand why she was so edgy, so tense, unless there was anger involved. And he didn't want anger from her. That was the last thing he wanted right now. He stopped the car and turned off the motor, but before he could get out, she said, "I keep telling you that you don't have to see me up."

She reached for the door handle, but he stopped her with a touch on her shoulder. "Lindsey?"

She was very still, and didn't look at him. "What?"

"What did I do?"

She shifted, breaking their contact, but this time she turned to him. In the dim light he felt the impact of her gaze, and his stomach knotted.

"You? Nothing, you did nothing."

She moved away from his touch and got out, and he hurried after her. He hated things that didn't make sense, and just about everything in his relationship with Lindsey didn't make sense. Except for the fact that he didn't want her to leave, to just walk away from him like this. He met up with her at the entry, and she went inside but didn't try to shut the door to keep him out.

She crossed to the elevator and tugged the cage up, causing the shawl to drop off her shoulders. She turned; he moved and had the lacy material. When she realized he'd picked it up, she silently turned and got in the lift, and he went after her. She pressed the button, as he pulled down the wire cage front. Then she stood staring straight ahead as they went upward.

"I told you I can't play games," he said as the lift stopped.

She lifted the gate, and would have gone to her door if he hadn't spoke again. "Lindsey, did you hear me?"

She turned then, the lights at her back, their softness haloing around her, and he ached deep in his soul with a sense that he'd truly be alone if she walked away.

"I'm not playing games. I'm going home. You're going home. You got what you want, I got what I want. We're even."

He moved toward her, so close that he could feel each rapid breath she took. "You don't know what I want," he whispered.

Her tongue touched her lips, and the action ran riot over his raw nerves.

"Yes, I do. You told me. You want here and now and not anything beyond that," she said in such a low voice that he wouldn't have heard her if he'd been an inch more away from her.

But he was close, close enough to reach out and frame her face with his hands, to brush the silky skin there with the balls of his thumbs and feel her tremble. He drank in each exquisite feature in the dim light. It was so simple, so painfully simple.

"I want you."

Had Cinderella been sure that midnight meant disaster, or had she thought that she was the one person who could change the laws? Lindsey stared at Zane and knew that nothing could change. He couldn't. She couldn't. And she wanted him. She wanted him with a passion that defied any logic, any sanity. But she tried to stop what was happening, tried to escape before she put herself in the path of sure pain.

"No...no," she breathed.

She knew Zane hadn't moved, but everything seemed to be shimmering, the world shifting in such a subtle way that it might never have happened if Zane hadn't whispered, "Tell me you don't want me, and I'll leave."

If she could have, she would have. If she could have told a lie of monumental proportions, she would have. But she couldn't. She tried. She opened her mouth and thought the words *I don't want you,* but they never came alive.

She came alive. She felt his lips come to hers, felt his touch on her shift from her face to the back of her neck, and the kiss killed all reason, all sense of self-protection. She was lost, and despite the knowledge that she was doing the most dangerous thing she'd ever done, she melted toward Zane.

She answered kiss for kiss, drinking him in, letting the sense of connection with him seep into her soul, and the glory outweigh the inevitable pain. The ecstasy won out over logic, and there was no turning back. His hands slipped lower, pressing to her back, bringing her closer still, breasts to chest, hips to hips. Heart to heart.

She felt them moving back and out of the lift, but the kiss never stopped. Not when the wall was at her back and Zane's heat was in front of her. She returned that kiss wildly, with a passion that almost scared her. This need to taste and explore an explosion of need that had a life of its own. Even when Zane moved back long enough to get the key she'd forgotten she was holding, and unlocked her door, she didn't let go of him. She couldn't.

If she let go, it might be over. She'd be lost. Then Zane had her in his arms, holding her to his heart and carrying her into the place that she'd called home for a year. But it hadn't been home until this moment—until she came into it with Zane, into shadows and silence. With Zane.

Somehow they found the bedroom area; somehow Zane eased Lindsey down to her feet, and still she held him. His hands skimmed over her, moving down her back, cupping her bottom and drawing her against his hardness. She tasted his throat, tugged at his tie, unfurling it, tugging it away from his collar; then, with unsteady hands, she managed to undo the buttons. His jacket slipped back and off his shoulders, the shirt opened, and she pressed her lips to the heat of his chest. She tasted him, savored him and pushed her hands under the shirt, around to his back.

It was then that she felt him against her naked breasts.

Her dress was down to her waist, her bra gone, but she had no memory of that happening. Skin against skin. Sensations were riotous, and she gasped when Zane touched her breast, his hand cupping it, his thumb finding her nipple, and shards of ecstasy shot through her. She gasped softly, arching toward the touch, moving backward, falling into the bed with him.

For a heart-stopping moment, Zane was gone, the world stopped, and she opened her eyes. He was over her, the shadows blending around him, and for a horrific moment she thought this was all a dream, a dream that was ending. Then he came to her, his clothes gone, and he was there again, slipping into the bed beside her.

The dream—because that's what it was for her, a dream, a time out of time—kept going. His hands found her, touched her, drew responses that overwhelmed her with pleasure and built her desire to a peak that was almost frightening. He touched her face, and she thought she felt him tremble slightly before his touch slipped down, feathered over her breast. Then it was her trembling. Her breath caught in her throat, and his hand went lower.

He eased her dress down, slipping it lower until he skimmed it off her legs and it was gone. His fingertips slid under the band of her lace panties, slipping them lower until they were gone, too. Lindsey turned toward Zane, toward the center of her universe. And he drew her to him.

She felt him against her, his desire as strong as hers. His arms were around her, and she was against him. She melted toward him, lost in the feeling of safety and oneness. She buried her face in his heat, and ached for more—a wish that immediately came true. He touched her, his hands slipping low, pressed to her stomach. Then he found her center.

She arched toward his touch, felt him enter her with his fingers, and the world shifted again. He was over her, his hands at either side of her, his legs between hers. She felt him touch her—the silky strength against her, testing her— and as she lifted her hips, he slipped inside her with aching slowness, filling her, and the connection was complete.

Zane settled deep inside her, and the sensations were beyond absorbing for Lindsey, surrounding her, filling her, embracing her. Then he moved and the center of the universe was them. She moved with him, thrust for thrust, meeting him, building higher and higher, almost desperate for the consummation. She'd never known that ecstasy had two sides, the pleasure and the pain, the joy and fear. This went beyond anything she'd ever known.

She held on to Zane and found a place that had never existed for her until him. A place where nothing mattered but him, where nothing existed but them, and she knew for the first time in her life what being one with another person truly meant. She melted into him, lost herself and knew that as the world fell away, he touched her soul.

There were tears of joy, a release that brought a sensation of peace unbounded, and she settled into Zane's arms. They sank into bliss and satiation, moving until Zane was behind her, pressed against her, his arm around her waist, his lips touching her shoulder.

"Don't ever tell me what I want," he whispered softly. "Ever." Then he pulled her more snugly against him, and his sigh echoed hers.

She didn't move. She didn't think. She just closed her eyes and let sleep come. And she stayed. For now.

It could have been a second or an eternity that passed before she stirred. She didn't know. All she knew was the sense of completeness that saturated her being, the feeling of Zane's body alongside her own, making her whole. She relished it, holding to it, not opening her eyes for fear that it would disappear.

She felt Zane move, his leg heavy over her thighs, and his hand stroking on her stomach. His fingers brushed over her skin, up to her breasts, then gently cupped one breast, his thumb finding her nipple. Any threads of sleep that lingered were broken when she moaned softly.

"I thought you were awake," Zane breathed by her ear.

Lindsey lay motionless as his touch aroused her, building a fire in her so quickly that she could barely absorb the sensation. God, she wanted him. She'd wanted him since that first moment she'd met his gaze, from the moment she'd seen the way his hair lay on his collar, the way his eyes narrowed with intensity. From the first moment he'd touched her.

She turned toward him, his lips finding hers as his hand went lower. Arching toward his touch, she wrapped her arms around him, holding on for dear life. She never wanted to know the feeling of his absence, of the emptiness she'd lived with all her life until now. But deep inside, she knew that she only had now. He didn't look beyond the present, and to be with him, that's all she had, now. She could dream of more, but those were dreams.

Zane shifted, spanning her waist with his hands and maneuvering her until she was straddling him, looking down at his shadowy face. A face she loved. A man she loved. She barely had time to realize the naked truth before he eased her higher, then slipped inside her, filling her, bringing that completeness again. And she soared with it.

She moved with him, higher and higher, deeper and deeper, needing this as much as she needed air to live. Needing this man as much as life itself. The ecstasy rose to heights that she'd never been to before, never dreamed existed, and when that moment of oneness came, when the world didn't exist, when reality didn't matter, she gave herself to him totally. They'd become one.

Sensation was everywhere, yet there were just the two of them, just her and Zane, just this moment, just this love. And she grasped at it with a passion so intense she didn't recognize it as her own. She held on to him, even as the feeling started to diminish, even as they rolled so she was on her side facing him. He didn't leave her until she sighed and snuggled into his chest. He eased back, then his arm was around her and she melded to him.

"This is what I want," he whispered, pressing his lips to her forehead and exhaling softly. "All I want...now."

Now. That was all he wanted. This. The moment. She closed her eyes tightly, fighting tears that came from nowhere. What had she been thinking? She felt his damp skin under her hand on his chest, felt the beat of his heart, the motion of each breath he took. This was it. This was all there would be. She turned away from Zane, but he didn't let her go.

He put his arm around her waist, pulling her against him, his chest to her back, his legs tangled with hers, and he kissed her shoulder. She made herself stay very still, and when she felt his breathing grow regular, when she knew he was asleep, the tears came. She felt a grief that made no sense, a feeling of loss that restricted her chest.

With the heat of Zane's breath warm on her bare skin, Lindsey admitted that the thing she'd feared all her life had happened. And she'd let it happen. She'd let herself fall in love. And she'd set herself up to never have that love. It was her fault. She closed her eyes tightly, balling her hands into fists on the linen. But that was her secret. That was for her to face...later. After Zane was gone for good.

Half an hour later Zane heard the distant sound of a phone. A strange sound. Muffled. But there. He shifted, felt Lindsey snuggled into his side, her hair tickling his face and his arm almost asleep where she was laying on it. The ringing continued, and he eased back, careful not to wake her, and turned in the darkness of the high-ceilinged space. The sound stopped. He sank back, but didn't turn to Lindsey again.

Just the feel of her against him was arousing. He knew he'd had his fill earlier, but that didn't stop the immediate response she awakened in him. God, he felt like some teenager, reacting on such a basic level. With no control. He skimmed his hand over her shoulder, thankful for the touch of moonlight in the room, its shadows on her skin. The way her hair was tousled.

The ringing started again, and his hand paused on her, even as he felt her start to stir.

"What's that?" she asked in a sleepy voice.

"I'll find out." He gave her a quick kiss on the shoulder, then twisted away and sat up. He reached for a light near the bed, snapped it on. In the low glow, he reached for the phone by the bed—but the ringing went on. He put the receiver back, and oddly the ringing stopped. "Do you have any other phones in here?"

"No." She pushed herself up in the bed, looking beyond beautiful with the sheets around her waist, her high breasts so inviting. Her lips softly parted. She rubbed at her eyes, but before he could reach for her, the ringing began again.

He looked into the darkness just beyond the glow and realized that's where the sound was coming from. His clothes had been tossed there. He got up, crossed to where his coat had come to rest on a side chair and picked it up. He reached into his inside pocket and pulled out his cell phone. It was lit, and the readout was the number at the hotel; the time read, two a.m.

He went back to the bed, pressed send, and sank down in the mussed linen. "Yes?"

"Oh, Mr. Holden, it's you. I've been calling and calling,

and when I tried to leave a voice-mail message, I kept getting cut off and had to keep calling back.''

"Mrs. Greenleaf?"

"Yes, I'm sorry to call, but it's the baby."

"What about Walker?"

He sensed Lindsey moving behind him, then sitting beside him, her hand on his arm.

"I don't mean to worry you, but he woke with a fever, and I called the hotel doctor and he's on his way up, but I—"

"I'll be right there," he said without even thinking about it.

He stood, closing the phone, but before he could get across to his clothes, Lindsey was there, right in front of him, naked.

"What's wrong?"

"He woke up with a high fever, and Mrs. Greenleaf called a doctor." He hesitated, the need to kiss her almost overwhelming, so he gave in to it. A quick, fierce kiss before he let her go and went for his clothes. He got dressed quickly, not bothering to do up his shirt or even reach for his tie. He pushed his feet into his shoes, turned, and Lindsey was there again.

She was dressed this time, in jeans, a loose sweatshirt and running shoes. "Come on. Let's go," she said.

"You don't—"

"I do," Lindsey said, looking at a very different Zane from the man who had carried her into the loft. This man looked tense, his clothes dishevelled, his hair slightly spiked. And she wasn't letting him go to Walker alone. "Come on. We need to hurry."

He didn't argue with her, just hurried with her out of the loft, down in the lift and out the front doors. By the time she got into the passenger seat of the car, Zane was behind the wheel, the engine running. He pulled out into the street, and the power she'd sensed in the car earlier was there full force.

Zane wove his way through the light traffic, barely stopping when he had to, before taking off again. She held on to the armrest, her fingers pressing into the leather, and she knew a real fear for Walker. Her heart broke thinking of him being sick, probably just wanting his mommy and being scared. But a part of her was vaguely pleased that Zane was so concerned. Maybe she'd been wrong about him and the boy. Maybe things were changing.

She looked at him, at the way his jaw was working, one hand gripping the steering wheel and the other never leaving the gear shift. They turned a corner, the wheels squealing slightly on the curve.

"What did this baby-sitter say exactly?"

"That he woke with a fever, and that the hotel doctor was on his way."

They reached the hotel, probably in record time, and Zane didn't bother with the underground parking. He pulled up right in front of the place, jumped out, and by the time she caught up with him, he was halfway across the lobby going to the elevators. He passed the first three cars and stopped at the far one, which went to floors fifteen and above. He jabbed at the call button, and the doors opened immediately.

They got in, and as the car started up, Zane looked at her. "Why do kids run a fever?" he asked.

"They're sick, have an infection, are getting teeth." She shrugged. "Any number of reasons. Sometimes it's nothing. It just happens, a fever spike, then it's gone, for no reason at all."

He rocked forward on the balls of his feet, glanced from the floor indicator to her and back. "Thanks for coming."

"I'm worried, too," she said, knowing she couldn't have let him go alone. Not in the state he was in. "He's so little, and being sick..." She exhaled heavily. "It's scary."

The soft *ding* indicated they were at their floor; the doors opened, and Zane took off toward the penthouse. The door was slightly ajar, and Lindsey followed him into the main part of the suite. The only light came from the extra bedroom where Walker slept.

"Mrs. Greenleaf?" he called as he crossed to the bedroom door.

When they went into the room, Lindsey blinked slightly at the light, then saw a lady dressed in a loose blue dress turn toward them.

"Oh, Mr. Holden, thank goodness."

A man was beside her, his back to them, leaning over the crib. Lindsey heard a sob, and saw Walker pulling himself up, his cheeks bright red. He was crying, a soft, heartbreaking sound.

Zane moved first, going past the lady to the crib, then touching Walker on the hand. The little boy looked up, then said, "Dada, hold," and Zane didn't hesitate. He reached for him and picked him up. "What's going on?" Zane asked the man.

"I'm Dr. Shennel," the slightly built man said. He had obviously been asleep himself, and must have dressed quickly in a polo shirt, jeans and boots. "He's running a fever, most likely from some teeth growing in. No congestion, no likely infection. I gave him some medication that should bring the fever down and probably make him a bit drowsy. My guess is, he'll wake up in the morning just fine. But take him to his pediatrician to make sure he's okay."

Zane listened intently, all the while rocking slightly from side to side to soothe Walker, who had snuggled into his shoulder. It looked so natural that Lindsey thought anyone who didn't know their background would think they'd been together forever. And Walker had called him "Dada." She crossed her arms to keep herself from going to the boy. He needed Zane. Not her. She'd be gone soon. She closed off the next thought—that Zane would be, too. The relatives would be found, and someone else would be there when Walker cried or got sick.

Zane started to rub Walker's back as the doctor spoke to him, and she had the same feeling of hope she'd had in the car. Miracles happened. It had been a miracle that Walker hadn't been in the car when his parents were killed. Maybe this was the way it was supposed to be. Fate.

Then Zane came over to her with Walker, and she let herself touch the boy, brush his hot cheek and whisper to him, "You'll be okay, sweetie. It's okay."

Walker turned heavy eyes to her, then leaned toward her, and she took him. She cradled him to her...one last time. While Zane went back to talk to the doctor and the baby-sitter, Lindsey carried the baby out into the darkened living room. She went to the couch that faced the extra bedroom door, sank down in the cushions and cuddled Walker to her.

He felt so hot against her, but he was settling, one hand clutching her sweatshirt tightly, the other up to his face as he found his thumb. He sucked softly as she crooned in his ear, humming "Rock-a-bye, Baby." Gradually he relaxed, sighing heavily, and finally she could tell he was asleep. She closed her eyes, just holding the child, letting sensations surround her the way she had with Zane.

She loved Walker, too. The idea came to her softly, but it didn't surprise her. It was just a fact. Another love, after a life without much love. And another passing love.

She scrunched her eyes to keep from crying. Tears

wouldn't do any good. She knew what she was going to get out of this: a raise for Amy, two new vans and drivers. No other promise had been made to her. None.

"Lindsey?"

She heard Zane's voice, and opened her eyes. For a moment she was sure she was in her dream. There had been blackness; now there was bright light, and Zane was coming toward her out of the light. Her dream. Had it been Zane all the time coming for her? The prince, coming to rescue the princess in the darkness?

Lindsey closed her eyes against that insanity. Prince? No. Zane. Rescuing her? No, but there was part of her that wanted to hope things could be different, that they might be different. Hadn't Zane rushed here when he heard about Walker? Hadn't he acted as if she belonged here? She stopped herself, afraid to continue. But she couldn't shut the thoughts out completely. Even though she knew how dangerous such thoughts could be. So dangerous. But maybe it was worth taking a chance. It was possible that Zane, and the man who had been in bed with her, was changing.

She felt the couch shift, as Zane sat beside her. She opened her eyes, and all she wanted to do was to touch him, to feel his reality—but she kept her hold on the sleeping child.

"He's asleep?" he whispered.

"Yes, and cooler, I think," she said, surprised that her voice sounded so calm. "I think he's going to be okay."

Zane blew out a breath. "I hope so. The doctor seems to think it's not anything serious."

"Where's the doctor?"

"He left. And Mrs. Greenleaf is changing Walker's crib, freshening it up. The doctor called in some medicine to the all-night pharmacy around the corner, but they can't get it here for an hour at least. It's just easier if I pick it up. Will you stay until I get back?''

She nodded. "Of course. Go ahead.''

He hesitated, then touched her cheek with his fingertips. Without saying anything, he stood and quietly left.

Chapter Fifteen

Zane had no sooner left than the baby-sitter approached her. "Here, miss, I can take him now."

Lindsey hesitated over letting him go. There was a growing protectiveness of Walker in her, and she had to force herself to place the child in the woman's arms. He barely stirred.

"Such a dear," the lady whispered. "So sweet."

Lindsey looked up at her, a real grandmotherly type, and saw there was a sense of caring about her. She'd do fine with Walker, Lindsey knew that. Then the lady carried Walker into the bedroom.

Lindsey stood and stretched, feeling almost chilled now that the child's hot body wasn't against her. She'd wait for Zane. She wanted to talk to him, to see if her crazy thoughts had any basis, except wishful thinking.

She crossed to what looked like a wet bar, turned on a light above it and blinked at the sudden brilliance. The mirrors behind the bar showed her pale face, her tousled hair, her lack of makeup. She looked like a little kid. And maybe she was—that little kid who wanted to believe in princes and in fairy tales. She looked away, turned to the room and saw the dining area.

The table was filled with papers, stacks of files and a

closed laptop computer. Zane hadn't been kidding about trying to work at home. She crossed to the area, turned on the light and saw the banner for LynTech on everything—files, papers, even stationery. She almost turned away, but stopped when she saw another familiar logo: the one she'd helped design for Just For Kids. It was a Valentine heart with ribbons flowing around it, and children dancing and laughing, holding the ends of the ribbons.

She touched her fingertip to the logo. A laughing child. A safe child. She sighed, then glanced at the typing below the logo. A status report. And the bottom line made her heart lurch painfully. *Projected closure date.* Right beside that was a date in March of next year. She picked up the paper, read it all, certain she had to be seeing it wrong, out of context. But she hadn't.

Zane had mandated a closure of the center in March. The plans were already in motion.

The coldness increased in her, and whatever stupid thoughts she'd had were gone. He'd known all the time. All the time.

Temporary. Everything was temporary with Zane. Her eyes burned, but there were no tears. The hurt went too deep for tears. And there was no way she could have him come back, have him be here, standing in front of her, looking for all the world like the man she loved, the man who had made love to her. No, not love. Never love.

She heard Mrs. Greenleaf singing softly to Walker in the other room, and she crossed to the door and left. She walked to the elevator, a bit shocked that her legs were holding her up. Her whole body was trembling now, and when she got in the elevator she wrapped her arms around herself, the only thing she could think to do that would keep her from shattering.

She barely remembered how she got home, but suddenly

she was walking into the loft and heading for the bedroom. She saw the bed, the mussed linen, and in a frenzy she stripped the bed completely, tossing the sheets and blankets into one corner. She stared at the naked bed. She felt nausea twist inside her and she turned away.

She started to go back into the living area, but saw something on the floor by the chair where Zane had left his clothes. *The pen.* The damn pen. She crossed to it, crouched and touched it. Closing her hands over the sleek gold only increased her nausea, and she tossed the pen away from her. It struck the foot of the bed, then skittered along the floor to come to rest partway under the dresser. She left it there and went back out into the darkened living area.

She crossed to the couch and collapsed into the cushions. Thoughts bombarded her. Feelings tore at her. She hugged herself tightly again and rocked slowly back and forth. But nothing eased her demons. Nothing stopped the pain. He'd lied to her. He'd used her. And she'd let him. He'd said he didn't play games. Another lie. And she'd willingly played his games.

She remembered what he'd said about negotiating with someone who was vulnerable. Damn it. He'd sensed her vulnerability, the way he sensed the vulnerability of his adversaries in business, and he'd gone in for the kill.

Joey jumped onto her lap, and at the same moment the sound of the entry buzzer cut through the stillness around her. Joey meowed, and she froze. The buzzer rang again, then again. Joey stropped her arm, but she didn't move. "Go away," she whispered. "Just go away. Leave me alone."

The cat meowed, and when the buzzing finally stopped, Joey curled up on her lap. She gave a tremulous sigh. "What am I going to do?" she breathed. How could she face Amy and the others? How could she possibly tell them that one man was going to tear their lives apart?

A sharp knock on her door startled her. Then another knock. George? Her neighbor kept strange hours, but it was past three in the morning. And she didn't want to see anyone right now. She stayed very still. The knocking came again, and she finally shifted the cat off her lap and went to the door.

"George, it's three in the morning," she called through the barrier. "Go away."

"It's not George. It's me, Zane."

She pressed her forehead against the cold wood of the door and closed her eyes tightly. "Go away."

"No, I'm not leaving. Let me in."

She stood back, took a tight breath and opened the door. Zane stood with the light behind him, a hulking silhouette of a man. No prince. Not even close.

"How did you get in?"

"George let me up. How did you get home?"

"A taxi." She was holding the doorknob so tightly that her fingers were aching. "Why are you here?"

"Why wouldn't I be? I thought you were going to wait until I got back with the medicine." He glanced over her shoulder. "Can I come in?"

She wanted to slam the door on him, but she couldn't. Nothing could be that easy with Zane. She stood back, letting him pass; he stirred the air with the freshness of the night and the scents that clung to him. Maleness. It knotted her stomach.

He was inside, the door swinging shut, and she turned to him, thankful for the shadows. He was less than two feet from her, looking for all the world like the man she thought she'd loved. The man she'd made love with. Sickness rose in the back of her throat.

When he reached out to touch her, she moved away from the contact, not trusting what she'd do if she felt his touch on her skin again. "Don't. How can you leave when Walker is sick?"

She moved to the couch before she turned, and he followed, then took away any protection the darkness offered by snapping on a side light.

He turned to her, stood over her. "First, Walker is sleeping and doing better. Now, tell me, what's going on?"

"How *could* you?" she said, hating the unsteadiness in her voice.

"How could I what? I came back, you were gone, you wouldn't answer your door. What are you talking about?"

She had to clasp her hands tightly in front of her to stop them from shaking. "The center. You planned on closing it all along, didn't you."

He was very still. "What?"

"I saw the evaluation report at the hotel. You're closing it in March, aren't you."

"Lindsey, listen to—"

"No," she almost screamed. Then in a lower voice, she said, "No, just tell me the truth. Are you closing the center?"

He didn't try to hedge or lie again. "Yes."

One single word, and it was devastating. "Damn you, how could you do this?"

His eyes narrowed, but he didn't move any closer. "It's business. It's not personal."

"Not personal?" Her voice rose again. "Not *personal?*"

"Listen to me, business is—"

"No, you can't get out of this with that lie. This is very personal. How dare you say it's not personal. It's my life, it's the life of everyone there, the kids—" She had to swallow hard to ease the constriction in her throat and chest.

"God help you, it's beyond personal, and you don't even know it."

"It's a decision based on—"

"Money, I know. I understand that. I also understand that you promised me Amy would get a raise, and we'd have two vans and drivers. And all the time you were having fun, weren't you. What difference did it make if you had to give away something for a few months, as long as you got what you wanted? Damn, but you're good."

He shook his head. "I was going to tell you."

"When the doors were sealed shut?"

"I would have let you know when it was possible to tell you."

He sounded so controlled, so reasonable, that it only deepened the hurt.

"You're leaving."

When she moved to go around him, to end this before it killed her, he grabbed her by both shoulders, stopping her dead in her tracks. But it didn't stop her pain or her fury. She twisted, but he pulled her around to face him.

"Lindsey, stop this," he said, grinding out the words.

She looked up at him, and it ripped her heart out to feel him so close but to feel, instead of the joy she'd known earlier, nothing but pain. "No, you stop it," she said, jerking back and free of his touch. Words came that she didn't want to come. Words that only cut her more deeply. "Why did you go to bed with me? Was it to soften the blow, to make me more agreeable when I found out what a manipulating, rotten son of a—"

She bit her lip, trying to stop the torrent, but it didn't work. "You're a heartless bastard without any redeeming qualities. The only man in the world walking around without a heart. You go around manipulating and using people, staying isolated so no one will find out the truth." Tears

came, and she hated them but didn't even swipe at them.
"You're destroying so many lives."

"You're attributing more power to me than I have," he
said.

She'd certainly given him power over her. "Amy's a
widow with a child and no job. What do I tell her?"

He shook his head. "This is why I never get involved
with the employees. You can't do what you need to do if
you get too close."

"Sex wouldn't make your list of getting involved, would
it?" she choked out. "My mistake."

"What happened between us—"

"Was nothing personal," she snapped.

"For God's sake, I wanted you and you wanted me. That
wasn't a mistake—nothing about that was a mistake. I don't
know what you want from me."

She knew then that all she wanted was for him to say
he loved her—and that only exposed her stupidity again.
He'd never once mentioned love. It had all been her—her
dreams and her needs and her loving him.

"I just wanted the truth," Lindsey whispered.

"I told you the truth. I wanted to be with you." Zane
frowned, jammed his hands in the pockets of his pants.
"You thought because we made love that I'd change everything, that I'd forget about the business and run rough-
shod over logic and reason?"

"No," she said. "I just thought that..." She couldn't
say it. She wouldn't.

He was closer but not touching her, and his voice
dropped seductively. "Lindsey, I can't make this all some
fairy tale for you. I am what I am. I told you right up front
that I'm not good at the long haul. You knew that. You
know that."

"You're right. You never lied about that." The tears

were gone suddenly, but it made things even worse. A certain sense of deadness was spreading through her, and that terrified her. "I knew that you took what you wanted. That you got what you wanted. That you didn't believe in anything to do with staying. You believe in going. You don't make anything personal."

"God, if I could..." He shrugged sharply. "I can't."

"I know. But what about Walker?" she asked.

He rocked forward, cutting down the distance between them even more. "I'm taking care of him for now."

"Until you can give him to some stranger who'll take money to watch him for you, like that string of baby-sitters and the nanny?"

"Damn you!" he said hoarsely. "How dare you judge me and what I do and what I am."

"At least you can get angry. That's a start at real emotions. Not a good one, but it's a start."

"You can't stop, can you," he muttered.

She couldn't stop loving him, she knew that. "Sorry. I'm saying all the wrong things again, aren't I. My mistake. I can't judge you. I don't know you well enough to know what you can or can't do. But I know that Walker deserves better than being passed from pillar to post. Children deserve our best, not what's convenient," she said. "Now, it's really time for you to go."

Zane was very still for a moment, then oddly seemed to retreat without even moving away from her. When she started to go around him, she feared he'd touch her again. He didn't. But he stopped her with his words.

"I want to stay."

She turned back to him. "What?" she asked in a whisper.

"I don't want to leave, not like this, not now."

"You want to stay until you decide it's time to leave."

"I want to stay for as long as it lasts," he whispered.

She was a convenience for him, exciting on some level but a temporary pleasure. She cringed inside at how she'd taken him into her bed, how easily she'd let herself be deluded by dreams and wishes. No wonder he thought she'd agree to some arrangement, some temporary affair.

"No thanks," she breathed and turned, crossing to the door and gripping the doorknob to open the barrier.

Zane came over to her, stopped, looked down at her. For one horrible moment she thought he was going to touch her. But he didn't. He left.

She closed the door, threw the lock and leaned back against the barrier. She heard the gate to the elevator go up, then down, then the low drone of the motors taking Zane away from her.

As the noise faded, she slowly slid downward until she was on the floor, her back against the door, her arms circling her legs, pulling them to her breasts. She pressed her forehead to her knees, and tears came again. Not silent tears, but racking sobs. And she could feel herself slipping into a dark, dark place—but there wouldn't be anyone coming to rescue her this time. There was no light.

ZANE FELT as if he'd been blindsided by a freight train. He'd never faced anyone so angry, or so frustrating. His first instinct was to go back into the loft and stay until he could make some sense out of what just happened. But he didn't go back. He left, got in his car and drove away from Lindsey.

By the time he got back to the penthouse and had checked on Walker to find him sleeping peacefully, he was even less sure of what had happened. Nothing made sense. He crossed to the table, saw the paperwork for the center on top of the stack and picked it up. *Closure.* He dropped it, letting it flutter down on top of the other papers.

It was business. It had always been about business. Nothing personal. He turned from the table, but couldn't get away from the thought that every moment he spent with Lindsey had been personal. Every second he'd been with her, touching her, kissing her, getting to know her. Very personal. But that was a separate part of his world. It didn't matter that he had come close to begging her to let him stay.

Damn it, none of this made sense. But then again, he knew that since he'd met Lindsey, not much had made sense for him. Except his need for her. And that would pass. It had to. Sooner or later, it would. At least he hoped so.

Thursday

NEAR DAWN Walker woke and miraculously the fever had passed. He was up and around immediately, running out of his room with Mrs. Greenleaf coming after him, and he went right to Zane at the table. He flew into Zane's lap, sending papers scattering, and Zane let them go. He picked up the boy, shocked at how relieved he felt that Walker was okay.

His emotions were crazy. Lack of sleep. Frustration. Stress. He had any number of excuses. He wouldn't use Lindsey as one of them.

"Hey," he said to Walker. "How about cartoons? Nice colorful cartoons on TV?"

The boy grinned at him. "Daddy, toons, peeze."

Daddy? Zane felt a shock at the word, something that had slipped past him last night. He looked at Mrs. Greenleaf. "I think we'll watch cartoons, and I'd appreciate it if you could call down for breakfast."

"Oh, of course. Anything special?"

"They know what I want, and for Walker, how about..." He realized he didn't have a clue what the boy would eat for breakfast beyond a bottle. "I don't know. Whatever you think would be good."

"Sure, I'll take care of it," she said.

"Thanks." Then he did something that surprised him. "I'll watch him for a while so you can take a break."

"Thank you, sir. I could use a shower and a change."

"Go ahead. I'll get the door when room service comes."

She hurried off, and he carried Walker over to the television opposite the couch. He turned the TV on, found some cartoons where a mouse was blowing up a cat, and sank down on the couch. Walker squirmed out of his hold, onto the cushions, but pressed up against his side, his eyes wide with wonder, perhaps that the blown-up cat had come back to life, looking perfect again.

The animal was damaged beyond repair—then miraculously, everything was fine again. A real fantasy. Walker slipped down off the couch, onto the floor and scooted closer to the television to get a better look.

He'd hurt Lindsey—he knew that and it made his gut ache. She thought he was cold and heartless, without humanity. Yet she made him feel painfully human.

Walker squealed with delight when the mouse hit the cat with a huge hammer, raising a bump on the cat's head that looked like a mountain.

"Great, contributing to the delinquency of a minor," he muttered. Another mark against his humanity. He glanced from Walker to his unfinished work on the table and wondered how such a little human being could make such a difference in his life. He hadn't even thought about going to the office today, and usually he went as early as he could. Now he was watching cartoons, waiting for room service and questioning his own humanity. But that wasn't Walker's doing, it was Lindsey's doing.

And he hated the sense of emptiness that had been born when he left her loft, and persisted even now. Her doing, too. She'd been in his life for such a short time, come and gone. But she stayed long enough to disturb him on so many levels, and make him start to think in terms of how things might have been if he'd been a different person. If she'd been different. If life had dealt them both a different hand.

There was a knock on the door, breaking into his thoughts. "Room service," he said to Walker, who didn't look away from the television.

Zane went to answer the door, but it wasn't room service. Matt was there.

"I know it's early, but I had to see you."

It shocked Zane that his first thought was that Matt wanted to see him about what had happened with Lindsey. But that was crazy. Matt didn't know anything about Lindsey. It was the meeting he'd come to find out about. Zane moved to one side. "Come on in. We sewed it up. He's ours. It's a done deal. Just paperwork left."

"That's great about Alberts. Knew you could do it," he said, but without much enthusiasm, as he moved into the suite, glanced at Walker, then grimaced at the cartoon that had escalated to the mouse setting the cat on fire. "Boy, I don't remember cartoons being that violent."

"I don't remember cartoons at all, so you can't prove it by me," Zane said.

Matt started for the table, but Zane waylaid him. "Let's talk on the couch, so I can keep an eye on Walker."

"Oh, no, Mrs. Greenmoss, or Greenbranch, took a hike?"

"Mrs. Greenleaf is freshening up. I'm just watching him for a little while."

Matt came over to the couch and sat down, putting his briefcase on the couch between them. "Okay, I'm not sure how to do this."

"Celebrate? What's wrong with you if you don't know what to do to celebrate this victory?"

"I'm not talking about that. This is personal."

"What are you talking about?"

"I got a call this morning from the attorney in Florida."

Zane glanced at Walker, something settling in him that he hadn't even known was there until now. "What did he want?"

"He got information—found a relative, as a matter of fact."

Zane darted a look back at Matt. "What?"

"Blood relative."

He absorbed it. It was over. Walker was leaving. But he didn't want that. He didn't know where it came from, but the idea of losing Walker, too, was not acceptable. The child was a crazy disturbance in his life, upsetting and touching. A man who had never in his life wanted a child suddenly wanted a two-year-old tornado. God, he was crazy.

"No," he said.

Matt frowned. "What?"

"He's not going."

"Zane, you don't know—"

"I won't let him go to some greedy relative. We've got the nanny lined up, and Mrs. Greenleaf is terrific. He's no problem."

That made Matt laugh out loud, startling Walker, who got up and hustled over to the two of them. "Daddy play?"

"Daddy?" Matt breathed, the laughter gone completely.

"He calls me that," Zane said, scooping the boy up on his lap. "Matt, listen, I owe Suzanne something for what I did to her, and I owe this kid. I can do it. I've got resources, and I want to."

"Where's the real Zane and what closet do you have him locked in?"

Zane smiled at that. "Maybe he just came out of hiding," he said.

"Well," Matt breathed as he raked his fingers through his hair. "This is going to be easier than I thought."

"What?"

"The attorney called because they found the paper trail, and the relative. Weaver wasn't Walker's father. He took that place—even put his name on the birth certificate. But Walker isn't his son. Weaver couldn't have children—a childhood disease thing."

Walker squirmed off Zane's lap, getting down to go back to plant himself in front of the cartoons again.

"What in the hell? There was another man? Someone Suzanne—" That made him sick. He thought he'd dealt with that—another man sleeping with her. But he hadn't. "Who?" he asked through clenched teeth.

"You. You're Walker's father."

Chapter Sixteen

Zane felt the world stop, almost the same way it had when Lindsey had pushed him out of her life. It ground to a halt and nothing made sense. "What?"

"You're the father. She was pregnant when she left. She met Weaver, fell in love almost immediately, and he wanted kids. But he couldn't. The blood type matches yours, and the attorney said that Suzanne's doctor knew all about it. He was bound by confidentiality, until her death. When they contacted him for background information, he felt everyone needed to know the truth. You're a father," Matt repeated.

Zane stood, not knowing where he was going, just feeling the ache in his throat and the blur of tears in his eyes and a need to move. He looked at Walker, his son. His. Part of him.

He stopped in the middle of the room, anything but breathing beyond him, especially rational thought. Oh, the pain he'd caused Suzanne—a pain he knew now had come from the fact that he'd never really known what love was, that she was having a child when he told her he never wanted one. God, his gut hurt. He'd never been able to really love her. Not the way he should have. Not the way he loved Lindsey.

His world shimmered and moved, and he absorbed the fact that he had lost again. He'd done it. He'd made it happen.

Walker turned, looked at him, frowned, then scrambled to his feet and ran for Zane. "Daddy," he whimpered, and Zane scooped him up, hugging the child to him. A little person who hugged him back. His son who knew something was wrong, but didn't understand any of it.

"It can't be," he whispered, but knew it was.

"Zane," Matt said from somewhere outside that ring of awareness that was surrounding him and his son. "It's true."

He knew it. He must have known it for a while. Somewhere in his soul, it had been there.

Walker pushed back, touching his cheek. "Daddy?" he said, his lower lip slightly unsteady.

"Yes," he whispered, and pulled him back in a hug. "Daddy." He focused on Matt. "What now?"

"You want him?"

"I wanted him before I knew any of this. Hell, yes, I want him."

"Then, we'll have to go through adoption. Weaver's the legal father. But it shouldn't be hard. We could get it done quickly, if you're sure."

"I'm sure," he said, letting Walker down when the boy started to squirm in his hold. He watched him run back to the TV, then he nodded. "I'm sure."

"Okay. I'll call the attorney back and set things in motion. Anything else?"

The only other thing he wanted was Lindsey—to tell her what had happened—but he knew he couldn't have that. "I'll do this. I'll take care of it," he said. "I'm going to Florida."

Six days later

LINDSEY HAD GONE BACK to work, pretending that everything was okay. The dreams had stopped. The nights were dark and long, but no dreams. She said nothing about the center closing, and kept up a facade of being in control. She pretended that things were okay, that they'd be fine. And the only contact from Zane had been the appearance of two vans and two employees to drive them.

Amy was thrilled. The others were impressed. Lindsey felt sick. And there was no contact from Zane. Word was, he was out of town on business, that he was "unavailable." And her one call to the hotel to check on Walker went unanswered. When the voice mail came on, she hung up.

Finally, Lindsey decided that she couldn't hide. She couldn't just wait until everything was over. She tried to think of options, and she came up with two. She had to accept that everything she'd worked for and everything she cared about was lost to her, or she had to change things herself.

Late in the afternoon, she went into her office, while Amy took care of the parents coming to pick up their children. She had admitted that the first option *wasn't* an option. So she reached for her private phone book, flipped to the *L*s, then dialed Mr. Lewis's home phone number, which he had given her at the start.

The phone rang once, then a man answered. "Lewis residence."

"This is Lindsey Atherton. I need to speak to Mr. Lewis, please."

"I'm sorry. He's not here right now. Is there any message I can relay to him?"

She didn't even know what to say, so she kept it simple.

"Could you just ask him to call me, Lindsey Atherton, at Just For Kids at LynTech?"

"I'll make sure he gets the message, but it might take a while. He's in Europe. Family matters. But I'll make sure to tell him when he calls in."

"Thanks so much," she said, and hung up the phone.

She sat back in the hard wooden chair. Europe? His daughter's engagement. She'd forgotten. Family matters. She closed her eyes, then sighed. She'd have to wait for him to call. Then she'd figure out where to go from here. If she could talk to Mr. Lewis, maybe somehow get him to step in... She didn't know if he kept stock in the company or what, but it was worth a try. Anything was worth a try.

She went back into the main room to help Amy, and saw Rita there with her two boys. They were getting their things, and when Rita saw her, she smiled. "Hello, there. The boys were just telling me that they have new vans for their pickup. That's great."

"Yes, it is great," Lindsey said.

"This place is so terrific. I don't know what we'd do without it."

She'd been worried so about Walker, but after her call she'd tried to push that away, along with memories of Zane. It all hurt too much. But she went closer to Rita. "How's Walker doing?"

"Oh, fine, I guess. Mr. Holden's still gone with him, to Florida, I think Mr. Terrel said. But Walker's with him, so he must be fine."

She could feel the blood draining from her face, and she groped for the nearest chair—a tiny tulip thing that was low to the ground, but she was thankful for the support. Amy was there, touching her forehead, talking to her, and she glanced up at the people around her. They all looked

concerned, but they couldn't know. Then she realized Amy
was asking her if she was okay, if she was sick.

She accepted the paper cup of water Rita was offering
to her, took a sip, then breathed deeply. ''I'm sorry. I…I
felt light-headed for a minute.''

''You looked as pale as a ghost,'' Amy was saying as
she crouched in front of her. ''You haven't looked good
for a week, and I've been worried, but…'' She touched
Lindsey's forehead again. ''Do you need a doctor?''

''No, no doctor,'' she whispered. Zane had taken Walker
to Florida to give him back. He would just give the child
away to strangers. She felt a horrible ache in her middle,
and leaned over a bit, pressing her free hand to her stomach.
''I'm just…just not feeling well. The flu…probably. I
think.'' A lie. ''I just need to sit for a minute.''

Zane had given the boy away. Of course, he had. Why
was she so shocked? He'd told her it was temporary, the
way everything was in his life. LynTech, Walker…her.

As the world settled, Lindsey cautiously stood. ''Do you
think you could close up?'' she asked Amy.

''Of course. But you can't ride the bus like this. I'll take
you home in a bit.''

''No, I'm not going for a while.''

Amy had her by the arm. ''You can't work. You go in
the office, lay down on the couch in there. Let me finish
up here, then I'll take you home and make sure you get
some chicken soup.''

''I'll lay down for a few minutes,'' she said, thinking
that maybe Mr. Lewis would try to call her back and that
she wanted to be there. ''But you go when you're done. I
can call a cab.''

''Are you sure?''

''Very sure.'' She just wanted to be alone. ''Finish up,
then go ahead and take Taylor home.''

She turned and went back into her office, left the door partly open and lay down on the couch. She put her forearm over her eyes and tried to breathe evenly.

"Damn him," she whispered. It shouldn't hurt so much. It couldn't. It had to end sooner or later. Just being here was painful, and all of the other things... She exhaled as she realized she had another option. She could just leave.

Her passion for the center was gone. Zane had killed it, along with so much more in her. If Mr. Lewis couldn't help her, she could leave. She had nothing holding her here. And she didn't want to witness the collapse. A chicken's way out, but maybe it was the only way she could survive.

"We're leaving," Amy said a while later, and Lindsey turned to see her friend popping her head in the door. "Are you sure you'll be okay?"

"Sure, fine," Lindsey replied, sitting up. "I'm just waiting for a phone call, then I'll be going, too."

"Okay, good night," she said. "See you on Monday. And don't forget Thanksgiving tomorrow at Jenn's?"

She'd totally forgotten, and she knew she wouldn't be going. But she'd call them later. She didn't want to face that right now. "Okay," she said.

She sat very still, listening to Amy leave: the door opening, then a shuffling, and the door closing. There was silence all around. She got up to call Mr. Lewis's place again in order to leave her home number, too—when she heard a noise.

Something fell. Something rolled on the wooden floor. Silence. Then something else fell. Someone was out there.

She went out the door, down the hallway and into the main room, finding the lights on and blocks scattered on the floor. This wasn't right. Amy always put the toys back and turned off the lights. She caught a blur of movement out of the corner of her eye. She turned just in time to see

Walker in navy overalls and a red T-shirt, running right at her.

She braced herself as he grabbed her around her legs—and she didn't understand anything. He looked up and grinned at her. A grin like Zane's. "Linny, Linny, me playing, Linny, me playing!"

Everything was off-kilter. He was here, but he couldn't be. And he looked healthy and happy. She looked up, as he turned and hurried to the blocks. He plopped down on his bottom and earnestly started to stack them. Then she saw Zane.

This was a dream. A crazy, wild dream. Zane couldn't be here. She was being haunted. But in this dream, Zane was very clear. The fact that he was in jeans and an open-necked chambray shirt and casual boots was painfully clear to her. So was the fact that his hair was slightly mussed, that there was a touch of sunburn at his forehead and that those eyes on her looked bluer than ever before.

"Zane?" she breathed, and she knew it wasn't a dream. It wasn't a fantasy that she'd concocted. He was coming closer to her, and she could feel the air stir as he moved.

"It's me," he murmured, his voice achingly familiar and almost as painful to hear.

"What are you doing here? What's Walker doing here?"

"I work here, and Walker's with me. Why wouldn't he be here?"

She bit her lip. "I...I heard you went to Florida, and I assumed—"

"See, that's your trouble. Never assume anything," he said.

"Zane, please."

"What?"

"What's going on?"

He shrugged. "I came to check out the center. I've been

told it's good, but it could be great. Also wanted to see how feasible it would be to relocate it to the bottom floor. You know, those conference rooms that are big enough to house a small country? I'm going to be needing it for Walker from time to time.''

She darted a look at the boy, who was intent on building with the blocks. God, she'd missed him—she looked at Zane—almost as much as she'd missed this man. ''Walker? I thought you took him to Florida to hand him over to some relatives.''

''That was the plan, wasn't it,'' he said. ''A good plan, actually, and I did. I went to Florida to talk to Edward Stiller, the attorney, and we worked things out—''

He came a half step closer to her, and it was all she could do not to back up.

''And I'm back.''

''You didn't leave Walker?''

''No. I actually ended up signing papers to adopt him. Stiller thinks there won't be a problem with it.''

''Oh, God,'' she whispered, and found herself fumbling for a chair again, sinking down onto it. ''You're really going to keep him?''

He crouched down in front of her and touched her for the first time. His finger barely made contact with her chin, applying gentle pressure to make her look up at him. She started to shake.

''I made several personal discoveries since you threw me out of your loft.'' She trembled, and he cupped her chin gently. ''The first one—I've got a heart.''

''Zane…'' she whispered tremulously.

''Listen to me. You have to have a heart to feel as bad as I did that night. You have to have a heart to hurt when you know that a little boy is going out of your life forever, to hurt when he's called you 'Daddy' and he's connecting with you. And you have to have a heart to regret hurting someone the way I hurt you. It hurt. It all hurt.''

"I don't...I don't understand," she said.

He drew back his hand but didn't move away from her. "I'm adopting Walker, and I was going to keep him if I could, even before Matt..." He took a slightly shaky breath. "He's mine, Lindsey. My child. Suzanne couldn't...no, she *wouldn't* tell me. And Weaver was willing to be his father. But it's me. She was pregnant when she left. She had to have known. We...we made love so seldom at the end, and that one time, maybe three weeks before she left, I guess that was it. I just never stopped to calculate time or dates, and probably would have thought she'd been with Weaver before she left.''

She'd never seen such pain and regret in one person, and her heart broke for him. "Oh, God, Zane."

"I know. It's all my fault. But it's okay now. He's here, and he's staying. I'm not sure how to go about this whole thing, but I'm going to try."

She knew she was crying, but didn't care. "You...you're his father."

"Yes, and when I found out, the only person I wanted to tell was you. And you weren't there." He touched her then, lightly brushing at her tears. "And I wanted you there so badly. So badly."

She couldn't say a thing. Her whole body was aching. She felt as if she were dreaming, as if she'd fabricated her own fantasy for Walker. A father. Zane. "You...you're doing okay on your own," she managed to say in a choked voice.

"I'm trying to do the right thing all the way around in this mess." He drew back, his hands pressed to his thighs, then he stood. "How about this?" he asked in a slightly unsteady voice, as she looked up at him. "This place, closing it—"

"No," she said, standing so quickly that she collided with Zane. For a moment she felt him against her, his touch on her, and she twisted frantically to get away. She stumbled slightly, caught at the wall, and when Zane would have helped her catch her balance, she moved even farther from him. "Don't."

He drew back, and when she turned, a good three feet separated them. But not enough space. She wondered if the whole world would be enough space to let her breathe easily and to not think about him.

"Okay, okay," he breathed.

"I won't let you close this place. I'll do anything, anything at all to keep that from happening."

She watched Zane studying her—a man who was slightly pale and looking very vulnerable at that moment.

"What will you do to keep this place open?" he asked.

"I put in a call to Mr. Lewis. I'm betting that he's got stock in LynTech, that that was part of the deal you made with him. And he loves this place. He won't let you destroy it, if he knows it's happening."

"No, he won't."

She wasn't sure she'd heard him right. "What?"

"He's got great ideas for the center. You were right, he loves it. It's a vision he's had, and you were the one making that vision happen. He agrees about relocating to the bottom floor, tearing out half of the conference rooms and expanding the facility. Giving it its own entrance at the back. Maybe a play yard, if engineering can figure it out."

She was getting lost in another fantasy, her fantasy for this place. And this man was giving it to her. "I don't understand."

"Robert and I have had several conversations, both from

here and from Florida. I asked about his visions for this place, and for the company. I never thought to ask before. I knew what it cost to run, what I could save if it shut down, but I never bothered to ask why he did it, or why he believed in it.'' He took a deep breath. ''I finally did.''

''And?'' she managed to ask.

''I think it could be very viable financially. Maybe even turn a profit if we go to the outside, offer the service to the people working in the area. What do you think?''

She couldn't believe what she was hearing. ''You aren't going to close it?''

''No, I'm not. And I'm staying here. I decided that building something is better than tearing it down. And I think that LynTech had a great start. Now it's up to me to keep it going. And Walker needs a permanent home, a place where he'll feel safe and loved and secure. No closets, no boogeymen.''

God, he remembered. He'd heard her.

''Linny, no cry,'' Walker said, coming over to her and tugging at her pants.

She crouched, pulled him to her and held him. ''Okay, no crying, okay.'' He let her hug him, surprisingly not squirming out of her hold. Then she held him back, and he smiled at her.

''Come on and play?''

Zane spoke, just behind her shoulder. ''You go play, scout, build something. Make something good with the blocks. Okay? And no wrecking it.''

Walker headed back to the blocks without a murmur, and she watched him reach for a big red block and very carefully put it on top of two blue blocks.

She closed her eyes for a moment and swiped at her wet cheeks. Two absolute miracles. Both from Zane. She turned and looked at him, his image wavering and unsteady. And all she wanted to do was hold him, touch him, feel his reality and know this was all true. That she wasn't imagining it. "Thank you," she said softly.

"Is that all you've got to say?"

"You've got a heart—" she said, her voice breaking on a sob.

He came closer, his image getting clearer and more disturbing for her. She loved him. She loved him for how he loved Walker, and she loved him for doing what he was doing for the center. But being close to him was something she couldn't do if she wanted to keep any semblance of control.

"I want to negotiate with you," he said, so softly that she wondered if she'd heard him correctly.

"Negotiate?"

"Negotiate. I enjoy it. And you're good at it. But the stakes have to be high. For it to be exciting, you have to really put something on the line."

She just wanted out of here. "There isn't anything to negotiate for now. Everything's the way it should be."

He took a step toward her, cutting any buffer of distance and acting as if she hadn't said a thing. "Okay, I'll name the stakes."

"You're crazy," she muttered.

Instead of seeming offended, he grinned at her. "I am crazy. And I'm going way out on a limb, here. If you'll give me a chance to prove once and for all that I have a heart, I'll…" He narrowed his eyes as if figuring out something. He said, "I'll give you forever."

She shook her head. "Oh, God, no…"

"Lindsey, here, feel," he said, taking her hand. When she tried to jerk away, he held onto her. "I'm not letting you go," he said in a low, rough voice. Then he pulled her hand to his chest. "Feel that?"

His heart beat against her clenched fist. There was heat, and she slowly opened her hand, pressing her palm against his chambray shirt. "Yes," she whispered.

"That's my heart. It's real. I finally found it." His hand eased its hold on her wrist, and he covered her hand with his. "And it's very fragile, being so newly found and all. Pretty damn vulnerable, actually."

"Zane Holden is vulnerable?" she asked, her voice quavering.

"Very. I've been alone all my life, even when I was with people. I didn't hide in closets. I hid inside myself. The only time I haven't felt alone, the only time I felt complete, was with you. I'm not a stupid man, and even I can put two and two together if you give me enough time. I'm not selling LynTech—although Matt thinks I've lost my sanity. I'm keeping it, and I'm going to watch it grow and develop. The center is safe. Walker's here, and for the first time in my life I'm really in love. And I'm in love forever."

She drew her hand back, clutching it to her stomach. Afraid to go any farther. She couldn't bear it. But Zane wasn't letting it go. He came even closer, and this time he touched her shoulders. Even through the cotton of her blouse, his touch brought fire with it.

"I'm not done, Lindsey," he said in a low voice. "Unless you say I'm done. I want peace in my life. I want to feel centered, and I want to know how to build instead of tearing down. I want Walker happy, and God help me, I want to be happy." His hands trembled slightly. "I want you. I want you in my life. I want you in Walker's life." He closed his eyes, then whispered as he looked at her again, "I love you, Lindsey."

She let herself hear the words now, and she felt them in the air between herself and Zane. She felt them filtering into her, seeping into her soul. And something spread through her that she had never known before. It was joy. Pure and simple. Joy.

She slowly slipped her arms around him and held him. Afraid to move. Afraid to do anything. Afraid that the dream would end.

But it didn't. Not even when he drew back, framing her face with his hands. His eyes held uncertainty, something she'd never seen before in Zane. "Will you have me...and Walker...forever?" he whispered hoarsely.

She smiled for the first time in what felt to her like an eternity, and touched his face with her fingers. Felt the roughness of a new beard, then a tension in his jaw. "Oh, yes, forever," she said. "I'll love you and Walker, forever."

Four weeks later

"A PENNY FOR your thoughts?" Lindsey said as she came into the office.

Zane turned from the work he'd been trying to finish up and smiled at her. Just the sight of him made something in her right. Very right.

"You should have negotiated for that," he said, his gaze flicking over the work overalls she'd been living in for the past two weeks during the center's renovations.

She crossed to him, and as he swiveled the chair toward her, she slipped onto his lap, put her arms around his neck and asked, "Two pennies?"

"No, no, you're supposed to negotiate down, not up."

She stroked the hair at his temples, and gently kissed him. "I'll remember that," she whispered. "Now, can we leave? Mrs. Greenleaf has Walker. She's on her way home with him, and we're going to meet them there." She kissed him again, lingering a bit before drawing back. "We've already had our family Thanksgiving with Amy, Taylor and Jenn. Hopefully that'll be a tradition." She smiled at him. "We had the wedding…"

He kissed her this time, then drew back. "You don't regret marrying me so quickly and not having a big ceremony?"

She touched his lips with the tip of her finger. "I told you, the wedding didn't matter, it was being together. Besides, it was perfect the way it was, in the loft, with just us, Walker and our closest friends. Even Joey was there. And, bottom line, I didn't want to wait."

"That makes two of us," he murmured.

"Okay, now that's settled, one more thing I don't want to wait for is a real honeymoon."

He touched her bottom lip and slowly traced the soft line, the simple action making her tremble slightly. "Oh, yes, the honeymoon. Two weeks late and with an entourage. You, me, Walker, Mrs. Greenleaf, Sol and Emma. Anyone else I forgot?"

"That's about it. But from what Emma's said, the Aspen lodge is huge and there's plenty of room for everyone." She slipped off his lap and looked down at him. "Now, let's go. I need to go over Joey's feeding with George and make sure he knows how to water the plants in the loft." She motioned to the stack of work on Zane's desk. "Matt's the C.E.O., too, he can take care of things. Leave it all and let Matt do it—"

"Let Matt do what?"

Zane glanced past Lindsey at Matt, as he strode into the room. "We're leaving and you're holding down the fort." He stood, and Lindsey moved back as he reached for his suit coat. "We've got a flight out first thing."

"Ah, the honeymoon."

"You got it." He glanced at Lindsey as he shrugged into his jacket. "Aspen until the New Year. If anything really important comes up here, well..."

He looked at Lindsey, and that grin came from nowhere, making her heart leap.

"Save it until we come back."

"Actually, there was one thing. Robert Lewis called and wanted to discuss something with us."

"Any idea what it is?"

"No, but he said it was a personal favor he needed, and my bet is, he wants us to take his daughter off his hands." He grimaced. "Poor guy. If you looked up *trouble* in the dictionary, you'd probably see a picture of Brittany Lewis."

"Well, whatever it's about, help him out. We owe him big-time."

Lindsey spoke up. "Matt, Amy's got things under control with the center's move and renovations, but if she runs into any trouble—"

"I'll keep an eye on things, don't worry."

Lindsey looked at Zane, as he gathered his things up to leave. God, she loved him.

"Ready?" he said.

"Ready," she echoed.

Epilogue

As Zane and Lindsey headed for the elevator, Zane scooped up the wool throw that they kept in the office for Walker to nap on.

Matt caught up with them by the doors. "You two have a great time. I'll see you next year."

"You've got it," Zane said.

The doors slid shut, and Zane looked at Lindsey. "How long do we have before Mrs. Greenleaf brings Walker back to the loft?"

"An hour, maybe longer."

"Perfect," he said, pressing the button to go down.

She motioned to the blue throw. "What's that for?"

He grinned at her, then, without a word, reached over and pressed the stop button on the panel. The elevator halted between floors, the lights flashed off, then back on, and everything was very still.

"We're stuck," he said.

She laughed, a soft, sexy sound. "Oh, we are, are we."

"I'm afraid so," he said, letting his briefcase and the envelope fall to the floor, along with the fabric throw. He took her into his arms. "So, we have some time alone—no one walking in, no one throwing cookies at a cat. And what good luck, we even have supplies."

She tipped her head back and smiled, but the expression

was a bit shaky. "You certainly have everything planned out, don't you."

"Oh, I hope so," he whispered. "The last time this happened, we wasted a whole lot of time talking. I don't intend to repeat that."

"Sounds like a plan to me," she breathed.

Just as his lips found hers, the emergency phone rang. He exhaled, then said, "Hold that thought," and reached for the phone.

"Hello?"

She watched him as he listened with a frown. Then a smile came and he cast her a slanted look. "This is Mr. Holden. No, there's no problem, but the elevator is going to be in this position for a while. Don't worry about it, and don't do anything about it. Understood?" He hung up and turned back to Lindsey. "John Olson is on the job. And we aren't going anywhere for as long as we want."

"Good old John, back on the job and as efficient as ever," she said. She reached to push his jacket back and slip it off, then she tossed it onto the blanket by her feet. "And if he does as he's told, I think I'll send him a present—maybe some chocolates."

"Good idea," Zane said.

She started unbuttoning his shirt. "Time. What a luxury. Time to be here, with you."

"Oh, yes," he said, and took a sharp breath as her hands found his bare skin.

"Then the honeymoon." She touched her lips to his bare chest. They had time, but that didn't kill the urgency in her, the explosion of desire that was all but overwhelming. The hunger in her for this man, her husband, was there, flaring into a white-hot passion. Clothes were discarded, the blanket was spread on the floor, and they found each other.

Lindsey lost herself in Zane, and at the same time found pieces of her soul that had been missing all her life. Zane and Walker were those pieces, and now she had both of them. Their bodies entangled, Zane's jacket a makeshift pillow, she snuggled against him—

The phone rang again.

Zane kissed her quickly and stretched to reach the phone. "Olson is going to be fired again," he muttered as he caught the receiver and brought it down to him. "What?" After a pause, he added, "Everything's fine, and we'll be down in a few minutes."

He hung up and turned to her with a frown. "That was Gordon this time. He's been waiting for a while." He grinned at her—that grin Walker imitated so perfectly. "We're busted."

He reached for his clothes and began to dress. While she did the same, he said, "Why don't we see about getting a bed put in this thing?"

She tugged on her coveralls, a bit worse for the wear, then pushed her feet into her shoes. "No, that would spoil it, take away all of the adventure." She bent down to get the throw and refolded it, then stood. Zane pushed the button to start the elevator on its way down again.

He slipped on his jacket and grabbed his briefcase. "Okay, the story, if Gordon asks, is—" he hugged her to him "—I'm in love with my wife."

"Works for me," she whispered.

"Forever?"

"Absolutely, forever."

*   *   *   *   *

Look for
THE C.E.O. AND THE SECRET HEIRESS,
as Mary Anne Wilson's JUST FOR KIDS
continues in October 2001,
from Harlequin American Romance.

There's a baby on the way!

HARLEQUIN®

AMERICAN *Romance®*

is proud to announce the birth of

AMERICAN *Baby*

Unexpected arrivals lead to the sweetest of surprises
in this brand-new promotion celebrating the love
only a baby can bring!

Don't miss any of these heartwarming tales:

SURPRISE, DOC! YOU'RE A DADDY! (HAR #889)
Jacqueline Diamond September 2001

BABY BY THE BOOK (HAR #893)
Kara Lennox October 2001

THE BABY IN THE BACKSEAT (HAR #897)
Mollie Molay November 2001

Available wherever Harlequin books are sold.

HARLEQUIN®

Makes any time special®

Visit us at www.eHarlequin.com   HARBABY

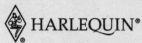

Harlequin truly does
make any time special. . . .
This year we are celebrating
weddings in style!

A
Walk
Down
the Aisle
WEDDING CELEBRATION

To help us celebrate, we want you to tell us how wearing the Harlequin wedding gown will make your wedding day special. As the grand prize, Harlequin will offer one lucky bride the chance to **"Walk Down the Aisle" in the Harlequin wedding gown!**

There's more...

For her honeymoon, she and her groom will spend five nights at the **Hyatt Regency Maui.** As part of this five-night honeymoon at the hotel renowned for its romantic attractions, the couple will enjoy a candlelit dinner for two in Swan Court, a sunset sail on the hotel's catamaran, and duet spa treatments.

A HYATT RESORT AND SPA   Maui • Molokai • Lanai

To enter, please write, in, 250 words or less, how wearing the Harlequin wedding gown will make your wedding day special. The entry will be judged based on its emotionally compelling nature, its originality and creativity, and its sincerity. This contest is open to Canadian and U.S. residents only and to those who are 18 years of age and older. There is no purchase necessary to enter. Void where prohibited. See further contest rules attached. Please send your entry to:

Walk Down the Aisle Contest

In Canada
P.O. Box 637
Fort Erie, Ontario
L2A 5X3

In U.S.A.
P.O. Box 9076
3010 Walden Ave.
Buffalo, NY 14269-9076

You can also enter by visiting www.eHarlequin.com
Win the Harlequin wedding gown and the vacation of a lifetime!
The deadline for entries is October 1, 2001.

HARLEQUIN®
Makes any time special ®

HARLEQUIN WALK DOWN THE AISLE TO MAUI CONTEST 1197
OFFICIAL RULES
NO PURCHASE NECESSARY TO ENTER

1. To enter, follow directions published in the offer to which you are responding. Contest begins April 2, 2001, and ends on October 1, 2001. Method of entry may vary. Mailed entries must be postmarked by October 1, 2001, and received by October 8, 2001.

2. Contest entry may be, at times, presented via the Internet, but will be restricted solely to residents of certain georgraphic areas that are disclosed on the Web site. To enter via the Internet, if permissible, access the Harlequin Web site (www.eHarlequin.com) and follow the directions displayed online. Online entries must be received by 11:59 p.m. E.S.T. on October 1, 2001.

   In lieu of submitting an entry online, enter by mail by hand-printing (or typing) on an 8½" x 11" plain piece of paper, your name, address (including zip code), Contest number/name and in 250 words or fewer, why winning a Harlequin wedding dress would make your wedding day special. Mail via first-class mail to: Harlequin Walk Down the Aisle Contest 1197, (in the U.S.) P.O. Box 9076, 3010 Walden Avenue, Buffalo, NY 14269-9076, (in Canada) P.O. Box 637, Fort Erie, Ontario L2A 5X3, Canada.

   Limit one entry per person, household address and e-mail address. Online and/or mailed entries received from persons residing in geographic areas in which Internet entry is not permissible will be disqualified.

3. Contests will be judged by a panel of members of the Harlequin editorial, marketing and public relations staff based on the following criteria:

   • Originality and Creativity—50%
   • Emotionally Compelling—25%
   • Sincerity—25%

   In the event of a tie, duplicate prizes will be awarded. Decisions of the judges are final.

4. All entries become the property of Torstar Corp. and will not be returned. No responsibility is assumed for lost, late, illegible, incomplete, inaccurate, nondelivered or misdirected mail or misdirected e-mail, for technical, hardware or software failures of any kind, lost or unavailable network connections, or failed, incomplete, garbled or delayed computer transmission or any human error which may occur in the receipt or processing of the entries in this Contest.

5. Contest open only to residents of the U.S. (except Puerto Rico) and Canada, who are 18 years of age or older, and is void wherever prohibited by law; all applicable laws and regulations apply. Any litigation within the Province of Quebec respecting the conduct or organization of a publicity contest may be submitted to the Régie des alcools, des courses et des jeux for a ruling. Any litigation respecting the awarding of a prize may be submitted to the Régie des alcools, des courses et des jeux only for the purpose of helping the parties reach a settlement. Employees and immediate family members of Torstar Corp. and D. L. Blair, Inc., their affiliates, subsidiaries and all other agencies, entities and persons connected with the use, marketing or conduct of this Contest are not eligible to enter. Taxes on prizes are the sole responsibility of winners. Acceptance of any prize offered constitutes permission to use winner's name, photograph or other likeness for the purposes of advertising, trade and promotion on behalf of Torstar Corp., its affiliates and subsidiaries without further compensation to the winner, unless prohibited by law.

6. Winners will be determined no later than November 15, 2001, and will be notified by mail. Winners will be required to sign and return an Affidavit of Eligibility form within 15 days after winner notification. Noncompliance within that time period may result in disqualification and an alternative winner may be selected. Winners of trip must execute a Release of Liability prior to ticketing and must possess required travel documents (e.g. passport, photo ID) where applicable. Trip must be completed by November 2002. No substitution of prize permitted by winner. Torstar Corp. and D. L. Blair, Inc., their parents, affiliates, and subsidiaries are not responsible for errors in printing or electronic presentation of Contest, entries and/or game pieces. In the event of printing or other errors which may result in unintended prize values or duplication of prizes, all affected game pieces or entries shall be null and void. If for any reason the Internet portion of the Contest is not capable of running as planned, including infection by computer virus, bugs, tampering, unauthorized intervention, fraud, technical failures, or any other causes beyond the control of Torstar Corp. which corrupt or affect the administration, secrecy, fairness, integrity or proper conduct of the Contest, Torstar Corp. reserves the right, at its sole discretion, to disqualify any individual who tampers with the entry process and to cancel, terminate, modify or suspend the Contest or the Internet portion thereof. In the event of a dispute regarding an online entry, the entry will be deemed submitted by the authorized holder of the e-mail account submitted at the time of entry. Authorized account holder is defined as the natural person who is assigned to an e-mail address by an Internet access provider, online service provider or other organization that is responsible for arranging e-mail address for the domain associated with the submitted e-mail address. **Purchase or acceptance of a product offer does not improve your chances of winning.**

7. Prizes: (1) Grand Prize—A Harlequin wedding dress (approximate retail value: $3,500) and a 5-night/6-day honeymoon trip to Maui, HI, including round-trip air transportation provided by Maui Visitors Bureau from Los Angeles International Airport (winner is responsible for transportation to and from Los Angeles International Airport) and a Harlequin Romance Package, including hotel accomodations (double occupancy) at the Hyatt Regency Maui Resort and Spa, dinner for (2) two at Swan Court, a sunset sail on Kiele V and a spa treatment for the winner (approximate retail value: $4,000); (5) Five runner-up prizes of a $1000 gift certificate to selected retail outlets to be determined by Sponsor (retail value $1000 ea.). Prizes consist of only those items listed as part of the prize. Limit one prize per person. All prizes are valued in U.S. currency.

8. For a list of winners (available after December 17, 2001) send a self-addressed, stamped envelope to: Harlequin Walk Down the Aisle Contest 1197 Winners, P.O. Box 4200 Blair, NE 68009-4200 or you may access the www.eHarlequin.com Web site through January 15, 2002.

Contest sponsored by Torstar Corp., P.O. Box 9042, Buffalo, NY 14269-9042, U.S.A.

PHWDACONT2

COMING SOON...

AN EXCITING
OPPORTUNITY TO SAVE
ON THE PURCHASE OF
HARLEQUIN AND
SILHOUETTE BOOKS!

*DETAILS TO FOLLOW
IN OCTOBER 2001!*

YOU WON'T WANT TO MISS IT!

PHQ401

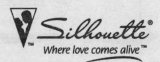